About the Author

Chris Bailey-Green was born in Suffolk in 1973. He spent almost twenty years in the police, both as a civilian member of staff and a police officer, before leaving to become a full-time writer. He has a degree in philosophy and lives in the heart of the Norfolk countryside with his wife and pets. *A Voluntary Act* is his fourth novel. He can be followed on Twitter @CBGreen9

A Voluntary Act

Chris Bailey-Green

A Voluntary Act

For Kerry

My old crew partner! Both now in different roles

Best wishes

[signature]

x

Olympia Publishers
London

www.olympiapublishers.com
OLYMPIA PAPERBACK EDITION

A CIP catalogue record for this title is
available from the British Library.

ISBN: 978-1-80074-154-6

This is a work of fiction.
Names, characters, places and incidents originate from the writer's imagination.
Any resemblance to actual persons, living or dead, is purely coincidental.

First Published in 2022

Olympia Publishers
Tallis House
2 Tallis Street
London
EC4Y 0AB

Printed in Great Britain

Dedication

As always, for Debbi, who makes it all possible and keeps the words coming

1

It all began when I decided to kill my wife.

It was all such a long time ago now. It becomes difficult to remember things after such a long time. I loved her. I remember that, of course. I loved her very much. I still do love her. Some people have trouble in believing that, but it is true. Some people always have trouble in believing the truth and in believing in what is right and what is wrong. Some people just have trouble believing. I know that now. I didn't know it then.

I write this now for my own benefit more than anything else. I live in the hope that by setting my pencil to paper and my thoughts down in writing, that it may aid me to make some sense of all that has happened to me. One day, when society is different, perhaps others may read this account and they may come to some kind of understanding as to the world that I inhabit — I was going to write 'the world that I live in', but I don't believe that anyone is actually 'living' here; they merely 'exist'; which is hardly the same thing; although it is often mistaken as being the same. The real tragedy is that they don't even know it. Whatever the legacy of this document may be, at the moment, it merely serves as a tool for me and I care for no other use.

I can still remember very vividly the events leading up to my wife's death. I am not a monster. I am just like everybody else, I still suffer the dreams, the nightmares, but worse than all of that, I suffer from the memories. I suffer from the results of an intellect. Of a mind that is capable of reason and of working things out. It is one of the worst curses that you can ever imagine.

It is not easy for me to keep my thoughts entirely in order. The luxury of writing is something that I have not had for a very long time now. It is something that I would not be able to do now, were it not that Alpheus secretly gave me these papers and a pencil, in exchange for me talking with him on the few chances that present themselves. It is a great risk for Alpheus, but this action gives me hope. I see so little that gives me hope these days that the smallest action can restore some of my beliefs, if only for a brief while.

As it is so long since I was able to express myself on paper, I must be forgiven for the rambling nature of my thoughts. I will try to stop this. I shall try to discipline myself. I shall start the story again from the very start. It is obvious that things really began before my wife died. It would make no sense to start this narrative with my wife's death, without being first able to explain the background to my story. If nothing else, for the reason that any reader of this will be able to understand why it was that I made the decision to kill my wife on a cold evening one winter.

***

Alpheus gives me a sheet of paper each day so that I can write for the hour or so before the light fades — to write by candlelight would obviously be too dangerous.

I fill my sheet up as much as possible and then whilst I am washing in the mornings, Alpheus takes the written sheet away and replaces it with a clean sheet. I will never see my written sheets again. It would be far too dangerous to have all the sheets with me in case I am searched. Alpheus removes them and takes them to some place that he says is safe. I don't know where this is and it is better that I don't know. I don't really want to know. At my age, I revel in the elements of ignorance that I can get after a lifetime of intellectualism.

'Alpheus' is not his real name, of course. I am not so stupid as to compromise him by using his real name. If they find out I have been helped, Alpheus will stand up to examinations and he will not suffer for his kindness, like so many others have done before him. Besides which, Alpheus suits him better, the records of the Ancients tell us it is a name that means 'exchange'.

I would like to go back to the time that I first met my wife. Her name was Eveline, but I can hardly remember anybody ever calling her by that name. She preferred to be called Evie and so that was what we called her. Evie was somebody that I think I fell in love with the first time that I met her. I have heard that said before, but until it actually happened to me, I thought it was something that had only been created by poets and the romantics, in order for them to get their plots moving all that bit more quickly.

Her hair was golden and it positively cascaded with curls as it fell down to her shoulders. When she laughed, she would throw her head back and toss her hair from her eyes. Her mouth would open showing her clean, white teeth and her eyes would sparkle with mischief and intellect. She was tall and elegant — even graceful. The first time that I saw her was when she was dancing with her father. It was at the wedding of a friend of mine that was distantly related to her family. I watched her dance for a long time as I sat at my dinner table, smoking a tobacco. People talked to me, and all around me, but all my attention was given to Evie. I could not have taken my attention away from this beautiful, graceful and elegant woman if the end of the world had been happening around me.

I shall never forget that night. After a while, I summoned up all my courage and with my heart in my mouth for fear of rejection, I asked her if she would like to dance with me. She had looked at me and her eyes had sparkled.

'Of course,' she had stated and we danced for the next three dances before we stopped, so that I could buy aqua vitae for us both. We then talked together for the rest of the evening, like two giddy schoolchildren.

That night was the first of many nights. We were both very happy together. We never really had all that much in common when we first met, but we still talked of many things and we never grew tired; or ran out of things to say to each other. We laughed about many things and there were also times when we would not talk, but would merely sit in each other's arms, as we watched the sun come up; or go down depending on the time that we were together. Later on, many years later, we would cry together and feel pain together; but that was all many years in the future.

It is unusual. Remembering her now does me good, but it also causes me pain. I remember the good times that we spent together and I smile at the memory of those times, but my heart also cries out in pain, because it knows that those times are gone and that they will never come back again.

The light is too dim now and I can't see very well. I shall have to leave this until tomorrow.

Because of my writing about Evie yesterday, all my thoughts today have been taken up with her. That is to say, even more than they usually are. What I loved the most about Evie was that she was a companion on equal terms. I had been out with girls before I met Evie, but they were never the same. We were never relaxed in each other's company. It was within minutes that the conversation would dry and very soon afterwards, we would grow tired of each other. It was not like that with Evie. We never grew tired of each other and I don't think we ever would have. It is the cruelty of life, that we never had the opportunity to grow tired of each other. Our life together was cruelly taken away before we had lived all that we could have.

Our relationship had a physical side as well; it was not just a meeting of minds. When I kissed Evie, it was the first time that I had ever kissed a girl and meant it. Every other kiss that I had experienced up until that time had been nothing. It wasn't until I met Evie that I realised that all the kisses of the past had been empty, cardboard kissing. All previous embraces had been nothing but empty-headed passion. Evie was the first woman that taught me how to love with my mind, body, and heart and with every essence of my existence. I think that is a very rare thing to have. I don't think that many people experience love like that and I feel sorry for those that don't. Not everyone can experience that intensity of love, because otherwise it would not be the rare delight that it is.

I would give everything I own to be able to be with Evie again: back as we were when we were happy. Everything I own? I own nothing. I wish no ill to anybody, and I don't believe that I ever have done; consequently, I truly wish that everybody — regardless of the Sphere that they come from — everybody should have the chance to love like we did; even if it is for only a short time.

There are times when it all seems so far away. It is almost as if the events of the past never happened. They are as distant as the remains of a dream after you have awoken. It remains there, but is distant and impossible to reach; always just slightly out of your grasp. Your dream remains the distant memory of a hallucination that you believed was reality until you woke-up, to find yourself back in the hallucination that we have come to know as reality.

There was a time when I was scared that I would forget Evie. Shortly after she died, I had trouble remembering what it was that she looked like. I would sit alone for hours on end, desperately trying to visualise her face in my mind, but it would not come. I would concentrate as hard as I could, but I would always be unable to focus on anything other than a blurred outline. It took me a while, but I was able to remember Evie in my mind once again. It must have been the initial shock of her death that kept me from seeing her. I am still frightened in case she goes away again, only this time never to return. I have already had to learn how to live without her in one sense, but I don't think that I would be able to do it in any other.

The memory of the last time that I saw her stays with me, as well as the first. This is a memory that has great pain for me and it is a memory that I will describe, but I should do it later. If any sense is to be made of this document, then I should at least make an attempt at some form of chronological order. I keep on making the presumption that what I know is what my reader also knows. I shall try to be as descriptive as my small amount of daylight will allow and I shall try not to leave out anything important.

I still have room left on this sheet — I try to write very small — but once, again the light is abandoning me. I must be thankful that it is summer; if it were winter, I would have no opportunity to write at all.

***

Last night I dreamt of Evie. Much of my thoughts, both waking and sleeping are taken up with Evie. Sometimes I have worse dreams. I might be asked if dreams and thoughts of Evie cause me pain. Yes, sometimes they do. Sometimes, however, a day or longer may go by without me thinking of Evie and then when I realise I haven't thought of her, I experience pains more than I ever did from a dream. I don't ever want to forget her. I will not allow myself to forget her. She doesn't deserve to be forgotten. Someone has to remember her and there are not that many people left who can remember her. Not now.

In my dream, we were both stretched out on some grass. Bright green and fresh. The sky above our heads was a clear blue with only a few clouds lazily moving out of our view. It was an idyllic time and there

13

did not seem to be a care in the world. Looking at my dream now that the daylight has broken, I have trouble in remembering if this was an actual memory that really did take place, or whether it was nothing more than pure fantasy. I have trouble making out the difference these days, but it seems to me, that such a place never really existed. The most painful thing was the fact that my mind managed to trick me in a dream that Evie was still alive and that we were together again. Sometimes, I wish that under these circumstances I might never wake up.

We were married almost five years to the day, when we first met on the dance floor. Evie was twenty-six years old and I was twenty-eight. The day was a happy occasion — as all weddings should be. The sun was shining and everybody was in high spirits. Despite the times that we had spent together, we were both incredibly nervous on that day.

It's strange. I've never understood why people can become so worked up over weddings. It's all part of our nature, I suppose. We seem to thrive on things to get worked up about and if we don't have things to work us up, then we go out of our way to invent things to get worked up about.

My best friend from my school days was groomsman. Simeon was in many ways different from me. He was always much more practical than I ever was. There were moments when he annoyed the hell out of me, and I am sure that there were many times when I annoyed the hell out of him. Annoyance was one of the greatest things that kept our friendship together. There were times when I believed that it was the very substance that our friendship was built on. Simeon was very good at business. He progressed far and fast. He was always far better at that sort of thing than I ever was, or ever could be. He was always somebody that I would turn to for advice; or just another person's viewpoint whenever I needed one.

I have not written very much today, but I must stop soon. I grow tired very quickly on some days. The light may still be strong and there may be plenty of room left on the paper, but there are times, when I just can't summon up the energy. I shall have to rest myself for longer tonight, and maybe, if all goes well, tomorrow I shall be able to make a better contribution to my narrative. I can then get round to explain to you why it was that this woman I loved so much was someone I had to kill.

2

I have not written anything for the last two days because I have been confined to the infirmary. It was nothing particularly to worry about, I merely came down with a bad cough and sore throat, but they cannot be too careful and isolation was a wise precaution. Subsequently, due to my isolation, Alpheus was unable to supply me with any writing materials and it would have been foolish of him to even try. My illness was, however, only slight and there was no need for concern. I'm now back to my usual quarters. Sadly, my brief illness has left me very weak, even more so than normal; so, I have no idea how long I shall write for tonight. This is unfortunate as I have something important to say.

A short while ago, I believe I stated in this narrative that I could not presume that my reader is entirely aware of all that I write about. I realise now that I have made one of the biggest presumptions of all. I cannot entirely rule out the possibility that this document will not be read until many generations have passed. Consequently, the society in which I was born, lived and will almost certainly die in, may no longer be in existence. All empires and regimes will eventually fall. Nothing lasts forever. This being the case, then what started out as a personal purge has now turned into a possible historical source for future academics. This may sound a little arrogant, but it is a possibility that I have to give serious thought to.

I have read in the books of the Ancients that the landmasses, on which we live, were once divided into different zones. Each of these zones had a name. They had their own people, their own languages and their own cultures and beliefs. It amazes me how this could be a productive relationship. How can so many peoples with such a vast contrast of their essentials get along in any kind of useful manner? There is nothing wrong with diversity, but it seems to me, that diversity to such an extent as this can achieve nothing and will only breed conflict. We do not have separate zones. We have one landmass where everybody speaks the same language and where all share the same beliefs — with a few exceptions. I will get to these exceptions in due course.

The only division that we, officially have, is one of social division. The peoples of our landmass are categorised into three sections. These are, from top to bottom, the Illuminati, the Median, and finally, the Residuum. I shall make the attempt to give a description of each of these groupings.

I suppose that I should start with the Residuum, although it probably doesn't matter. The Residuum are the lowest form of peoples in our society, they are also in a majority. The Residuum are chiefly the workers. Their purpose is to do all the jobs that nobody else wants to do, or those jobs deemed too dangerous for anybody else to do. The Residuum are expendable. The Residuum are vast. Their numbers far exceed either of the other groups; which is just as well, because members of the Residuum are the highest of our mortality rate. Any members of the Residuum that make it to their late twenties or early thirties, may consider themselves to be very lucky and extremely old aged. Although the truth is that few ever do live that long and the lucky ones are really those that die early.

Conditions amongst the Residuum are very bad indeed. Disease is the natural order of things. They live in the poorest, most crowded areas of our habitats. They have appalling sanitary conditions and anyone from outside entering this world takes their lives in their own hands. Not only is the risk of infection high, but also crime stalks freely. The members of the Residuum have no moral values other than those which enable them to survive. This is not entirely their fault. The Residuum receives no education of any kind whatsoever. They are not encouraged to think and it can be believed that because of this, they don't think; or at least I think that is what a lot of the rest of us would like to believe to reassure ourselves. Theirs is a hard life, and if the truth be told, like many others, their conditions were not something that I gave a moment's thought to until I had to go amongst them.

The jobs that they do are basic and mundane, requiring no more than the simplest of motor skills to complete successfully. All that they do is to work for the majority of the day — eat a very basic meal, sleep (for four hours, or so, a night) and procreate (in order to combat the mortality rate; procreation for pleasure is a doctrine that is entirely alien to the Residuum). That is all that they do and nothing more. There is nothing more for them to do.

They are put to work as soon as they are old enough to hold a tool in their hands. Males and females alike are sent to work in the fields or the factories, and many are dead before they are nine years old. Others last longer. The majority never make it out of their late teenage years.

From the time of their birth, some females are selected for light duties. They will be given jobs that are not too demanding so that their early life will be relatively easy. However, as soon as they reach maturity these girls are expected to bear the young. From as early as ten to twelve years old, they are expected to have a baby as often as every year. Almost all of these girls, with hardly any exception, die in labour. Those that are unable to have any more children are immediately sent out to work, and invariably they die quickly, because they are unused to the harsh conditions. Furthermore, the concept of relationships is something that is not encouraged within the Residuum. The Residuum do not mate for life, they do not have partners. Procreation takes place with whoever is available at the time of need.

I know that the conditions for the Residuum are harsh and I can also see now that it is not fair. I have to be careful, that is a dangerous statement to make. It matters not to me now, however, how dangerous my comments may be perceived to be. They can do nothing to me that they have not already done, or that I would not welcome them to do to me.

This situation with regards to the Residuum is not only wrong but outrageous. We are so immoral and yet we are blinkered to it, because it suits us to see only what we want to see. We would rather make excuses than face the truth. All of us, even the Residuum, are raised to accept things for what they are. Complaints and dissension are hardly ever heard of, not even from the Residuum who are deliberately kept in ignorance so that they won't have the ability to reason. Revolution requires intellect to succeed. It needs people to understand an injustice before they rebel against it. This is the very cunning of the Illuminati that they are able to keep the Residuum in ignorance of their own plight. It is an injustice, but it is ingenious when you think about it.

You reading this now from wherever and whenever you are will probably think that it is barbaric to have some of our people quintessentially in slavery. How did we allow this to go on for so long? It is rather impossible to say. Being conditioned to a situation, it is harder to rebel against that which seems the norm. I am sure that if your own society were to be examined, then there would be fault that could be found in it, just as much as our treatment of the Residuum.

What excuse can I offer? Only that of familiarity. We grew up to accept the Residuum as the way that they were. We didn't see any great injustice in their position, or the way that they were treated. They were just a necessity.

It is wrong though.

***

I have been foolish. After my short illness, my return to the writing of this narrative, placed a great strain on me and I became ill again. This time I was kept in the infirmary for a week and it was touch and go for a moment as to if I would be allowed out when I was. I fully realise the dangers that illness can lead to and I know that precautions must be taken. I must be more careful and take things easier in future. I, perhaps more than many others, know the danger of illness.

Last time, I wrote about the Residuum. Due to the gap in time between my last writings and this, I can't remember what it was that I said about them. I think I said all that I intended to and I am loath to repeat anything unless I really have to. I shall just have to be forgiven if my account of the Residuum is not as comprehensive as I intended it to be.

The next group of people that I should talk about are the Median, but that is a subject that I shall have to leave until tomorrow. I was late returning from the Infirmary today and even though Alpheus has been as faithful as usual, the light begins to dim and there will not be enough time for me to tell all that I want about the Median tonight.

Also, I should rest. I don't want to risk my health any more than I have to.

***

All of my recent illnesses have placed a great strain on me and I am now much weaker than I once was. I must continue with this narrative though. Alpheus is particularly persistent at placing importance on the need to record our stories so that future generations may have some insight into what it was that we did and how we lived in a society that may well be both familiar and yet alien to them. I think his motivation for this is the belief that one day there will be change and these records of a fallen regime will be essential for future generations to learn from our mistakes.

I personally started this account so that I might be able to record the reasons for why I killed my wife, and also explain, why I decided to opt for the course of events that followed, which eventually led me to being in my present circumstances. However, whatever my personal reasons for this narrative, I now realise that I must devote time to explanation of our society, otherwise this document will be of no interest to future academics, other than as a quaint rambling of an epoch dead and of events that can be of no importance to anyone else.

Have patience with me, reader. These may be but words on a page to you that you might even be only semi- (or less) interested in, but please remember, that I too was once a living, breathing creature, like you; and yet, perhaps not like you at all. It might be possible that we shared the same emotions, the same fears and maybe even the same ambitions. It is almost certain that our faults are similar — for all of us who tread this planet, past, present and future make the same mistakes time and time again. Read well and learn anything that you can.

But enough of that for now. Today I must tell you something of the Median. Well, as the name suggests this section of our peoples comes in the middle of our social scale. The Residuum are the lowest, the Illuminati are the highest, but the Median are somewhere in the middle of the two.

Life for the Median is very different from life for the Residuum. The Median make up numbers that are perhaps equal to half of the numbers of the Residuum. It is difficult to tell for certain, since nobody actually knows what number the Residuum are; but if I were to guess, I would say half is perhaps about the right number; perhaps a little more.

The Median work, but they do not work in the same jobs as the Residuum. Some members of the Median are Overseers, which is as close as anyone else gets to the Residuum. The task of the Overseers is to literally oversee the work of the Residuum. The Overseers may be the people who own or manage the factories that the Residuum works in; or, they may be the farmers that own the land that the Residuum toils. The task of Overseer to the Residuum is not a job that is widely coveted among the Median; but it is widely believed that the task of an Overseer is not something that can be given to any member of the Residuum, and it is certainly not a task that would be undertaken by any member of the Illuminati.

Secondly, and more widely, the Median work in jobs that require skilled training. Some are doctors and other medical types; others are lawmen; there are those that have been skilled in the sciences and there are others who are employed to provide entertainment for the rest of the Median. There are many jobs that are open to members of the Median. Almost all jobs that require reading skills, writing skills and thinking skills are open to the Median.

As you will have noticed, this fact means that the Median, unlike the Residuum, receive an education. Members of the Median start their education at the age of five. From that age until they are thirteen, they are given a basic education in all the major disciplines. From the age of six onwards, they are given detailed examinations each year in order to determine their progress, strengths and weaknesses. On the basis of these examinations, at the age of thirteen they are assigned a career that best suits their abilities in ratio to what is available and required. For the next three years, they study the dynamics of their assigned career in minute detail. At the age of sixteen they then begin their working lives. There is no choice allowed to the Median about their own career. Nobody chooses the job that they want. Why would you want to when the system is so fair and done for the better of society?

Due to the better conditions of the Median, they live longer than the Residuum. An average member of the Median can expect to live well into their fifties and maybe even their early sixties. This is the average age, of course, there are those that live longer.

There are those that would hold that the Residuum are harsh on their females and young. In a sense they are, and in another sense they are not. Male and female are both treated as equally bad in the Residuum, with the exception of those that are expected to bear the young. In the Median there is some level of equality, although it is not unknown for males or females to be selected for jobs that suit their gender rather than their individual merits. All females in the Median are allowed to bear children. A formal marriage between two people is the norm and the two people will stay married to each other for the rest of their lives. Marriage is very important in the Median and great emphasis is attached to it. Initially, couples are allowed to marry who they like and when they like, but if a member of the Median is unmarried by the time they are thirty, then they are forcibly matched to another person, whether they desire it or not. Subsequently, it is desirable to find your own partner. Each couple is expected to have at least one child — indeed it is a civic duty to do so. There are no limits to the number of children a couple can have.

Work for the Median can be hard — although not as hard as the Residuum. Something that the Median can enjoy, that the Residuum cannot, is the ability to relax when the work is over. There are many forms of relaxation and entertainment available to members of the Median. After your work day you may choose to spend some time reading some work of fiction from a favourite writer; you may choose to associate with friends; or you may desire an evening out, in which case you may go to the Performance currently playing, or perhaps a concert or a dance; perhaps even — on rare occasions — a trip to view the latest Cinematograph.

***

My narrative today brings me around to the Illuminati. The Illuminati are the last of our recognised divisions in our structure. There are others in our society however, but I will tell you more of these people after I have told you something of the Illuminati.

The Illuminati, as I believe I have already mentioned, are the highest and most elitist of all those in our society. Life for the members of the Illuminati is a very privileged affair. Disease is something that is very rare among the Illuminati. That is not to say that they don't suffer from illness, but their illness is nothing, compared to that suffered in the ranks of the Residuum. Due to the elitist nature of the Illuminati, their numbers are smaller than either the Residuum or the Median, but that does not stop them from being the most powerful on the landmass.

The Illuminati are workers; I would not wish to give the impression that they are so elite that all they do each day is sit about on their arses doing nothing. The main task of the Illuminati is to govern. I believe that I have already stated that we are a people of one landmass with one language and one culture. We do not, however, all live in the same place; such an event would not be practical. We live in communities known as Populaces that are distanced by about three hours walk from each other. Some are located further away. One of the tasks that are unique to the Illuminati is the job of governing each of these individual Populaces across the landmass.

The governorship of the Illuminati is not something that I regard as autocratic, but others of my time, and you reader, of a different age and different culture, may think differently to me. The main job of governing is to ensure that all laws are maintained and that the correct form of justice is passed out on those that may break the law. They are also responsible for the day-to-day running and decision making of each Populace.

I should mention, whilst talking of law, that this is a procedure that only really refers to the Median. The Illuminati do not commit crimes; or at least they never have done to most people's knowledge. The Residuum may commit crime, but nobody concerns themselves with giving them a trial; it is something that is purely seen as a waste of time. If a member of the Residuum is believed to be guilty of a crime, the responsibility for justice falls to their Overseer to enforce. The Overseer, therefore, has complete control over the Residuum that are their responsibility and they have the power to act arbitrarily. More often than not, the punishment for crime is that of death. Subsequently, trials and lawmen are reserved for the Median. I would not wish to give the impression that crimes are always being committed. We are not a lawless society and we are not a perfect society; we are merely a society.

There are some who will not allow too much examination and criticism of society. It is my privileged position to be able to criticise the way things are because I have nothing left to fear. All that can be done has been done and the only thing that I have left to take from me, is my life, such as it is. Our society is not perfect, no society is. Therefore, because it is not perfect, criticism of it is legitimate. If the criticism is justified then it should be heeded and acted upon; if the criticism is not justified, then it should be argued against.

I now believe that criticism is justified. I think it is the job of any thinking person to criticise their governors, and to hold them to account for their actions, or their lack of actions. It is their responsibility to justify themselves to us. This, as you can imagine, is not a particularly popular view. Some people do not like to rock the boat. They prefer things to go along without any challenges from them. I suppose I can understand this point of view, even if I no longer agree with it. It is important to challenge and question. Our lords and masters must be held to account.

The work of the Illuminati is not just limited to that of being our leaders. There are also those that study and specialise in a particular discipline so that they may become expert in that area; for example, a member of the Median may become a doctor that practises general medicine, whereas a member of the Illuminati that studies medicine will know general medicine, but will additionally study a specific area of medicine devoted to the study of the heart, eyes, brain or whatever it is that they prefer.

This leads me to the education of the Illuminati. Like those in the Median, their education starts at the age of five. They receive a similar foundation in the basics, only when the Median break at thirteen so that they may study their career, the Illuminati continue a far more detailed study of the major disciplines until they reach the age of sixteen. At this age they study the subject that they will be working in. This study is an advanced and complex study that lasts five years. When the student reaches the age of twenty-one, they begin to work in their career.

It is worth mentioning that there are those in the Illuminati that devote themselves to study and even teaching. Members of the Median may teach other members of the Median throughout that person's education and members of the Illuminati until the age of thirteen, after this age, they are taught be members of their own Sphere. Those that choose to work in the academic field study the philosophy of the

Ancients, or other such academies of thought that may enable them to come to a better understanding of the world around us.

Due to the almost luxurious conditions in the Illuminati, they live longer than anyone else. Members of the Illuminati may expect to live until their seventies and even eighties.

There are no restrictions on marriage and there is no preference over gender — all are equal. One thing that may be of interest to some is that the Illuminati are encouraged to spend their time on matters intellectual rather than sexual. Subsequently, sex for the Illuminati is for procreation rather than pleasure. It is expected that the Illuminati get pleasure from knowledge. The mind above the body. It seems to me that the Median are the only ones that get pleasure out of sex for sex's sake.

The Illuminati do relax, however. They are intelligent enough to realise that intellectualism constantly is a strain. The forms of entertainment that they opt for are similar to that of the Median, but often, more elite in style and content.

I must leave off now for there is no more room on this sheet of paper. Tomorrow I will tell you of those in our society that do not fit into the groups that I have mentioned and whose very existence is still denied by some.

3

As much as some people might like it to be, the world is not a textbook and things do not always fit so easily into rules, guidelines and laws. I may have painted a picture of the Spheres of our society that makes things look very much as if they are from the pages of a textbook. In some regards they are like that. People are in their separate Spheres and for the majority, they stay in those Spheres; but there are instances that occur when people break from their Sphere of their own free will, or those that are born to a Sphere in which they do not belong and cannot exist; these last peoples are then forced out of their Sphere by their would-be companions.

Those that are forced out of their Spheres become the Pariahs. They are outcasts that are considered anomalous and not to be tolerated. The Pariahs are usually those people from the Median or the Illuminati, who early on in their education demonstrate a lack of the intellectual requirements of the Sphere. As they are academically useless, they are exiled. You may ask why they are not placed amongst the Residuum so that some use may be made of them, but I do not believe that the Illuminati would like this kind of knowledge to leak through to the Residuum, or indeed to anybody else. As I have said before, revolution requires intellect to succeed and although a Pariah may not have enough intellect to stay in their own Sphere, they could possibly have enough intellect to sow discord among the Residuum.

The only reason why I am privy to this information is due to the fact that the course of my story has led me to gain knowledge that is not in wide circulation, and with that knowledge, as with all knowledge, comes a certain degree of pain.

The Pariahs, with no social Sphere of their own, consequently become a Sphere of their own making. They cannot live any longer on the main land, however, so they are sent in exile across the Waters to a smaller landmass. They are then marooned there. None of their sailorjailors ever set foot on the island. The knowledge of this island is a closely guarded secret. Few know that it exists, even less know where it is. I shall speak more of this island later, for it plays a larger role in my story.

There are those that acknowledge that the Median produces Pariahs on the odd occasion, but you would be hard pushed to find many that would admit to the same coming from the Illuminati. It is certainly something that the Illuminati have never admitted to. They would wish to have all believe that they are pure in intellect and do not produce delinquents. They do exist. For I have seen these so-called delinquents.

There is a sub-division of the Pariahs. It also happens that amongst the members of the Residuum are occasionally born those of an intellect above their position — a natural intelligence. Members of the other two Spheres are quick to realise the danger of an intelligent member of the Residuum. The Residuum are kept subversive, but if a member could stir aggression, the whole Sphere could erupt into revolution as easily as a spark from a tinder box could start a fire.

Subsequently, the Overseers have strict orders to watch carefully for anyone showing Pariahan tendencies. Anyone suspected may immediately be executed by their Overseers. With this threat of arbitrary death hanging over them, it is not surprising that the Pariahs from the Residuum seek refuge in an underground existence where they may escape all influence from the Spheres. These people live in a secret existence. They live by resistance and by black-market profiteering. There are members of the Median that are, in extreme circumstances, prepared to go to these people should they need something that cannot be obtained elsewhere. This is by no means an everyday occurrence, for it is dangerous to communicate with these people and prosecution awaits any member of the Median caught communicating with them. However, the Resistance (as they like to be called, in order to distinguish themselves from their exiled cousins), have many contacts among the Median and, so it is rumoured, even masquerade as members of the Median on certain occasions, a disguise that they seem to find effortless, if dangerous. They work themselves into positions where they may serve the Resistance and any member of the Median that requires their assistance will probably find that it is not very long before a member of the Resistance finds out about it.

How else do you think I am able to record this narrative?

**

I think I have almost said enough about the formation of our society and I will soon return to the telling of my story and that of Evie; but before I continue my original narrative, there is one other thing that I should mention and now is perhaps as good a time as any to mention it.

There is something that unites all of our people together, regardless of the Sphere that they come from. That unification is fear.

There is a fear that covers our land and clouds our history. I have already mentioned the risk of disease that can be found among the Residuum; but I have not mentioned an illness that cares nothing for class barriers. We call it simply, the Virus — although there is nothing simple about it.

The Virus is a disease that we know next to nothing about. We do not know how people contract the disease, but there is much speculation as to the possible means — few of which have any grounding in medical fact. These speculations are allowed to grow, however, chiefly because of the fact that despite their research, our medics are not able to provide us with any information. Truth be told, I don't think that amount of research has been done into the Virus. Too many people are too scared of it to want to look at it so closely. It is something that breeds fear.

This is something that I have since discovered is of enormous frustration to the Illuminati, who feel that they should have the answers to everything. This ignorance is something that they really do not like to have to admit to. The most intelligent will admit that they are ignorant of some things; nobody can know everything, but this is not a philosophy that the Illuminati adhere to.

So, we are not entirely sure how a person may become infected with the Virus, but when they are, it soon becomes obvious. The symptoms are not always the same and there are cases when a person may be infected, but the Virus will remain dormant for many years; so those infected, may for years, show no or only gradual symptoms. Subsequently, there are people who can continue to play an active part in

27

society, consciously or unconsciously subjecting those around them to possible infection also. It is this fact that causes the most fear in the majority of people.

Subsequently, whenever anybody develops even the slightest illness, a panic may result for both the patient and everybody else. More often than not, these illnesses would turn out to be nothing more serious than a cold. But in the past, many possible Virus carriers were lynched by frightened mobs before this could be determined. We have evolved a little since then; but not much.

Some fifty years ago now, our medics developed a blood test where they are able to determine if an illness is the Virus or not. Anybody who becomes persistently ill, or has an illness of any duration which is not easily diagnosed is expected to turn up for this test. It has to be said that it is statistically proven that the majority of those tested prove to be negative carriers. However, every now and then somebody will test positive. There is nothing that can be done to help these unfortunate people. They may live with the illness for many years (cases have been reported where the patient lives for up to fifteen years) or they may die quickly. To die quickly is the best that can happen.

There appears to be no reason for these attacks. At the beginning, the medics were entirely incapable of treating the Virus because of the sheer ignorance as to the correct procedure. People in perfect health, from all manner of strata, suddenly began to have burning sensations; their eyes became bloodshot, inflamed and sore; ulcers appeared in their mouth and their breath became unpleasant. Next, the stomach was affected with pains and frequent vomiting occurred with great pain and difficulty. The skin became covered in ulcers and lesions that would appear and then disappear over a long period. The skin became highly sensitive so that even the lightest touch of clothing could prove unbearable. Many, in these early days, died, by plunging themselves into cold water to relieve the burning sensation, and subsequently drowned due to the inability to save themselves.

All of the time they are afflicted with insomnia, night-sweats and the feeling of aching bones which made them restless and uneasy. From here, the Virus descended into the bowels, producing painful ulceration and uncontrollable diarrhoea. As a result, much weight was lost and, in some circumstances, hair began to fall out for reasons that were not apparent. It was as if the body was rejecting everything in an attempt to rid itself of the parasite.

From here developed mental illness. Dementia set in; immense fluctuation in temperament and even in some advanced cases, full-blown insanity. In lesser cases people lost their memory, faculty for reason, use of sight or simply became catatonic. All eventually die. With no exceptions.

It is now known that the Virus manifests itself in various forms and not all of the symptoms above may be experienced by a sufferer; likewise, there are many kinds of peculiarities that seem limited to individual cases that I have not included. Many attempts at finding a cure have been attempted, but what did well in some cases, did harm in others. Those who are strong are no more able than the weak to resist the Virus, which carries away all. The Virus has no care for our social Spheres and will take Residuum and Illuminati alike. Death is the only equality that exists.

The Virus is terminal. There is no cure. There are no forms of medicine that will slow the procedure or even help to make the patient more comfortable. With each passing stage of the disease, the sufferer will begin to feel increasing pain. Some will reach the level of insanity before relief finally takes them over in the form of death, but in an ironic way, insanity is a relief from the Virus.

Those that test positive are immediately placed in isolation carriers. They are then taken to the north of our landmass and they are left at the path of a mountain range. Across the mountains is the aptly, albeit unnecessarily melodramatically named, Valley of the Damned. Here, far from any populace, live a small tribe of Virus sufferers. Damned never to see a healthy person again. The luckiest ones, are those suffering from the advanced stages of the Virus. They climb as high as they can and fling themselves to the rocks below and there they are left to rot and for carrion birds to feed upon. I am told the stench is almost unbearable. Rotting corpses in various states of decomposition.

Although we are not completely sure as to how the Virus can be contracted, medical theory gradually began to teach us that it probably wasn't by direct contact with another person. Logic dictated that it wasn't airborne — otherwise we would all be dead by now. For many years it was believed that it could be contracted somehow via touching an infected person, but this has been proven to be false. How many people does one-person touch in a day? If this were how to become contaminated then the numbers of those suffering would again be higher. It has never stopped the hysteria though and the over-reaction to the illness that people have who feel that they have come into contact with someone who suffers from it.

Over the years, these points have helped to relieve the hysterical fear that was felt for so many years; it would be wrong to say that it has entirely taken it away, however. In some cases, it has swung the other way and there are even those now who have adopted the attitude of 'if you are going to get it, you are going to get it, and there's nothing that you can do about it'. This may well be true, but that only makes risk of random infection all the more frightening.

So, although we are almost positive that you won't be infected by being in the same room or by physical contact with an infected person, there is still much that is not understood about the illness. This is why even today, the sufferers are still sentenced to the Valley of the Damned, an action born of an inherited fear.

***

If my story becomes a little confused from time to time, I must apologise, but I am finding it difficult to remember what I have already written down. There are times — mainly at night — when a sudden flash of information comes to mind and the desire to record the information is great, but there may be no paper left; so, I just have to make a mental note to include it at a future date. I forget to, of course, and when the same piece of information is recalled in my mind at a later day, I have trouble distinguishing between that which I have already recorded and that which I meant to record, but didn't. Subsequently, a reader may find that in some places I am repetitive and in other places I leave out vastly important facts and events. I recognise that this is something that may be the cause of much annoyance and frustration, but please try to remember, that it is no less annoying and frustrating for me. Few, if any, of us are actually perfect.

I feel that I have strayed from my story for too long and it is about time that we moved on. I realise that it was important for you to know about the life that we live and I have tried to give an impartial view of what it is like. No doubt there are many questions that you would like to ask on matters that I have or have not covered; matters that are perhaps of a personal interest to yourself. I apologise. I have no intention of writing a textbook. I can only do what I can, the way that I can to the best of my abilities.

If I remember correctly, the last event that I narrated for you was our marriage. It is probably of little interest to anyone but myself for me to embark on a detailed description of the life that we led after our marriage. With that in mind I shall refrain from doing so. There is, after all, little point in narrating such events that are only incidental to the main events that were to follow later. Suffice to say that after our marriage, there existed an epoch of idyllic life or at least, that is how it seems to me now. We do so often tend to look back into the past with a rose-tint in our eyes; but in this case, I do feel that it was the happiest time of my life.

On saying that, I am entirely unable to exorcise the memories of Evie from my mind. She continues to haunt me to this day and it is a haunting that I could not be happier with than I am. I remember fragments of memories that I am unable to place in a period or context. Running along after being caught unexpectedly in a rain shower. Sitting in front of a log fire in a cabin somewhere in the mountains. So many memories. So few to follow.

This entry today will not be a long one, because I have spent too much time tonight reflecting in self-indulgence. The only thing that it is important for me to mention in this entry is Doctor Asa.

Asa was a great man. He was Evie's uncle. Asa was a tall, well-built man with broad shoulders. He could easily have been an athlete or something, but instead, showed a natural talent towards medicine. He was a big man, but he was very nimble and moved with the grace of a cat walking through a display of china ornaments. The man had 'presence'. You knew that he had entered the room, even if you were not facing the door. He was also a very gentle man. I don't believe, that in all the years I knew him, I ever heard him raise his voice to shout; he never needed to. On the rare occasions that people — perhaps irate patients — felt the need to shout at him, he would simply stand impassively meeting their eyes with his own fixed, slightly myopic gaze. Eventually the other person would run out of steam and grind to a halt. At that point, and only at that point, would Asa explain in a quiet, reasonable voice the logic of the situation and a solution would be found. He was not someone that it was easy to argue with.

Doctor Asa was a man that was probably too intelligent for his own good. When you met the man, you were immediately aware that he seemed to know more than you did. He didn't need to say anything (indeed I never heard him boast that he knew more than anybody else and he welcomed discourse with people with experience not his own), it was just a state of mind that you became aware of, the moment that you looked into his eyes. There was a natural calmness and intellect about him.

The reason I'm telling you about Doctor Asa is because he is to play an important role in this story. His importance first came into play when I arrived home one day after a particularly arduous and mundane day. I was looking forward to a relaxing evening with Evie. Nothing was particularly planned but I thought it would be an opportunity to do what we liked to do best; which was spending time together.

As I walked into the hallway after closing the door, I immediately knew that there was something wrong. Asa was standing at the end of the corridor with a look of concern on his face that I had never seen before. This immediately made me worried. I put down my things and approached him.

'What is it?' I asked, as I slowly walked towards him. 'What's the matter?'

For a moment he did not answer and looked at me with concern and I gained the distinct impression that he was trying to work out the best way to tell me something.

'It's Evie,' he finally fumbled out.

'What? What about her?'

'She's ill. I think it's serious.'

4

We had been married for twelve years when Evie had suddenly developed an illness that was to prove persistent. She had never been this ill before and it came as a great shock to the pair of us. The moment that I had stood in the hallway and was told the news by Doctor Asa, I was shocked to the core. Immediately, of course, I became deeply worried that it might be the early signs of the Virus. Old prejudices will haunt us.

Standard procedure when encountering illness is to firstly identify what type of illness it appears to be. For instance, if it is a cold, or something slight, then it will have cleared up within a few days and there will be no need to worry. If it doesn't clear up, or becomes worse, then a doctor must be called who will take the blood test. If the test is positive then the next course of action is as I have already described. If the test is negative, then the doctor will be free to diagnose an appropriate course of action to combat the minor illness.

Thankfully, the panic because of illness these days is far less than it used to be. It is logical to remember that there are many illnesses out there and not everyone who becomes ill has the Virus. Anxiety is limited mostly to the patient and their relatives. Sheer logic dictates to us that if a victim of the Virus infected everyone they came into contact with, then there would be no doctors left alive. There are, of course, those that will panic at the thought of even being near a possible victim, but these are just the kind of people that will panic at anything. They are also the same selfish individuals that care only for their own unlikely danger of contraction and not for the very real danger that the potential victim might be in.

The major concern for the family of a victim nowadays, is not the risk of catching the Virus themselves, but the welfare of their loved one should they test positive; for not only will they suffer great pain, but they will also have to suffer the law and be exiled from all and everything that they have ever known. There has never been any suggestion that the law is fair, or just.

Evie was a very strong-willed woman and almost always was able to manipulate me into doing whatever she wanted. Subsequently, when after three days her symptoms had not cleared up, she absolutely forbade me to call in the doctor. I consented to this, even though you may think it very wrong of me to do so; but you never knew Evie and my devotion to her, meant that I would have done anything for her. We were aided a great deal by the fact that Asa was a doctor and could assist us, although the morality of him acting as a doctor for a relative was something that was strictly forbidden.

After three more days, I persuaded her that we should call in her uncle. It seemed logical that we should get the blood test out of the way so that we could discount the Virus and proceed with the treatment for the real illness. She agreed and now the two of us stood facing each other in the hallway.

It was late in the afternoon and the sun was setting. He had given Evie as thorough an examination as he could and said that he would return first thing the next morning to conduct the blood test. I could see by the look on his face though, that he already expected the worse.

During the course of that long night, we lay together with me holding her and comforting her as best that I could. I don't think that either of us slept all that much during that night.

The following morning, Asa arrived at nine. Overnight, despite the lack of sleep, Evie had started to show some marked signs of improvement. Consequently, be it because of a professional belief, or because of deference to his niece, Asa did not conduct the blood test. Instead, he prescribed that Evie should be given plenty of liquids and he would return each morning and evening to check on her progress.

We did as instructed, and much to the delight of everyone, Evie was back to her normal self again within a few days. We all heaved a great sigh of relief and continued with our everyday lives. The incident was momentarily forgotten and we laughed at how foolish we had been to think that there was something more serious going on.

***

It has been some time since I have had the chance to write. Alpheus informed me that he had managed to get word that a security clamp-down was about to take place. It is supposed to be policy that all guards are given a search as they leave and enter the compound; however, because this is a very time-consuming process, it is hardly ever done, otherwise Alpheus would never have been able to start this process in the first place.

From time to time, the compound is subject to an external inspection. If the slightest thing were found amiss then the governor would be in serious trouble. Fortunately for the governor, word usually reaches him when an inspection is about to happen. Although the exact date is hardly ever known, it is usually possible to be within a few days. So, when an inspection is expected, the whole compound is placed on a tighter security regime and the rules are strictly abided to. Subsequently, for the last ten days I have not had the chance to continue my account.

These inspections really are the most pointless of exercises. The inspectors are surely not so stupid as to believe that the way the compound is perceived on the day of their visit is the way the compound always operates. During a visit, all members of staff are on a higher level of alertness. All the rules are obeyed with the utmost diligence. They all pay such meticulous attention to detail that if they were to do so all the time, the job would never get done. Less than forty per cent of them would make it passed the main gate in the morning before it was time to undergo the process of going home.

It has also caused me much amazement that an inspector could seriously hope to inspect anything during the course of one day. It can't be done in such a short period of time. If you are going to have inspections, then the inspectors should stay longer and live with the staff. Observe everything. Otherwise, it is a farce. It always was and I imagine that it always will be. Stupidity and a distance from reality is part of the policy of the ruling classes.

Still, I must be thankful that they don't spend longer here; otherwise, I would be separated from my writing for an even longer period of time. As it is, I have become very frustrated at the time lost, because of this latest, external, fact-ignoring expedition.

It strikes me that the writing of this account has become something of a comfort to me. I find some degree of solace in these pages that I shall never see again. That surprises me; I would never have thought that it would be possible to become so engaged. It just goes to show you that even when you think that there is no hope there is always something that can take you by surprise.

***

What is the most painful: to lie to a loved one, or to have a loved one lie to you? To me it seems to be a very close-run contest. Ultimately, it depends upon the nature and content (and indeed, context) of the lie.

We are taught for the sake of morality that truth is always the best policy, but there are times when to tell the truth, will cause too much pain. It is usual for the person about to tell the lie to be the one in pain, either physical or mental, or both. They may choose to lie because they know that the truth is something that will only cause pain to somebody else. One person in pain is bad; what sense is there in spreading the truth if it means that two people will be in pain because of it? Under these circumstances, it is better for the one who holds the truth to protect the one they love from a situation over which they have no control.

In love we may lie to protect our loved ones from pain; yet each time we lie, we cause ourselves more pain. Yet, truth always seems to have a way of working itself into the open eventually. It is usually at this stage that the situation turns. The person who has been lied to receives double the pain. First of all, they share the pain that the other person has been hiding, and to this, is added the pain of realising that you have been lied to.

Evie lied to me.

She kept the truth from me for three years. She lied because she knew that she was ill and she knew that my knowledge of her illness would not ease her suffering, but could only serve to increase my own.

Evie never made the full recovery that we believed she did after her initial illness. She chose to keep secret her growing illness and her own diagnosis that she had, in some way, contracted the Virus. Many will say, and have said, that her secrecy over this information was highly wrong and immoral. I have said that the reason she kept her silence was because she did not wish to burden me with her sorrows until there was no alternative. Others have stated that she kept silent because she feared that I would have her ostracised.

This is not true. Evie would have known that I would never have betrayed her. She knew that I had sworn to be by her side, and such an oath would have meant us both leaving society hand in hand, or staying together and damning the law. I have always attempted to be a law-abiding individual, but without any hesitation or qualms, I will always place the woman I love above any law. I would rather betray humanity, than betray my wife; any lover would do the same, and I loved Evie more than I loved my own life and certainly more than I loved the society that I lived in. If you would not do the same, then I pity you and suggest that you examine the relationship that you are in more carefully, for it may not be all that it seems.

Due to the fact that we do not entirely understand the nature of the Virus, it has been argued that Evie's silence could have resulted in her contaminating me. I would she had. Evie was an intelligent individual. She knew the risks and she knew even more of the prejudice and ignorance that surrounds this disease. If Evie had felt, that her remaining with me would endanger my life, she would have left without another thought; were it not also for the fact that Evie knew that her leaving me would cause me far more pain than any that would be caused by illness.

All is academic now. Evie chose to keep her illness from me and I understand why she did so. I do not condemn her for this action; I could not condemn her for any action. Evie kept her silence for three years after her first signs of illness. Many people believe that I must have been aware of her illness during this time. It is not so. Perhaps I hid the facts so that I would not have to confront them. However, in my defence — should I feel the need to offer one in these circumstances — the illness only became more pronounced after this time and during this three-year period, Evie took great care to ensure that no subtle signals gave her away.

To begin with, I was the only one that was in a position to notice the signs of her illness when it became more pronounced. Later, the signs would become more apparent. I confronted Evie, not out of any fear for myself as has been callously suggested, but out of fear for Evie. She told me of the full nature of her condition and we talked until the small hours of the morning and then as the sun rose on the next day, we cried in each other's arms. Each crying for the other, with neither of us giving a thought for ourselves.

It was then and there that we decided to take no action in this matter. We would wait to determine how events unfolded and then we would decide what the best course of action would be. In some cases, no action is the best action. Subsequently, at this precise moment, in the eyes of the law, I became as guilty as she was supposed to be.

The law means nothing in these circumstances. The law does not understand the nature of love. It does not recognise the acts that will be done in the name of love. The law is a heartless, callous machine and it is nothing to me. Only those who have loved can understand what love really means. If anyone reading this is on the side of the law in condemning us, then all I can say is that I feel pity for you. It is obvious that you do not comprehend the nature of the greatest and most essential quality of existence.

***

It was not so very long after the worst was known that Evie approached me about a subject that took me by surprise and caused me great anguish, both at the time and ever since.

Late one night as we lay together, she turned to me.

'You know that there will soon reach a stage where this illness is going to become very painful and also impossible for me to conceal any longer.'

'For *us* to conceal any longer,' I corrected her. I wanted to remind her that we were in this together, rather than because I had a need to correct her grammar.

'For us,' she acknowledged as she lightly touched me. 'I cannot bear the thought of being sent away from you. From being ostracised for the rest of my life.'

'I will come with you,' I replied, as I stroked her hair.

'You can't do that. You know that don't you?'

'Yes, I know,' I admitted. It is true that they would not have allowed me to join her. The law has no compassion in these matters.

'They will use every force that they can to stop you from going after me.' I couldn't deny the truth in this.

'Before it reaches that stage, before the worst happens there is something that I want you to do for me,' she continued. She obviously had something on her mind.

'I would do anything for you, you know that,' I replied. She nodded her head as if to admit that this was something that she had always known.

'Yes, I do. I want you to do something and I know that you may find it very hard to do, but I need you to help me with it, because I am just not strong enough on my own.'

'What is it, my love?'

'I want you to help me to end my life.'

What could I say or do? At that precise moment I froze and my entire body turned to ice. I could not even consider the possibility of killing Evie, or even standing by as she died by her own means. I would sooner have given up on my own life.

I was in a situation that had no possible way out. How could I help Evie to kill herself? How could I kill that which I care more for than life itself? Yet, how could I stand by and watch Evie suffer an agonising, ignoble and painfully slow demise? Who is the person that would precisely and immediately know what to do if they had been in my situation?

The prospect terrified me and I hugged Evie tightly as I realised that this was a subject and a situation that she had been living with for such a long time. This was no idle thought for her. This was the painful admission from somebody that had spent months deliberating on the subject. How many times had she wanted to broach this subject? How many times had she backed down because the moment was not right? For how long had she lived with her terrible knowledge eating at her soul? Desperately, she must have wanted to talk to me, in order to help ease her suffering. But she always held back, because her first thought was always for my well-being, just as mine was for hers.

This was not the rashness of someone who was unaware of their situation. We both knew that her condition was not going to get any better. We knew that there was no hope for a recovery and that the only thing that lay in store for her was pain and persecution. Under these circumstances perhaps her thoughts were more rational than you might think so from someone else.

I held her in the darkness.

'I have always done whatever I could for you and I will continue to do whatever is best and whatever you ask,' I whispered softly to her. In the darkness, as we held each other tight, I would be hard-pushed to state which of us felt the most pain. What is certain is, that in all of the fifteen years of our marriage, we did not cry as much as we did that night, but not as much as we would cry before our marriage was over.

5

We agreed that the wisest course of action would be to keep Evie's condition as secret for as long as possible. However, there are some secrets that require the help and advice from others. So, just as Evie reached the stage where she had to tell her secret to me, we realised that there would be at least another two people that would have to know about the tragedy that had befallen us. The question of trust was obviously of paramount importance, but we both knew that we would not be able to face the days ahead on our own.

Firstly, we would have to let Evie's uncle, Doctor Asa, know of the situation. Asa's love of his niece was higher than the love of the law and he would have done nothing to cause her any harm. We would need the knowledge of a doctor to keep Evie as comfortable as possible until the time came. We would also need somebody to falsify the death certificate and avoid an after-death medical examination. We knew that Evie's sudden death would raise suspicion and on examination, would have shown that she had been suffering from the Virus and that she has died from unnatural means.

Asa would also be able to help to fabricate some non-fatal illness that Evie could be said to be suffering from so as to explain her withdrawal from public life; otherwise, people may have started to become suspicious that she was not about so much. Obviously, there were illnesses that existed that were serious enough to warrant a degree of isolation and recuperation without being illegal.

Secondly, if Evie were to be helped to die then it would be necessary to obtain some kind of deadly poison that was strong enough to kill a person. Such substances are not available to purchase in everyday life. However, such illicit substances are available through the Resistance. It is known that some members of the Median indulge in the highly illegal activity of recreational substance assimilation. These substances in a vastly reduced form are still harmful — if taken over a long period —

but for the immediate consumption, provide a brief period of elation. I have never felt the need to indulge myself, but I am aware that it goes on.

Subsequently, I would have to find out the way in which I could contact a member of the Resistance and then find out the best way of getting enough of the substance required to kill Evie. Understand that this thought process and later course of action was not easy for me to take. It is not even easy for me to relate the events now, so many years later. If I sometimes sound cold and dispassionate when talking of these times, it is only because I must give you fact as well as emotion. Do not doubt that my heart was breaking at that time and do not doubt that it is still irreparably cracked, even to this day. My plan was not so easily formulated either. For quite some time, I could think of nothing to do and was a total mess and entirely unable to organise any kind of thought. My rational plan, as it may seem now, was something that I gradually worked out carefully over a period of time.

Until this time, I had had no contact with the Resistance in any shape or form whatsoever, so far as I was aware. Yet, if the wheels were to be set in motion (for it was unknown how long it would take to obtain the opiate required, or indeed how long it would be before it was required), I would have to take somebody into my confidence as soon as possible. The only possible candidate that sprang to my mind was that of my life-long, best friend, Simeon.

I knew Simeon to be as like-minded as myself. I knew that the knowledge of both Evie's illness and our intended course of action would not send him running to the authorities. He would either pledge to help us or he would pledge to have no more to do with us. I hoped for the former and I dreaded the latter. I was entirely confident, however, that he would not turn us in.

We met one night and we both indulged in a liberal quantity of aqua vitae, but not enough, I hasten to add, to dull our senses. With my courage backed up by the spirit, I told Simeon of all that had taken place and what Evie had asked of me. He was naturally very shocked, more so by the knowledge of Evie's illness rather than her request. He was quiet for some time whilst the enormity of the situation sunk in before he finally replied.

'Yes, of course I will help you.'

When I informed him of my problem, he exceeded all my expectations of hope when he told me that this was a matter that he felt he could, in some part, help out with. It was indeed fortunate that he was able to help me in this matter, but I wish with all my heart that the day had never come when I would have to seek his, or anybody's help, in such a dreadful matter as this.

Simeon informed me that he knew of a man in the Resistance that would be able to supply the quantity of opiate required. A meeting could be arranged between the two of us when I deemed it necessary. I did not, at this time, ask how it was that Simeon knew this man. I merely accepted that my path was set and I began the painful journey to bring myself to being resigned to the fact that one-day soon, I would have to kill my wife.

**

Obviously, I have no idea of what kind of person you are that is reading this. I have no idea as to the kind of society that you live in and speculation upon the subject is a futile activity that will gain nothing. All I can say — if I haven't mentioned it already — is that the kind of activity that Evie and myself were contemplating, was highly illegal. We had broken some laws already, but that was only the start. The first law to be brushed aside was the concealment of Evie's illness. A considerable number of years ago it was decreed illegal to conceal infection by the Virus. If you have read this far, it may well be obvious to you that Evie and myself had absolutely no problem with breaking this particular law.

It is also illegal to commit suicide, but to me this law has always been ineffectual. You can only punish somebody that has failed in their attempts to kill themselves. How can you punish somebody that is successful in their attempt? Suicide is considered to be a transgression of the morals of society. It is forbidden for an individual to take their own life, but it is not forbidden for the lawmakers to take that life from you, if they so decree. Those that particularly wish to do so, will revel in the moral double standard of this situation. It makes a mockery of those who make the laws.

Punishment for attempted suicides is to place the individual in solitary confinement, where they are slowly starved to death. Some may think this a harsh penalty, but after all, it does give the criminal what they were ultimately looking for. How many punishments are there that reward the criminal with that of which they broke the law to achieve? Also, by slowly starving the criminal to death they have plenty of time to contemplate the error of their ways. To die quickly means that you do not have the luxury of contemplating exactly what death may mean. By this punishment, you are able to learn too late exactly how precious life really is. That is the rationale behind the thinking of this law, at any rate. I will leave you to draw your own conclusions on what you think of it.

As for those that are successful in killing themselves? In this instance their family is forbidden the normal rights of burial as they stand. The rights of mourning are denied to the family and death faces them if they breach this law. The corpse is then taken and displayed in selected areas throughout the landmass. It is left there to rot. Anybody that takes it down to bury it becomes subject to the laws of execution. These laws are strict, but as we are used to them, they do not appear as harsh to us as they may to those of a different society; or perhaps by your standards these penalties are very light.

An equal punishment is that given for murderers. Any person found to have unlawfully killed another would be either executed or detained for life, depending upon the nature of the case. There is no case of appeal for convicted murderers. Life means life and death means death. There is no hope of release, other than that afforded by death. If Evie and I were to go through with our actions, we would be breaking both of these laws. Evie would be guilty of attempting suicide and if I help her in any capacity, I would be guilty of murder. If I were being truly lawful, I should have notified the authorities that she was contemplating the crime of suicide so that she could have received treatment. The sheer fact that I had kept this secret, meant that I was already guilty of having committed a crime in the eyes of the law. Betrayal of Evie was the only crime that I was concerned about; besides, if I had of told the authorities what she was contemplating then the nature of her illness would have become public. Naturally, I had no intention of telling them anything if I could get away with it.

Even though Simeon had pledged to help us, we did not act

immediately. The situation was not yet that grave. Simeon and I would often sit and talk about the moral implications of what was taking place. That is not to say that Simeon was having a change of heart, or attempting to change mine. It was just that the philosophical nature of what we were doing gave us something to talk about. If anything, the intention was to try and convince ourselves that we were doing the right thing.

In a sense, the four of us — Evie, Simeon, Asa and I — were all guilty of breaking the law by knowledge of the situation. Evie and I were committed to the situation and there was no debate to the contrary. Asa was needed because, if we were to get away with it, we would need his medical skills and knowledge, qualities that Asa very quickly lent us along with his full support, the moment he realised what was actually going on. Simeon would provide the contacts in the Resistance, but that was all I would allow him to do. It would be I that would buy the opiate. I could not risk Simeon being traced to buying these illegal substances. If we were all caught, there might still be a chance that Simeon would escape with no one aware of his part in the 'crime'.

I still am unable to call it a crime in all seriousness. As far as I am concerned, the law is incorrect on this point. It is a crime, however, to stand by and see your loved one suffer when there is something that you can do to prevent that suffering. It is a crime to willingly permit your loved one to be exiled to a terrible, miserable end. It is no crime to love. I would never have agreed to help Evie, if there had been any chance of her recovering from the illness, but this was not to be. The condition is terminal. The Virus is a killer and it has no mercy.

***

The days went slowly by. Eventually, the days added up to weeks, the weeks accumulated into months. Evie's progression of illness was slow, but marked. To another less attentive observer, the signs may not have been so prominent, but I believed that I was able to detect them. I know that Evie was trying her hardest to lead as normal a life as is possible, for anyone who is living under a sentence of death. She shrugged off all help offered, only giving way to receive help for those tasks that even she had to confess were now beyond her abilities. She did not require pity. She required dignity; and I was doing all that I could to ensure that that was what she got.

Gradually, the physical signs of her illness began to manifest themselves; however, it was not yet time for the opiate. Evie was not prepared to give in at the first hurdle. The physical ailments at first were very slight. I suppose that the first physical sign was a slow loss in weight; nothing too drastic and noticeable. It was, however, clear to both Evie and myself, that she was gradually, but steadily, losing weight.

Secondly, there appeared the first of the lesions of the skin. These were really only very slight at first. They started as tiny, dark blotches, no bigger than a fingernail. These first appeared on the torso; it was therefore, easy for Evie to keep them concealed from everyday scrutiny.

It was not so very long after this time that Evie began to grow tired. Sleeping was difficult for her, despite the tiredness. She would desperately crave eight hours of solid, uninterrupted sleep; but her condition did not make this possible. Consequently, the feeling of extreme tiredness was to become enhanced by the growing lack of sleep. Strenuous activity of any kind was fast becoming an impossibility for her.

The manner in which I have listed these symptoms may make it sound like Evie had quickly gone from her normal self to the state that I have described. I would ask the reader to remember that this was a gradual transformation over a long period. The symptoms advanced so slowly that those who may have seen her each day and not known her condition would not have noticed any marked change in her. The change was really only noticeable to those that had not seen her in a long time and those like myself, that knew what to look for.

Being isolated from general life as she had become, would obviously increase the danger that when she did, on the rare occasions, come into contact with someone from the outside world, that they would be more likely to notice that there was something wrong. This was the kind of thing that made everyone suspicious of everyone else, as everyone was a potential informer and everyone was a potential "criminal". This is the life that we led.

I also would not want to disgrace her memory by suggesting that she handled this situation in any other way than the best she could. I never heard her complain once. I never heard her curse or blame anybody for the condition that she was in. I truly believed that the only thing that she took issue with, was the fact that she would be leaving me alone. Other than this fact she seemed resigned to her fate. It is as if she had long ago come to terms with the fact that this was her fate and as there was nothing that could be done about it, the best course of action was just to continue for as long as was possible. I doubt that I ever knew, or will ever know, a braver person than Evie.

Although I tried my very best not to think about it, I was aware, at the back of my mind, that the day was approaching when I would have to get hold of the opiate that would be needed. We didn't talk much about what was going on. Some of you may say that we were living a life of denial, but we never really looked at it in those terms. It is true that we did live under pretence, but it was really the only way that we could successfully move from one day to the next.

Even though we were living a pretence, it would be false to say that we were not changed by the situation. We didn't go out as much as we used to do. It had been agreed early on that it would be wise to prevent as many people as possible from discovering Evie's condition. Thus, Evie lived under a form of self-imposed exile from the rest of the world. On a sub-conscious level, I now realise that we were going out of our way to spend as much time with each other as we could; whilst we were still able to. It was not evident to me at the time, but looking back now, I believe that it motivated us a lot.

***

Eventually the time came, as we knew it would, when I decided that it was necessary to obtain the opiate that would be needed. Although Evie did not yet require the dose of opiate, I considered that it would make more sense to obtain it now. My chief reason for this was because there may have been trouble obtaining the substance and I could not stand the thought that Evie would be suffering sustained pain because I am unable to provide the opiate. With all of this in mind, I contacted Simeon and informed him that the time was right for me to meet his sources in the Resistance.

Two weeks passed after this time. Each day, I contacted Simeon, in the hope that he had some news to tell me, but each day, there was no news. Simeon was having difficulty getting the message through to his contact. He explained to me that it was more usual for the Resistance to contact him than the other way around. Simeon could always be found by somebody in the Resistance, but because he did not know the specific location of any Resistance member, he would be unable to betray them should he be arrested. Whenever, like now, he needed to contact them, he would leave a message at a pre-arranged location that would be spasmodically checked.

Eventually, Simeon was able to inform me that his source had been in contact and that he had explained my requirements to him. No answer had been given straight away. Presumably, the Resistance would be doing some research into my background to discover whether or not I was likely to be a threat to them. All that could be done now was to sit back and wait to see what would happen next. All in all, I seemed to be doing little else but sitting around waiting. Thankfully, although Evie was still ill, she was not so bad that the need for the opiate had reached a necessity. I was glad that I had not waited until the last moment before requesting Simeon's help. The thought of all this helpless delay whilst Evie writhed in agony, was more than I could have stood.

Simeon had originally suggested that he should be the one to obtain the opiate personally; he would then pass it on to me. I rejected this plan, however. I could not bring myself to place Simeon in any further danger than he already was by helping us. If Simeon had been caught with the opiate on his person, I don't think I would have been able to live with myself for the consequences that would have followed. It would be much better if I were to take the personal risk of making direct contact with the supplier. I also suspect that this was partly because I was slowly being driven crazy by my inactivity. Everybody else seemed to be doing something, and I felt that if I didn't have a task to occupy my mind, then I would have surely run mad. Also, it would be necessary for someone with Simeon's contacts to stay safe. If I were captured, then somebody else would have to make a second run for the opiate; and if Simeon had been captured first, I would not have known the contacts.

Thankfully, it was only a few days later that Simeon informed me that a meeting had been arranged between me and a member of the Resistance called Azarias.

6

My meeting with Azarias was to take place the next day. Simeon provided me with an address that was located firmly within an area frequented by the Residuum. I have to confess that I felt a certain amount of trepidation about having to go so very deep into Residuum territory, but all fears were quenched by the fact, that what I was doing I was doing for Evie, and I would have gladly walked into worse places for her.

I don't have the time or space to tell you of my journey to meet Azarias; I am also not convinced that it bears any real relevance to my narrative. Nor do I particularly wish to provide any detail that will help those who are against me find and persecute those who have helped me. I should perhaps just leave it at the fact that I travelled among some of the harshest conditions that I had ever seen at that point in my life. There is no form of mechanical transportation that is prepared to penetrate so deeply into the Residuum. Consequently, the bulk of my journey had to be made on foot. This was not particularly hard, but it did take me almost half a day to reach the address that I had been given.

I managed to pass reasonably unnoticed by trying to disguise myself as an overseer, so that I might not draw too much attention. The most difficult thing that I found was walking in this unusual place and trying to make it look like it was something that was natural and that I was used to. My disgust was something that I found very difficult to hide, but I hoped that I pulled my role off sufficiently, so as to not draw any suspicion to myself.

The address was what would normally be assumed to be a derelict building by many people, myself included; but I have come to learn that among the Residuum, there is no such thing as a completely abandoned building. The Residuum lives where they can and how they can. The Residuum cannot afford the luxury of allowing anything to go to waste. Everything can serve a use. Although there appeared to be nobody about, I could hear shouts coming from somewhere. What came as a surprise to me was that the shouts were not those that were raised in anger or even in anguish, but were those of what I imagined to be children playing. It was the most unexpected and alien sound that I ever imagined I would hear amongst the Residuum. Life continues and develops in all manner of circumstances, regardless of how appalling those circumstances might be.

The building itself was a large block with small windows. The building ran around a large area that appeared to have been designed at some point for recreational use. This area was now mostly filled with rubbish and abandoned, useless possessions of the long-since dead that couldn't serve a use, even among the Residuum. Across this courtyard from one building to the other, could be seen the occasional washing line that could be reeled in from whatever side you were on. There were many staircases and ladders running up and across the buildings allowing access to the individual apartments that were housed therein.

The staircases did not appear to be entirely safe. It certainly appeared to me that it had been many long years since they were last maintained; if indeed they ever had been. I had come too far, however, to back away at such a silly obstacle. I therefore began to climb the staircase that was fixed to the outside of the building. I climbed for a long time and passed many floors, all of which appeared to be totally deserted. I assumed that the occupants were either at work somewhere or were asleep in preparation for their next shift.

I passed the walls which were chipped with large sections of plaster that had fallen and been left in disarray. Clearly, there was no need for anything within the Residuum to be repaired. Things decay in nature, it is what happens, yet it is our vanity that makes us repair and patch things up. To try and make the transient last forever. This was something not followed by the Residuum, who left the rot and the decay to take its own course.

Eventually, I arrived at the correct floor; it was, like all the others, totally deserted. I looked over the balcony and noted that I was many stories up from the courtyard and for a moment I felt giddy at how far up I was and how dilapidated the infrastructure was that I was standing on. I consulted the piece of paper that Simeon had given me, and I worked my way along the floor, until I came to the door that had the correct number chalked on it. I knocked on the door and it opened at my touch. I pushed it open further and was immediately hit with a stifling heat which was almost unbearable. I looked into the room and was rewarded with the view of a shabby room that had piles of laundry in various states of wash scattered about. Several lines of washing criss-crossed the room from wall to wall. I cleared a path through the washing and found a woman situated in the epicentre, engaged in the task of sorting through the garments. She looked up at my approach and, not seeming to be the least bit surprised by my appearance, immediately returned to her work; as if I were of the least significance imaginable.

I was so taken aback by this lack of action or response to my appearance that I could do nothing but stand there feeling extremely foolish. Realising that my companion was not going to take the initiative, I coughed and informed her that I had come to see a man called Azarias. She merely nodded her head and without a single word, indicated a small door in the corner of the room that I had not previously noted. Aware that I would not gain anything else from her, I nodded my thanks and worked my way across the room to the door.

The door opened on to a small room that contained a number of bundles of material on the floor that I realised served the residents as beds. Aside from these, the room was entirely empty with the exception of a ladder in one corner that led to a small hole in the ceiling. As there didn't appear to be any reason for staying in the room, I cautiously climbed the ladder.

The ladder led up to an attic that was much larger than I would have expected. I realised that this was because the attic must have run the length of many apartments, not just the one that I had passed through. The ceiling in the attic was low and punctuated by the odd tiny hole that allowed just enough light through to permit vision — although not enough to completely see to the corners of the attic. I could not, however, conceive of any immediate circumstance that would make me want to see into the corners of the attic; I didn't know what was there, and I didn't really care, so long as it chose to stay there.

A few seconds after I had climbed into the attic, a man appeared out of the shadows. He was dressed in black, wore a tightly-cut beard and was smoking. He came within two or three lengths of me and then stopped. We faced each other for a few moments as we sized each other up.

'Why have you come here?'

'I'm looking for a man called Azarias,' I replied.

He asked me why I had come to this place. I told him.

'What is it that you want from this Azarias?'

'I'm hoping that he might be able to give me something that I want,' I realised that I was going to have to be jumping through a number of hoops. I suppose that I could forgive the element of caution.

'And what is it that you want from him?' I told him. 'Such things are illegal and difficult to obtain. Were you to have such an opiate then it would be both dangerous for you and for this Azarias, of whom you speak.'

I chose not to say anything, but waited, prepared to stare him out if needed. It occurred to me that he might need to be cautious and not reveal too much, but I had already revealed a great deal about my intentions if this were proved to be a trap. Without anything else, there would be enough information to land me in very serious trouble.

'Who sent you?' I replied to this question as well, not giving Simeon's name, but an alias that Simeon had told me to say.

He then proceeded to ask me a series of questions, many of which were of a personal nature and related to Evie, which although it made me uncomfortable to be talking like this to a stranger, I felt that I had no option but to answer any questions that he chose to ask me. After an interrogation of some ten minutes or so, he nodded his head and stood looking thoughtful for a few moments, motionless, with the only exception of his continuous smoking of his tobacco that never seemed to extinguish. He continued to spend a great deal of time weighing me up before coming to his own conclusions.

'I am Azarias.' I had never thought anything different if I was honest, but I nodded my head.

He reached into his inner pocket and withdrew a long, thin, flat box. He paused once again; obviously making a final evaluation before he reached the point of no return. He opened the box and withdrew a small vial of clear liquid. He replaced the box in his pocket and handed me the small vial in his outstretched, yellow-stained hand. I was doubtful that the contents of the vial would suit my purpose, and he must have guessed so by the expression that I gave.

'There's enough for what you have told me, providing that what you have told me is the truth.'

'It's the truth.'

'It's unlikely that you will need more then; besides, if you require more, it will take more time to acquire.'

I pocketed the vial and handed over to Azarias the correct amount of credit that Simeon had told me to bring. He nodded, pocketed the credits and without saying another word, withdrew into the shadows.

It was like he had never been there.

***

Considering our business to be concluded, I made my way back down the ladder to the room below. Upon reaching the bottom, I was more than a little surprised to notice that the beds were now all occupied. I had not been in the attic for very long, but during the course of my brief meeting with Azarias, the workers had returned and had immediately gone to sleep.

I stood frozen at the foot of the ladder for some minutes, but none of the occupants of the room seemed aware of my presence and I strongly felt that if they had seen me, they would not have cared in the slightest. I feared them, but they could not have cared less for me.

Nevertheless, as quietly as I could, I crossed the room and opened the door that led to the room I had first entered. This room was slightly different as well. Much, but not all, of the washing had disappeared along with the washerwoman as well.

Outside it was already beginning to grow dark. I shivered slightly in the early evening air and replacing my hat, I began the long climb down to the street below. As I began my descent, I was aware that the voices I had heard on my way up were no longer to be heard. As a matter of fact, there was nothing, but deathly silence, which unnerved me greatly. By the time I had reached street level, the darkness was setting in.

At the level of the street, there appeared to me to be an even greater silence. I had never fully realised until this moment that there are so many different grades of silence. My hearing seemed to me to have become super-sensitive. I strained through the silence, desperate to hear a sound, any sound. At that moment, I actually believed that even a sound of danger was preferable to the emptiness that I was experiencing.

The mind likes to play tricks on us from time to time. There are moments when it likes us to believe that we are in danger when no such hazard actually exists. At other times, it likes to lull us into a false sense of security, allowing us to believe that we are in no danger, when in reality, our very existence rests in the balance. However, such knowledge and understanding of the tricks that can be played by our inbuilt paranoia did not help me to discover which situation I was now in. I desperately wished for a sound to be made. If I was to hear a sound of danger, I would at least be able to focus my mind on dealing with the problem that was being presented. This silence that I heard, merely served to fuel my over-active imagination, into worrying about a whole host of dangers, that probably didn't exist.

I hurried through the streets with the advance of night approaching steadily. I do not mind admitting my fear that I was experiencing at that time. My fear was two-fold. It was certainly true that I was fearful for any threat that might be presented by the Residuum; although I admit that there wasn't any actual evidence to suggest a threat from the Residuum, it nevertheless did not lessen the fear. It is even possible that the absence of any threat was more worrying than any actual threat. I suppose I had just been conditioned from an early age to somehow expect the Residuum to present me with some kind of threat.

My second fear was more pressing. Up until this moment, even though I had broken the law with reference to my part in the concealment of Evie's illness and my contact with Azarias, these were offences that may have been possible to deny under a plea of ignorance. However, if for any reason I was stopped and searched by the authorities, the discovery of the opiate on my person would cause serious complications. The opiate is a highly illegal substance and it weighed heavily in my pocket. It might well be thought that my fear of discovery was for my own safety; I admit that this may have been part of the fear, but I was also very aware of the fact that Evie was depending on me. If I should be caught at this time, I was more fearful for what would happen to Evie.

As it happens, and I am grateful for it, my fears were unfounded. My journey home was as uneventful as my journey out; with the exception that I was now carrying the means of killing my wife.

***

Over the weeks that followed, Evie's illness became more pronounced. By this stage, it had become virtually impossible for her to hide the true state of her condition. This, naturally, caused her some difficulties. She hardly ever ventured outside any more, and on the days that she did go out, it was only on her best days, and even then, she was heavily disguised. It became necessary for her to shun the majority of her friends and acquaintances. Nobody ever saw Evie that we couldn't trust, but even then, only Doctor Asa, Simeon and I knew the true nature of her condition. I now suspect, however, that there were some kind-hearted, un-superstitious people that secretly suspected the truth, but never once mentioned their suspicions or asked questions that might have been difficult to answer. There were also, possibly, those that decided that they would not keep silent forever.

Once or twice I discussed Evie's condition with Doctor Asa, but never in her company; Evie still refused to talk about her illness. Her determination to carry on as best she could and as normally as she could, was still as strong as ever. The news from Doctor Asa was never good. Evie's condition was indeed growing worse day by day. It was really only a matter of time now.

On the times that Asa, Simeon and I would meet, we would often just sit in silence; each of us isolated to our own individual thoughts and hopes. Hope had not entirely left us. It may seem strange, but even though we all knew that Evie's condition was terminal and that there was absolutely nothing that any of us could do to reverse this; we still clung to our own hopes that some miracle would happen and everything would once again return to the way that it used to be.

Looking back now, I strongly believe that this belief in hope, even a forlorn belief, was the only thing that held me together and enabled me to keep moving through the darkest period of my life.

Subconsciously, I must have been aware of the fact that even though

I could cling to Doctor Asa and Simeon for support and Evie could cling to me, eventually it would only be me that went to give Evie the lethal concoction that would end her misery; whilst continuing mine.

Evie knew that I had been able to obtain the opiate, but it was a subject that was never discussed. It was there for when it was needed and that was all that any of us needed to know. Evie herself was not about to give up until she was placed in the position that gave her no further choice. She wanted to hang on for as long as she could. The pain meant little to her and she had no fears about bracing the pain until the end; but she also knew, that as her condition grew worse, the physical symptoms of her illness would become permanent and prominent.

At the present moment, Evie's physical symptoms fluctuated in their appearances. Lesions would appear one day, but were just as likely to disappear a few days later. Evie knew that Asa would have trouble denying that she had died from the Virus if the physical symptoms that are unique to the Virus were too prominent after she had died. Even in her worst hours, Evie was thinking of how the rest of us would cope. Also, it must be said that one of Evie's few voiced fears was that dementia would set in before she died. It had always been one of Evie's fears that she might one day lose control of her brain faculties. She once told me that she wanted to die knowing who I was and feeling the same emotions for me as she had always done.

It was with all of this in mind that Evie woke me up one morning with the devastating news that she considered the time had come for me to help her to die.

7

I have spent many hours running through events in my life, trying to determine that I did what was the right thing, and if I didn't act correctly, trying to work out if there is anything that could be done to remedy the situation. Many will point out that this kind of activity is fruitless. There is no way that we can turn back the clock and do things differently, no matter how much we may wish that we could.

One of the most difficult things that it is possible to do is learning how to live with yourself inside your own mind. Regardless of all else, we are ultimately answerable to our own minds. We make our choices throughout our lives and we always strive to do what we think is right and moral. We make attempts to ensure that our conscience is clear so that we can sleep well at night. All else may rest easy if we can convince ourselves that we have done everything in our power to do what we believe is right.

However, there are times when despite it all, we can't be sure that we have done absolutely everything that was in our power at the time. In many circumstances, it appears to be a case of act now, repent forever. Therefore, it is illogical to waste time thinking about how different things could have been. This is all true and I do not deny it. We are not, however, a logical species. Regret, or if you are in denial, reflection, will eventually catch up with us and win in the end. As you may imagine, Evie occupies my thoughts a lot, both now and regularly over the course of the past fifteen years or so. At the time, I was completely convinced that I had done everything that I could to ensure that the right thing was done, but the sheer magnitude of the situation, unlike anything I had dealt with before, made it impossible for me not to keep running the situation over and over in my head.

The bottom line is that I miss Evie and I would do anything possible to bring her back again, and to have things the way they were before all of this started. It is so often the case that we desire the most that which we cannot ever hope to have. The greatest pain that love can bring is that caused by having to learn how to live without it. Some of our great academics choose to write long papers on how it is better to have loved and then lost, than it is to have never loved at all. So, these great minds proclaim upon a subject that I have great trouble believing that they have ever experienced outside of their ink and their papers. I have great trouble with this hypothesis of theirs. I have great trouble with these writers who write the life rather than actually living it.

I am not convinced that I am entirely better off having lost my love than never having had it. It is true that Evie brought me the greatest happiness that I have ever had, and where as I wish everybody could be as happy as we were, I would not wish the pain I feel now on my worst enemy. I cannot help but feel that if you have never loved, then you do not know what it is that you are missing, and although never having loved may generate pain of its own, it can never be as great as that suffered by loss. You can't miss that which you have never had.

We must therefore, all learn to live with our choices and with the consequences of our choices; although it is certainly true to state that we can never completely be aware of the consequences of our choices at the time when the decision is made. Many things may result as a consequence of our actions and what may seem like a simple decision at the time, may generate a whole wealth of consequences that we could never have dreamed of.

As I believe I have already mentioned, Evie had chosen the best time to end her life when it would be easier for those of us left to cover up the nature of her illness and subsequent manner of death. The truth, of course, was that no matter when or how it was handled, it would never be an easy task to undertake.

Some may wonder why it was that Evie did not just decide to take her own life without any assistance from the rest of us. There are a number of reasons for this. As I believe I have previously mentioned, suicide could have some dire consequences if caught. I believe that Evie cared little for herself, but did not wish that I should have to suffer the ignominy of witnessing her starve to death in a cell if she failed in her attempt; nor that I should be refused the rites of mourning should she succeed. Evie, therefore, needed me in case the attempt went wrong and

Doctor Asa for the necessary certificates afterwards. Everything must be handled correctly; I certainly had no desire to see Evie's corpse hanging in public as an example to others. I couldn't have cared less what they did to me.

Yes, I suppose she could have flung herself from a tall building or done something that would have made it easy for her to act alone, but we were a couple. We did things together. I am sorry if that is not easy to understand.

Many people will put forward the opinion that we had already violated our moral conduct code, but if there is one thing that I have come to understand, it is that morals are unique to the individual. Each of us must act on a set of principles that we are comfortable with, not those set down by others; it makes no sense for anybody to be forced to follow morals that they find immoral, it defeats the nature of morality. We must set our principles and then live by them and live by the consequences of them.

I have learnt that there are many doctrines that we can fundamentally agree with and which look nice when written down, but which we are quick to discover can fall apart when put into practice. For example, one of the Ancients' doctrines, was that we should always sacrifice the one to the needs of the many. This doctrine seemed perfectly reasonable and valid to me once; but if I were to live by this doctrine, I should instantly have denounced Evie so that she could have been ostracised to secure the safety of the many. Many may still think I should have done this; but it is a cold-hearted individual who will sacrifice the one he loves above the fate of the faceless multitude. Given the opportunity of betraying the multitude or betraying Evie, the multitude will lose each time. At the end of the day, we must all live with and answer to ourselves.

Soon I shall be describing to you the events that took place the day that Evie had made her choice and I had to make mine; but I have recorded all of this beforehand, so that you know in advance that this was not a decision that any of us involved were treating lightly. We all spent many sleepless nights before and after the events of that cold, winter night so long ago and yet so very recent inside my own mind.

It might be considered selfish by some, but there are times when I cannot help but weep when I think of how alone I have become; but I know that if Evie could see me like this, she would weep as well. It is never a consideration when you first meet. You are both taken with each other and everything is wonderful and exactly as it should be. It becomes natural for you to consider that you will be spending your whole lives together. It never occurs to you at the time, that one of you may be left to live out the long remaining years alone.

Evie died when she was forty-two and I was forty-four. When she died we had been married for sixteen years. I have now lived for fourteen years without her, but each day in that time, had appeared to me to be tenfold its actual time.

***

When Evie told me in the morning that the time had come, she had in mind the fact that we would be able to make the most of our final day together. Evie did not want to have to make the decision suddenly so that we had no, or little, time to say our goodbyes to each other. It would be a painful process.

It was her reasoning that by this way, everything that needed to be said could be said and everything that needed to be done was done. It was also at the back of her mind that the day would serve as final preparation to the event. Although some would have no doubt have preferred no build up, she knew that both of us, myself more than her, would need to build up a tremendous amount of courage to carry through the events that the evening would bring us. The trouble is that there really is no preparation that can be done, to sufficiently cover you for the task of surviving the death of a loved one. Naturally, there are many more added complications that no preparation can cover when it has been deemed that you are to take an active part in that loved one's death.

Evie remained deeply concerned as to how I would cope with events before and after her death. She hoped that I would be able to draw on enough courage to be able to see me through the darker days ahead. I immediately tried to counter this by pointing out that Evie was the one who would be requiring the most courage. She diffused this argument by making an appeal to intellect. On many occasions during our marriage, we had talked of the ultimate reason for why the world had been created and why we were working our way across it. Evie pointed out to me that since the dawn of time, people had tried to unravel these great mysteries, but the answers were not so easily forthcoming as the questions were. Evie pointed out that courage was not needed to make this final leap, for if the answers were ever to be found then the only place that ultimate knowledge could be found, would be on the other side of life.

Evie saw life as partially being the means to gain as many questions and as much secular knowledge as possible, before it was time to move on to the next stage of the learning. Evie emphasised that this didn't mean that she was eager to leave me and this world; but she pointed out that I should not feel fear for her. None of us knew what would happen after death, or if anything would happen, but Evie promised me, that if there was an existence she would be waiting.

Evie did not want this final day to be one of regret, remorse and premature mourning. She rather intended that the day should be spent in the celebration of her life and in a celebration of our marriage. It may have been possible that Evie could have lasted a few weeks longer before she was entirely consumed by the onset of the final stages of the Virus, but the decision was hers to make and she rightly opted to make that decision whilst she was still able to rationally do so.

There are a number of people that have argued that even if the taking of one's own life were not unlawful, a person such as Evie should not be allowed to make the decision to die. These people claim that at a certain point during illness, rationality leaves the mind and rational decisions are not possible. I have difficulty in following this view.

From experience, I am of the mind that each person should be allowed to make the ultimate decision of their own life or death for themselves. You wouldn't really expect me to say anything else under the circumstance. People attempt to remove the responsibility from the individual so that we no longer have the right to life and conversely, if we have the right to life, we also must have the right to death. I have heard people use arguments such as if you take your life a cure might be discovered for your ailment or you may just get better naturally.

In my opinion this is just blind optimism. It is hanging on desperately in the hope that something magical will cure the incurable. The decision of life or death of an individual should rest with that individual. At the end of the day, it is their life to do with as they choose. Conversely, there are many recorded incidents when those who have commanded armies have been very free at throwing away the lives of other people, but there has been no criticism of these people. In my view, each person should be responsible for making the decision as to if they should live or die. What we should outlaw are those people who take it upon themselves the responsibility for making decisions as to whether other people should live or die; or whether other people should have the right to live or die.

Briefly, in the morning of that final day, Doctor Asa and Simeon came to visit Evie and without making it obvious, said their final farewells. It had been agreed that when Evie died, I would be the only one with her. In the eyes of many, this would be a scene of a crime and the fewer people that were implicated by their presence the better it would be. Before leaving, Asa instructed me in the correct procedure for administering the opiate. Ideally, Asa told me, he should have stayed in case there were any complications, but I persuaded him that for the sake of appearances, it would be better if he acted as if he knew nothing of Evie's condition until the time that I sent for him later in the evening, so that he could complete the necessary death certificates. If need be, it might still be possible for me to feign that I was the only one that had knowledge of what had taken place and the others could be innocent bystanders.

Upon the departure of Asa and Simeon, Evie and I found ourselves alone. As Evie was now too weak to leave her bed, I sat beside her and held her as we talked over our reminiscences. I was worried that we would slip deeply into melancholy at this stage, but Evie desired that this should be a time of celebration and we soon found that we were laughing deeply at the reminiscences that we were coming out with. It may be suspected that the laughter was hollow and contrived, but this was not the case. By some miracle, we had been granted the dignity of celebrating the last hours of Evie's life in the manner that she had lived it. I was pleased that Evie had been allowed this small epoch of peace so that she could prepare herself for her death in the manner that she dictated. This was particularly important to me in view of the events that immediately followed.

***

Simeon and Asa had been gone for some time when the first signs of evening began to make their appearances. Although it was winter, the night was calm, even though it was very cold. Evie and I had spent the majority of the day talking over our shared memories. As the first of the stars appeared in the sky, I drew back the curtain so that Evie could see them from where she lay. She gazed at them in wonder of the infinite nature of existence. She wondered what lay beyond the stars and if it were really true that they were the homes of the dead. She told me that the stars were most likely to be her destination. From that point, she could look down on me and I could look up at her, and regardless of what happens in the future, I would know that she was always looking out for me. If I were ever to feel lonely, all I had to do was look up at the stars to know that she was with me. The thought gave me some comfort.

I closed the curtain and silently hoped that Evie's sentimental view was the correct one. There was really no delaying now. This was the moment that we had both known would eventually be upon us. I had believed that I had done all that I could to prepare myself for this moment, but now that the time had come, I suddenly realised how futile all preparations had been. I quaked at the knees and my stomach turned over. I was working fully to keep everything under control and not show fear to Evie. Whatever I was going through, it must have been worse for Evie; but even at this point her strength, courage and determination amazed me. I drew strength from her and we began to place in motion the plan that we had so carefully worked out.

Firstly, I once more hugged and kissed Evie and she assured me that we were doing what was right. I then left the room to fetch the dosage of opiate. This was where the difficulty lay. The opiate was an unpredictable substance. The opiate reacted differently to each person that it came into contact with. One dose may be enough to cause unconsciousness in one person, but instant death in another. It was for this very reason that it was illegal. There were those that heavily watered down the substance and used it for recreational purposes, but even in this state, there was still a high chance that it could have fatal results for the user. With practice and experience it was possible to develop a more detailed knowledge of the kind of dosage that would be required to suit your purposes. The problem was that I had neither the experience nor the means to practice, in order to discover what would be correct for the purpose that we needed it for. I hoped that there was enough provided to give Evie her peace in a quick and painless manner, but I was scared, in case the dosage would not prove enough to defeat Evie's constitution. You might suggest that to have been on the safe side I should have acquired as much of the opiate as possible, but the opiate is both rare and expensive. I had brought as much as I could afford, and I just had to hope that it was enough.

I removed the opiate from where it had been hidden and took it back to Evie. She indicated to me that she was ready — we had passed the stage for words; all that could be said, had been said. I nodded and uncorking the vial I handed it to Evie. It had been agreed that Evie would be the one to actually take the opiate and that I would remain on hand in case anything went wrong. Evie looked at me and then in one swig, swallowed the contents of the vial.

For a few moments there was no result and I feared that the effort had been a failure. However, soon Evie began to cough; slowly at first, but with increasing violence. She then began to choke and struggle for breath. It became very apparent that the opiate was only of sufficient strength to cause a violent and possibly prolonged reaction. Evie was aware of this and through tear-stained eyes, she looked at me pleadingly as she writhed in pain. It was a look that would have pierced any living being to their very core. It is a look that I had wished that I had never seen and it is a look that I will never forget for as long as I live.

I could not stand it any longer. I rushed over to her and grabbing a pillow, I pushed it over her face and pressed the entire weight of my body down to drain the air from her. For a short while, Evie continued to cough, but then her arms grabbed me around the shoulders, not in defence, not in attack, but in a last embrace. Then all movement ceased and she lay still.

At this point, all my emotions flooded out and I cried into the pillow and wailed for forgiveness for what I had done. For some moments I remained like this until I had the courage to remove the pillow. Evie's arms fell from me and I looked once more on her face that could no longer see me.

With tears streaming down my face, I slowly closed Evie's eyes and kissed her. I sat holding her, slowly rocking backwards and forwards. All of my grief, all that I had hidden from Evie from the moment that I discovered her illness up until this moment, flooded out and I could do nothing but cry and begin the mourning that I have still not completely come to terms with.

I looked through my tears at Evie's face and was startled to see the radiance that she still possessed, even in death. She looked as if she was now finally at peace. All of the pain had gone. I can close my eyes — even now, all these years later — and I can still see the peaceful expression on Evie's face. Though my grief was manifold, I consoled myself with the belief that Evie had finally found the release that she had so deserved. Perhaps, at last, Evie was beyond the stars.

At the back of my mind, I was aware of the fact that I should contact Asa, but for the moment, all that I could do was hold my wife for the last time. It was then that the realisation hit me that I no longer had a wife. For the first time in over twenty years, I was without Evie. I had killed the one person that I had ever loved above all else and I was completely and utterly alone.

8

They are becoming suspicious again. Alpheus has just informed me that one of my fellows here tried to escape this morning. The punishment for this is severe, but it is only natural really. If you are going to confine someone against their will it seems only natural to me that they will have a duty to attempt to free themselves. Conversely, I have not sought my freedom, because I have no reason to want to be free. What have I left? Freedom, for me, can only now exist within the limits of my own mind; perhaps it is the only place that we have ever been free, but I had not rationalised it until now. The outside world holds nothing of any attraction to me.

We may view it as a duty to escape, but the powers in charge take a very different view of the matter and anyone caught trying to obtain freedom, will be rewarded be being freed of their life; which in an ironic sense would probably make a lot of them very happy; or at the very least, happier. Either way they get to be released. It is just another example where the system has no logic to it. The thing is, the law rarely has any logic. It is designed by men who think they know better than anyone else. They control the world from little rooms and pass judgement down on others who will always show more courage than they ever did.

The problem that faces me is that the measures to tighten security after this last attempt, could result in problems for Alpheus in removing these pages that I write. I recognise the importance that my recording of these events has for Alpheus and his people. I know that he is prepared to take more and more risks to ensure that I am allowed to record my story.

Up to this moment, I have just recorded the events connected with Evie, but none of us could have foreseen that the death of Evie was not the end of my troubles; but just the start of them.

Evie was dead.

Dawn slowly began to approach and with it came Doctor Asa. I told him of the events that had taken place the night before and tears filled his eyes, as he searched for words that he might be able to use to comfort me. At such a time as this, words become superfluous. The common bond of mourning binds us all and we share the empathy of the situation that renders words inadequate, hollow statements.

Asa ordered me to go into the other room and make myself something to drink whilst he completed the paperwork that would register Evie's death and make the arrangements necessary to have the body taken away. I left the room with the knowledge that I would never look on Evie again.

It was at this time that the real shock of the situation completely kicked in. I sat in a dazed state; only vaguely aware of the gradually increased activity that was taking place around me. I became distanced from the whole affair. It was as if I was no longer taking part in the situation, as if it didn't concern me. People I did not know came to consult with Doctor Asa. They signed forms and discussed preparations. I was an actor with no part left to play.

Nobody talked to me. I was dimly aware that as I sat in silence, Evie's body was removed from the house and that somebody was changing the bed sheets. It seemed bizarre to me that somebody would think to change linen at such a time as this. It seemed bizarre because it was, with hindsight, a rational thought, and at the time, I was as far from rational thoughts as it was possible for me to get.

I suddenly became aware that Simeon was sitting opposite me. I honestly had no idea how long he had been there. We sat, again without the need to say anything, each with his own private thoughts. Later in the day, the authorities came to talk to me and ask some questions about Evie's death. I answered their questions and told them that Evie had been suffering from a long-term illness that had unexpectedly claimed her life. This was, of course, very close to the actual truth. If you are going to lie, it is safer to get as close to the truth as possible. It also helps to have a good memory.

Asa had falsified Evie's medical records to show that she had been suffering from a mild illness that had irreversibly damaged her internal organs. Asa went on the record to state that Evie had chosen to keep this fact limited to a small number of people, a perfectly legal choice considering that it was a disease not harmful to anyone else. Asa also informed the authorities that Evie had undergone a blood test and it had been negative. Asa also showed surprise that her death had come so suddenly. He cursed himself and told the authorities that if he had known she was this close to death, he would have insisted on some form of medical care. The authorities told him that he was not to blame and offering me their condolences, left satisfied.

We had kept as close to the truth as possible, only lying — or as Asa phrased it, showing economy with the truth — on two matters. Firstly, concealing the true nature of her illness and secondly, the nature of her actual death. Two minor points that could see us all hang.

That night both Asa and Simeon offered to stay with me rather than see me left on my own, but I insisted that I would rather be alone. Reluctantly, they left with the promise that they would return in the morning.

That night I didn't sleep much. I lay in my bed that now seemed too large and listened to the rain as it lashed against my windows. My tears ran down my face as if they were competing with the rain that was streaming down outside; and all the time, I was over-consciously aware of the seemingly, screaming silence of the empty space next to me that would never again be filled.

***

Some of you may ask why it was that I didn't decide to take my own life at this time. This is a matter that I have spent much time thinking about over the years that followed that winter's night. I could spend time weighing out the different moral arguments for and against such an action. As I have already mentioned, suicide is an act that is against all of our laws, but really, such an observation as this is a meaningless comment. All of us were already so far outside of the law it really wouldn't have mattered what I did with my own life. As a matter of fact, my suicide at this stage would probably have counted towards me, rather than against me.

There are those that are of the opinion that the taking of one's own life is an act of great cowardice, but I am personally of the opinion that suicide is an act that requires a great deal of courage. True, it may be viewed as being the coward's easy way out of dealing with situations beyond their control, but I would question the use of the word 'easy'. Surely, whether suicide is an act of cowardice or not, it doesn't diminish the fact that either way it is far from the easy option. Indeed, I think it takes a certain degree of courage to voluntarily launch oneself into the great unknown. None of us truly can be certain of what it is that lies in wait for us after this life. Indeed, we are not even sure that there is anything waiting for us at all. The only thing that we can be certain of is that once we have made the decision and carried it out, there is no turning back.

My reasons for not taking my own life are probably three-fold. Firstly, it is true that I think I lacked, and still lack, the degree of courage needed to take my own life. When it came down to it, I lacked the courage that Evie showed. However, of course, others would argue that I showed greater courage by keeping my head in the situation and not taking the option of suicide. Both hypotheses are correct; both events require different types of courage.

My second reason is because there are those amongst the Illuminati that have long preached that anyone taking their own life will never be reunited with their loved ones, in any kind of existence that may continue after death. Rationality makes me think that this is only a device that the Illuminati use to keep the masses from transgressing the law. However, even though I am not really a superstitious person, I decided not to take the risk of not being reunited with Evie.

Logic, of course, kicks in to inform me that there is no guarantee of meeting Evie at any rate. If there is an existence after death, what judgement will it take on Evie who attempted suicide, and myself who to all intents and purposes, murdered her. There are no secular answers to these questions, but I see no reason to make the situation any worse by taking my own life. It occurs to me that it may be of ironic amusement to some that I was debating the moral implications of taking my own life, when I had just killed my wife.

But the third, and perhaps most important reason for why I did not take my own life, was because of the suspicion that this might raise. I may have been able to pass Evie's death off as being natural, but it was very unlikely that the authorities would believe my death to be natural. An investigation would have been instigated and the possible consequences for Doctor Asa and Simeon may have been grave, literally. Both of my friends were already deeply embedded in this situation, but it would have been an act of sheer madness to do anything to draw attention to them and make their position more precarious than it already was.

All of these factors were important reasons for not killing myself, but this last one was perhaps the most important and immediate of the considerations foremost in my mind. My friends had betrayed the law to help Evie and myself and I was not about to do anything that would betray them.

The times that followed Evie's death was especially difficult, needless to say. For a long time, I must have been deeply in shock, for I cannot remember too clearly what followed that infamous night. There were moments when I actually believed that all of it had been nothing more than a dream. I would go to bed at night and toss and turn, unable to sleep. On the few moments when sleep did not escape me, I dreamt that I was once again back with Evie and everything that had happened over the past few months had merely been a nightmare. At such a time, I would wake and realise that I was living the nightmare and that my dreams were nothing but false hopes.

As time passed by, all I wanted was to be in the bliss of my dreams of Evie, but I soon came to realise that although my dreams created happiness for me whilst I was asleep, upon waking the pain of realisation grew to be too much to live with. So, eventually I even tried to shun the happiness of my dreams in an attempt to make reality more bearable. All is an illusion, of course, and no matter how hard we run and how much we try to disguise it, reality has a habit of catching up with us and making us face the true nature of our existence.

There are those in this life that strive for greatness. There are those that crave the desire to be celebrated. There are those that allow ambition to get the better hold on their lives and direct them to new heights of accomplishment. For as long as I can remember, all that I ever wanted was to be with Evie. I know that there was a time before I met Evie, but when I look back now, I find it very hard to remember a time when Evie was not in my life. It is silly, I know, but it is like she has always been there. It is indeed very strange the way that memory plays these kinds of tricks on us.

Now that my one life's ambition had been taken from me, I was at a complete loss to know what I was meant to do with myself. I had lost all sense of direction and purpose. Some might think that I have a very shallow existence to desire only to be with the one I have loved, but I am not particularly impressed with the idea of being high in the public eye. Perhaps it is true that fame and greatness brings us a great number of rewards, but it also seems to me, that it brings us a great deal of baggage as well, and robs us of some of life's essential qualities. There is a certain amount of privilege and security that comes with leading a life of relative anonymity. I can speak with relative authority on this matter as I have had the bliss of anonymity with Evie and the hell of infamy afterwards.

***

Evie was dead and the realisation of this fact didn't really completely set in until the time that had been set to one side for her funeral to take place. I must confess that I had no hand in the organisation of this event; I was too much wrapped up in my own remorse and feelings of guilt. I can only assume that it was Asa and Simeon that lifted this particular burden from my shoulders.

I had no desire to be seen in public. All I really wanted to do was to crawl away into a deep, dark corner and remain there forever; isolated from everyone and everything. Once again, I can have no idea of the rituals associated with death that your society follows. I can only state that for the society in which I have lived, it is not always considered normal for people to become so completely isolated after a death. There is some form of morbid curiosity that exists where people have to see other people's grief. It makes me sick, for I have always considered grief to be a very private matter, but society insists that we must place ourselves on show at the funeral.

I considered myself to be alone in thinking the entire thing abnormal and abhorrent to nature. I needed my own space to come to terms with Evie's death; not only the fact that she was dead, but also the manner in which she had died. No matter how I tried to intellectually convince myself that I had done the right thing, I could not control my passion from the realisation of what I had actually done. No matter how many good arguments were advanced, I could not come to terms with the fact that this was a black shadow that I would have to live with for the rest of my life.

Many things have happened since that night, but my mind is always pulled back to it. Even now, I still find myself running the events through over and over again in my mind. At times, during the darkest hours of night, I relive those final hours with Evie and I find myself remembering things that happened and very often remembering things that did not happen. Such are the tricks that our minds play on us that it is possible to remember with crystal clarity, events that never actually took place. Since that night, I have run through everything that I am positive did happen as well as several scenarios that I can only describe as 'What if...?' situations. If only I had done this, if only I had done that. Constantly I shift my position, trying to place the blame for the entire situation onto somebody. Society cries out and teaches us that somebody must always be found to blame for everything that goes wrong. Society is always quick to deliver the blame, but I have had to come to terms with the fact, that there is nobody really to blame; but such is our nature and our upbringing, that we must always find somebody whose responsibility it is.

If anything, my final conclusion must be that it is society that is to blame. Society is to blame for being afraid of the Virus and all things associated with it. Society is to blame for not empathising enough. Society is to blame for being selfish and hiding behind its prejudices and archaic laws. Society is to blame for not understanding us and society must be condemned for not helping us when we needed it the most. Society had become everything that I hated. Society represented all that I loathed. Society was responsible for the loss of everything that I had ever held dear.

***

Then came the day of the funeral. The time was upon me and there was no longer to be any delaying, I would be finally forced to show myself in public at the most private of times.

I awoke the morning of the funeral and having washed myself, although not shaved, as is our custom in mourning, I placed on the clothes that had been provided for this instance. Having thus prepared myself to the best of my abilities, I straddled a chair and smoked two consecutive tobaccos as I watched the world pass by my window. It seemed strange to me that there was a world that existed outside. People still went by on their own particular business and spared no thought for me. The world still continued as it had done for countless generations, although I could see no good reason why it should. I felt like shouting out to those passing in the street below, demanding why they were bothering to continue in their everyday lives, when it was so obvious that they must by nature die and none of what they had done or could do would ever matter. Fortunately, I was able to restrain myself from actually doing this.

Simeon and Asa arrived together and came into the room before me.

'It's time,' Asa said as he handed me my overcoat. I nodded.

'Then we should be going,' I replied, as I stood up and we all left to oversee Evie to her final rest.

The funeral was a haze for me, overcome with grief as I still was. Somehow, I managed to make my way through the entire event. I listened to what was said, although I can't really say I heard it; just the usual tributes being uttered by somebody that had never actually met Evie in his entire life. I stood by the graveside and I threw my handful of dirt over the casket and I tore my clothing in the manner of our custom.

Afterwards, many people came up to me and said comforting words to me that I did not hear, but I nevertheless smiled and expressed my thanks on behalf of Evie. People told me that with time, things would get better and I would learn how to live with my pain, but these people are fools and know nothing of life.

There used to be moments in my life when I would become so involved in the wonderful nature of being, that I would just revel in existence. I would look at the world on a sunny summer's day and glory in the wonder of this mysterious creation that appeared to have been created for no other purpose than to bring me enjoyment. At such times

I gloried in being alive. There was nothing else that I would rather do and nothing else that I would rather be.

But that was all in a time of my life that has now long since gone. My glory with creation is something that died with Evie and I suspect it is an emotion that I will never regain; nor do I wish to regain it if I am being entirely honest.

Evie was enclosed in the dirt forever and all I had left were those memories of her that I tried so hard to keep from forgetting. Most of all I remember the smell of her hair. It was the most adorable scent that I have ever come across in my entire life. From time to time, I capture a similar scent and I am fooled into believing that Evie and myself are together again; but it is, of course, not so and I am only being fooled by my senses. Nevertheless, I catch a suggestion of the same fragrance and it is as if all the intervening years had never happened.

Evie was buried in the cold dirt and our separation was complete. It was our hope that we could put behind us all that had happened to us so that we might at least make pretence at continuing with our lives; for what they were worth.

It was not, however, to be. It was not so very long after the funeral that Asa and Simeon came to me and informed me that they had good reason to suspect that somebody had discovered the true nature of Evie's death.

9

Mourning for Evie had been cut short by the necessity to place our thoughts to the situation that we now found ourselves in. Asa and Simeon came to see me a few days after Evie's burial to inform me that they had heard through sources in the Resistance, that the nature of Evie's illness and the manner of her death were known. It was unlikely to be too long before the authorities learnt of this as well. How this information could have been found out was a mystery to us, however, there are those that are always prepared to inform and spread gossip.

Simeon had formulated a plan.

'I think that the only option is that you have to flee,' he stated, as we all sat down to debate the situation. 'You must take refuge elsewhere.'

'I don't see why that should follow,' I replied.

I saw no reason as to why I should flee. Undoubtedly there would be a heavy punishment in store for me if I were captured by the authorities, but my escaping for this reason carried no weight with me. If I were to face punishment for my alleged crimes and possibly death, then that would be my destiny. At the very least I should hopefully be reunited with Evie again. As a matter of fact, death at the hands of the authorities would have been more of a welcome release than a punishment.

'If you are caught,' Asa took up the argument, 'then you will have to stand trial and in such a situation, even though I know you would not intentionally do so, you may be placed in such a position where you might also betray us as well.'

This, to me, was a very different situation. I knew that Asa was not really bargaining for his and Simeon's safety, but rather that he knew that this was the one argument that was most likely to convince me. When one has only oneself to consider, a different path may be forged than when one has to consider the welfare of others. Particularly when those others have already placed their life and liberty on the line to give assistance to me at a time when I needed it the most. At the end of the day, loyalty to my friends and family speaks louder than loyalty to my society and its laws. Condemn me for this belief if you must, others have and there will no doubt be more.

***

'The plan is simple,' continued Simeon. 'I will contact Azarias again and the three of us will leave this landmass with Azarias as our guide.'

'Three of us? You mean four?' I asked.

'I'm not coming,' stated Asa.

'Not coming? But you must. You can't stay here.'

'I'm an old man. It really doesn't matter what happens to me. Besides, if I were to leave as well it would spread even more suspicion over what actually happened to Evie.'

'I don't like the idea of us splitting up,' I countered. 'We should stay together. All stay here together; or all leave together.'

'Think logically for a moment,' he continued. 'I'm a well-known and respected member of society — whatever we may think of it. If I were to leave it would draw far too much attention.'

'I'm not happy with the idea at all.'

'My mind is made up on this.'

Asa's mind was set and when his mind is set there is no way to talk him out of it. I nevertheless tried, but it was obvious that he knew what he was going to do. As I'm sure you can appreciate, we didn't have too long to discuss the matter. A decision had to be made there and then. As I was still trying to cope with my own grief, I allowed myself to be swayed by the others after only a semblance of argument, for I was still used to following the wisdom of those that had guided me thus far. At that point in my life, I was so grieved that I could have been swayed by the slightest persuasion.

Simeon left in order to contact Azarias. Asa stayed with me for some time to offer me words of comfort and reassurance that he would do all he could, to cover our tracks after our departure. I was still not happy about leaving Asa behind and I would like my protest to go on record now, particularly in view of certain accusations that were made against me later on. Eventually, Asa informed me that it was time for him to go. If it were at all possible, Simeon and I would be leaving the landmass the following day. My farewells to Asa had a certain degree of finality about them and a great cloud of sadness hung over the pair of us. It was as if each of us secretly believed that we would never see each other again.

***

Later that same night Simeon returned.

'It is arranged,' he stated, as he drank deep as his arrangements had obviously made him extremely thirsty.

'Where are we to go?'

'It is better that you do not know until we are safe away. As a matter of fact, I do not even know where we are going.'

'You don't?' I was slightly shocked by this.

'No. Azarias is the only one who knows where we are going and it is better for all that it remains that way. For the time being at least.'

I was not entirely sure that I was happy with this arrangement although I could not be entirely certain as to the reason why.

'If either of us are caught then we will not be able to betray the destination of those that have been able to get away.'

'There are others?'

'Oh, very much so, my friend. You are not as alone as you may think you are.'

He was very wrong in this statement though. Since I had lost Evie, I had been alone and I couldn't imagine that I was ever going to feel any different about it. There is a loneliness that exists that runs so deep that you can feel alone, even when in the densest of crowds.

There was little time to lose. Azarias was already waiting for us at the coast. I packed a few things together and left the bulk of my possessions behind. It was then time to leave. I took a last look around the home that Evie and I had made together and then I closed the door on my physical remembrances of Evie forever.

It was a dark, rainy night, but on the whole, our hurried flight to the coast was an uneventful one. In answer to the question; no, I did not feel a traitor turning my back on society and running as a fugitive. I felt something of a traitor at leaving Asa behind; but I knew that Asa's decision to remain was something that he was compelled to do. There would be little gained in making myself feel any guiltier than I already did.

We arrived at the coast a little after midnight. Azarias met us in his usual cloak-like manner.

'We should leave at once lest the authorities catch up with you,' was the only greeting that he gave us.

We boarded an old ship that, like us, looked as if it had seen better days. Without much further ado, we set sail and left the landmass that I had always known as home, but would never truly be able to call home again. From this time onwards, I would always consider myself to be a homeless man. A citizen of no society; but that which I created about myself.

With as little hesitation as possible, we set sail and left the landmass behind. I am no expert on the art of sailing; indeed, I had never been to sea before. What need had there been before this night to go to sea? However, by close observation I was able to notice that the captain of our vessel altered his course several times; perhaps with the intention of losing any would be pursuers; or perhaps the intention was to confuse us passengers as to the direction in which we were travelling.

When we were some distance from the landmass, Azarias came to inform us of his intentions.

'The journey will be long,' he informed us. He seemed to pause for dramatic effect before continuing. 'We will be going to the land of the Pariahs.'

'The Pariahs?' I said, feeling slightly shocked.

'Do you have a problem with that, opiate man?' he asked. I shook my head quickly.

I experienced mixed feelings at this news. I felt some trepidation at the prospect of having to live amongst these peoples, but my intellectual curiosity was also aroused, at finding out what the Pariahs were really like. Despite everything that I had been through there was a conditioning that I had been grown up with that was difficult to shake off.

The calm waters continued to the next day when it was succeeded by a breeze from the west. The wind left us to variable light airs and calms, so that we were apprehensive of being carried back again by the currents. Retarded by contrary winds, calms and currents we were three days trying to make any progress. It seemed that the authorities had somehow managed to harness the elements and were trying to stall our progress. Constantly I was watching the horizon that we had left behind, in case I should spot a distant sail that would indicate a pursuit. I could not help but wonder what activities were taking place back where I had once called home.

We were at sea for no more than a week when I began to notice that Simeon didn't appear to be his usual self. I questioned him and he admitted to feeling slightly lethargic and sluggish. He stated that all he really felt like doing was going to bed. I advised him to do this, and reassured him that it was probably only seasickness; after all, none of us were really used to a life on the sea. Simeon went to his cabin and assured me that he was certain to be feeling better in the morning. We had both read reports from the Ancients of times when sea travel was commonplace; there were often sailors that were taken sick because of the unnatural movements of the ship. Simeon swore me to secrecy; he did not want the rest of the crew finding out about his afflictions and making fun of him.

The next day, upon waking Simeon still complained of feeling extremely tired, even though he had slept long and soundly. He also complained that he was aching in his muscles, particularly around his thighs and loins. He didn't feel he had the energy to get up. On the one attempt he did make to get up he had trouble walking. I advised him to rest, but I certainly could not hide my concern. Simeon told me not to be so silly. He had obviously contracted some sea virus due to the unnatural close quarters that we found ourselves in where the air was so stale. He assured me he was sure to be fine after a few days' rest.

There didn't seem to be anything else for me to do. All Simeon needed was some peace and rest. I left him to sleep and went up on deck. The weather seemed to me to be harsh as I went on deck and lent against the rail where the captain was. I told him that I thought it was harsh.

'This is nothing,' he smiled indulgently at me. 'What we have here is no trouble at all.'

I remained unconvinced and I was certain that the manner in which the ship was being thrown about was the cause of Simeon's illness. The rest of the day passed without any incident. Leaving Simeon to his rest, I talked with our captain. He told me of old sea stories of the Ancients. He told me of a time when a race of people known as Pirates ruled the oceans. In such times, sea travel was a regular activity and the Pirate race would sail without any home, robbing ships on their journeys. All was long in the past now and no such people were around today.

We continued on our long voyage.

***

The next day we encountered stormy weather and I began to understand the mocking nature of the captain when I had thought it harsh weather before. It seemed to me that all the elements had combined together against us. The captain ordered me to remain below deck as there was a very real danger that the inexperienced might be swept overboard. I suspect that he just didn't want me underfoot. I spent my time looking after Simeon whose condition had worsened. He was now having extreme difficulty with his breathing. Even the slightest movement seemed to make him lose his breath. The pain he had experienced in his thighs continued; only now, his thighs had swollen and they became marked with red, brown and purple blotches that were hot and livid. His face had turned to a pale brown hue.

My concern grew at the sign of these symptoms. The symptoms were not really the same as those experienced by Virus sufferers, but as you can imagine, I was particularly sensitive to this subject at the time and my initial reaction was that somehow, and against all the odds, Simeon had contracted the Virus from Evie. Logic, of course, makes nonsense of this hypothesis.

However, whatever Simeon was suffering from, it was now no longer possible to pass off his illness as purely seasickness, for what form of motion sickness could cause such ailments? I informed Azarias of Simeon's condition and he came to inspect him. There was no doctor on board and we were still some distance from our destination. There could be no considerations of turning back as the authorities would certainly know of our disappearance by now, and besides, Simeon would not tolerate any talk of turning back. We were all at a loss to know what to do. We could really do nothing, but sit tight and hope that whatever the sickness was would soon pass.

I sat up with Simeon all that night. His gums became swollen and he complained that they ached and throbbed. The slightest pressure on them caused bleeding. His teeth no longer seemed to fit the gums and they became loose so that there was a danger of them falling out, indeed some of them did just that. Eating or drinking, therefore, became an activity that caused him a great deal of pain. He complained to me of pains all over his body, both internally and externally.

Towards dawn he began to cough up blood. The storm had passed over and the captain came down to see Simeon, as it was no longer possible to stop word of his illness from getting about. The captain was unable to offer any form of help other than that there was something peculiar in the confined and polluted air of the ship. He had seen similar illnesses amongst seamen before and he greatly feared for Simeon's chances.

'In the time of the Ancients,' he said, after he had inspected Simeon. 'A person in as serious a condition as this friend of yours would probably have been thrown overboard, rather than risk infecting the rest of the crew.' I must have looked horrified by what he had just said as he quickly continued. 'Of course, it is not a practice that is employed today.' It would seem that in some ways we are humane, but in others, we still have a lot to learn.

Within three days Simeon's gums grew worse. They began to give off a stench and became inflamed with blood oozing from them. He was no longer able to eat anything, the pain that eating caused had become too extreme. His teeth loosened further and they became yellow, black and decayed. By this stage his body was almost covered in putrid ulcers that seemed to respond to no treatment that we could devise. Simeon tossed and turned complaining of gnawing, stabbing pains which moved swiftly from one part of the body to another.

In the few remaining moments of clarity that Simeon experienced, he was able to tell me not to blame myself for his condition. It seemed that he had become resigned to a fate that he had had some advanced warning of. He told me that he had willingly helped Evie out and if this was the situation he found himself in as a result of his help, and then so be it. If he had to do it all again then he would do everything exactly the same. We had become rebels against our own society. Our society had turned its back on Evie and we had responded by turning our back on society. The needs of the one had overridden all preaching of the needs of the many — as it always does.

***

Our voyage continued and Simeon's condition went from serious to almost certainly terminal. On the ninth day of Simeon's illness, he broke into hot and malignant intermittent fevers, which resulted in vomiting, diarrhoea and dysentery. He began to slip in and out of consciousness and his few waking moments were racked with extreme anxieties and convulsions. He flew from one extreme to the other, suffering sudden fits of trembling followed by paralysis.

I spoke to the captain about Simeon's growing illness, but we were at a loss to know what to do. It seemed now that the end was inevitable; all that we could really do was sit and wait. The captain informed me that we were but two days from land and if we could make it in time there might be some hope that Simeon could be treated. However, I believe we both secretly knew that Simeon was unlikely to make it to see land.

Once again, I found myself in the hopeless situation of watching someone I cared about, being struck down by serious illness. After the death of Evie, I had hoped that I would never again have to watch this process taking place. I could have had no idea at that time that I would have to go through it all again so soon. The situation was hopeless; once again, I was reduced to a situation where I could do nothing of any weight to help. I have always considered myself to be a relatively active person. Whenever I have been faced with a problem, I have always attempted to quickly move to resolve it. In the case with Evie and now Simeon, I found myself confronted with a problem and there was nothing that I could do to try and solve it. Events were very much out of my hands. All that I could do was be with Simeon and offer what limited amount of comfort there was to offer. Hour by hour, Simeon was slipping away from me and we both knew it, even though we never spoke openly of this fact.

Simeon's strength was admirable, like Evie he knew what the result of his illness would be but he never gave in to it. He clutched to life for as long as he could. During these dark hours I found myself wondering if I would ever have the strength that seemed to run through Simeon and Evie's veins. I hoped that I would never be in a position to find out.

During that night, Simeon experienced a brief moment of clarity, during which he actually apologised to me for the state that he was in and the trouble that he was causing. I told him not to be so foolish, but he was convinced that in some way, he had let me down. I did my best to convince him that this was not the case. He had never let me down. As a matter of fact, it was entirely the opposite; he had been there for me when I had needed help and without his and Asa's help, I would never have been able to cope with the death of Evie. This in some part relieved him, but I could sense that he still felt that at the end of the day, he had failed both Evie and myself. Shortly after this, Simeon slipped back into his restless unconsciousness.

Some members of the crew suggested that it would be wise not to spend so much time with Simeon in case his illness was in any degree infectious. This was certainly a possibility, but I had no intention of deserting Simeon at this late stage. I acknowledged that there might well be a risk of contamination. Consequently, although I stayed in attendance of Simeon, I disassociated myself with the rest of the crew. At this stage I cared very little for my own welfare and in a morbid sense, would have probably even welcomed death if it made a claim on me; yet still I was unable to bring myself to the act of taking my own life.

I continued my bedside vigil of Simeon, offering him whenever possible the few remaining words of comfort that I could think of. I talked constantly to him, although intellectually I was convinced that he could no longer hear what I was saying. I recalled the many times when we had held discussions on the meaning of life and the nature of death. In a sense, the pair of us had been amateur investigators into the grey areas of existence. I could have used this time to talk to Simeon and reassure him that he was not going to die, but I saw no reason to delude him. If he could hear me, then he certainly knew that he was going to die at any rate, and if he couldn't hear me, then surely it made no difference what I said to him.

I found myself informing Simeon that he was not to worry about dying. He was merely about to make the next step into solving the answers that eluded us during life. One way or the other, death was the only way that we would be likely to find out if any of our assumptions were true. I talked endlessly, sometimes slipping into incoherence, mere rambling from thought to thought with no logical order. I said that death was not to be feared. If death brought us nothing but a void then there should be no fear. What is there to fear from nothing? If we are annihilated, we would have no knowledge of this fact. If, on the other hand, death was to bring us some form of after-life then this was not to be feared either, for this could only be the start of a great journey of discovery. I realised later, of course, that I was saying these things more as a comfort to myself than as a comfort to Simeon.

Simeon was now beyond any comforting that I could offer; for shortly before dawn, Simeon died and I found my words yielded little comfort for me.

10

It may seem very strange, but it was Simeon's death that launched a chain reaction within me. It had taken all of my ability to keep myself from falling apart after Evie had died. It was the added trauma of Simeon's death that pushed me over the edge. Looking back now, I can clearly remember what I felt, but I can remember nothing external of these feelings.

The full weight and significance of my loss finally hit me. Perhaps for the first time, I became truly aware of what an existence without Evie would actually mean. It finally occurred to me that there was no point in continuing without Evie. Evie had meant everything to me. She meant more to me than I actually imagined she did and I suddenly found the prospect of living without her to be the hardest thing imaginable. She gave me the most precious thing that it is ever possible to give and receive. For a period of my life, I achieved a level that I will never reach again. At the end of the day, she was snatched away from me and lost forever.

I began to ask myself what it was that I should do now, but the very concept of 'now' was lost to me. There was no 'now'. There was only heartache and pain as I desperately struggled to come to terms with my loss. A very small part of me was trying to suggest that I should carry on, but a belief in carrying on and actually executing the means to carry on, are two very different things. It would have been so very easy for me to have curled up in a corner and given in, but the prospect of giving up, was one that I did not find to be too attractive, besides I did not believe that Evie would have wanted me to give up. We all must find ways and means to carry on through the pain. There is no formula; there is no set plan. Each individual must find what the best motivation for them is and then take the gigantic step of putting it into action.

Somehow, I struggled to pull myself together and push my way forwards, but even now, I still feel a pain that I have never found any relief for and perhaps I should not even try. This pain has, by now, become as much of a part of me and my character as any other characteristic and trait that I have. It has become so that I would probably not be able to live without it now. It serves as a reminder to me. I will never be able to love again. I would never be capable of loving again and I would never want to love again. I only have one heart and that was something that was broken a long time ago.

I learnt, perhaps too late, that it is important to cherish every moment, because that moment will never come again. There are brief moments in time that are never to be repeated. It is just unfortunate that we never learn to cherish those moments whilst they happen and then, before we know it, those moments have gone. Slipped between our fingers like water, never possible to pick up again.

I've had time to reflect on this and I am still never sure what is best; to forget, or to remember. I look back on the key memories of my life, most of which are centred on Evie. I cannot bring myself to say whether I would banish those moments forever if I had the power to do so. Sometimes I even find myself wishing that those intimate memories had never happened, purely because of the pain that they cause me now. That is a very selfish comment to make. Of course, I don't really wish that those moments had never happened. Those memories are at the very centre of my existence, I would be nothing without them. It just becomes difficult to live with the pain at certain moments, even if the rest of the time I can look back on them with affection.

The problem that I seem to have, no doubt a common problem that I share with the vast majority of my fellows, is my ability to over think a situation. I am quite convinced that life and the majority of situations would be far easier to cope with if it wasn't for the fact that our thinking over the situation only seemed to create a bigger problem. If I had developed the ability to take things as they were without searching for any form of hidden meaning — or the like, I am certain that my mind would have rested much easier. However, it is our ability to think the smallest trickle of a problem into a gargantuan flood that sets us apart from those less capable than ourselves.

This is a common myth. Those that live their life without encountering, or feeling the need to encounter, the biggest problems of existence are probably far better off than we would care to admit. We could so easily think any situation to contain good or bad elements if we tried hard enough, regardless of whether there are good or bad elements there in the first place.

Due to the nature of his death, it was decided that the best course of action would be to bury Simeon at sea. My memory of this burial service is only a haze in my mind; I was at that point wallowing deep within my own pit of depression. All that I remember clearly was the fact that Simeon now lay at the bottom of the sea and that I wished with all my heart that I was there instead of him.

***

Events are quiet at the moment, which always leads me to be suspicious — but there again perhaps I am drawing too much into the situation. Why it is that I cannot just accept things to be the way they are, I shall never know. Perhaps it is because experience and instinct have taught me that there is usually more going on than is at first apparent anyway.

Alpheus continues to come and talk to me as well as providing me with a means of continuing this narrative. At times, I am too frustrated to continue. The claustrophobia of this place is intense and I know that I will never live to see again the sights that I have seen. Never be free to feel the warmth of a summer day on my skin again. Never feel the coolness of a shower of rain. Never again feel all of these luxuries that so many people take for granted. Just as it took me the death of Evie to realise how impossible life would be without her, it took my being in this place to realise the importance of the simple things in existence that I now miss so dearly.

Life is, however, all about loss. From the moment we are born, we begin the process of coming to terms with that loss. We counteract by trying to gain as much as possible on the way through life, but the end result will always be the same. I don't pretend to be the first person to discover this. I merely state my opinion so that perhaps someone out there will be able to piece together these ramblings and come to a better understanding of myself and why I have done the things that I have. I know that this all sounds very depressing, but this was very much the way that I viewed events at the time, and also how I considered things to be for many years after the events that I describe. Reality hurts. It is not my intention to depress anybody, but as far as this narrative is concerned, I have no real intention other than the recording of the facts as I remember them. Alpheus continues to remind me that this account will be invaluable to generations to come. I fail to see this and it is certainly not part of my intentions. If anything, I am writing this account for my own salvation and to partially explain why things happened the way that they did.

***

With the death of Simeon, I fell into a very reflective period, some might say depressive period. It amounts to much the same. I had lost my wife and my best friend. There seemed to be little point in going on. I realise now that there is always a point in life. We may never be able to see it, but I would like to think that all things happen for a reason. This is all very well said now, but it meant nothing to me at the time. At the time, there was absolutely no way that I could be consoled. At the time, I believed myself to be the most miserable person alive, but this sentiment is nearly always a fallacy.

For most of our lives we are just concerned with our own problems and ourselves. At the time when we are in trouble, our problems seem to be the biggest and most complex that they could be. It is only afterwards that we can truly reflect and realise that these problems are in reality, never as problematic as we thought at the time. There are, of course, exceptions; there always are. However, the gigantic problems that we are confronted with as children, the kind that cause us frustration in our impotence at dealing with them are problems that we can only look back on and laugh at in adulthood. Sadly, this is nearly always due to the fact that one problem or situation is replaced by a far more complex and impossible one. It is the problems that have grown in complexity, rather than ourselves that have grown in competence. So, the world continues to revolve.

I look back on my childhood now and I am not sure if it is because of the fact that I am looking back with the knowledge I have gained or whether I was truly aware of it as a child, but it seems to me, that I was always something of an outsider. I was always aware that there was something wrong with the society that I lived in. Then, like now, I was impotent to do anything about it. I wonder if there is anything that anybody can do. Perhaps if we all think that we cannot change things then things will not change.

The privileged are the ones that will do all they can to ensure that there is no change, while it is the under-privileged that desire and deserve it the most. Change only takes one person, but there are very few people who are willingly prepared to be that one person. At other times, the one person that steps forward seems to be a reluctant person who just happened to be in the wrong place at the wrong time. Circumstances stand to dictate for most of the time what the future will hold. The people that play so grand a part in the future are usually just caught up in the circumstances. Cynical, perhaps, you may think so, but experience is the father of so many things.

The point of it has to be that the society I inhabit is wrong. Maybe I wasn't aware of it during my school days, but I should have been. Day after day, we sat in rows of seats and the wrong things were pounded into us. Society would rather have laws that were fixed, enforced, but wrong, than laws that were ethically correct, but always changing. Our treatment of the Residuum is an obvious example. I cannot be the only one that regards their situation as unethical, but the majority of people are prepared to live with this situation as it is, rather than attempting to come up with a better solution. Enforce the laws of society even if they are wrong, for the simple reason that they are the laws of society and cannot be wrong. Too few people are prepared to question the situation. Too few people are encouraged to and too few know how to. So much is wrong. So much is left wanting.

I stepped outside of our society and its laws the moment I chose to keep Evie's illness a secret. Since that day, I have uncovered more and more reasons for staying out of it. It never ceases to amaze me, however, that there is such a large number of people that are prepared to play the game. By the law of society, I should have immediately handed Evie over to the authorities for something that she could have no control over. By the law of society, Simeon should have handed me over for concealing her illness. Yet we all realised that this was a basic law of society that was wrong and that we could not obey. It makes me wonder how many other laws of our society are wrong and that the only ethical course of action, is open disobedience. It also makes me wonder and gives me hope if there are other people disobeying these laws. Surely, I am not the only person that has turned away from society in favour of a loved one. Perhaps, however, others have been too much assimilated by society and its education that teaches us to place society before all else. In a sense, I was always a Pariah, even before I legitimately became one.

***

We were always told that education was a wonderful thing. The truth of the matter is that our education was a controlled thing. We were only taught what they wanted us to learn. Unrestricted access to knowledge is a wonderful thing, but it is also a very dangerous thing. One of the biggest concerns of our society is to prevent people from being in a situation where they can ask dangerous things and think dangerous thoughts. This is why I have always considered myself to be something of a Pariah. I have always considered it would be an ideal society where everybody would be entitled to have their say in how things are run. I have never voiced these opinions to anyone of course. Our educators taught us that the best system is for total control to be handed over to the Illuminati.

Firstly, they state that the Illuminati are the only ones that can have an understanding of such complex matters as running society and taking responsibility for it. Secondly, the opinion is hammered into us that if everybody had a say in how society was run, chaos would exist. Everybody would only be interested in matters that related to them and there would be no concern for the greater good. There may well be some degree of truth in this statement, but I am sure, as in the case with Evie, there are moments when we must act for ourselves against the greater good. Besides, it is also an opinion that I have that the Illuminati don't act for the greater good; they only act on what will be good for the Illuminati.

Society is fundamentally flawed, of course. I don't limit this statement to just my own society, I would imagine that somebody would be able to find fault with any society, even the most perfect society that could be created. There is no such thing as a perfect society, somebody, somewhere, somehow is always prepared and able to find fault.

My education was designed to steer me away from all of these thoughts; it obviously didn't work. We were led to believe from a very early age that everything was perfect and that there were no problems with the world. Even as a child, however, I was aware that this was far from the truth. I knew that bad things happened in the world and I knew that there were bad people as well. However, in my child-like, idyllic state I pushed everything bad from my mind. Seriously believing that if I ignored the bad things then they would simply go away. My educators would have been proud of me for such an action. There comes a time in everybody's life, however, when it is no longer possible to keep on ignoring the bad things. Sooner or later, we must take the responsibility of standing up and facing these things head on.

11

We had finally arrived at the island of the Pariahs.

A strange island that was to become my home for the next two years, although I had no idea that it would be at the time, of course. The captain left Azarias and myself on the shore of the island and having replenished his stock, left again for the mainland. This appeared to be his relentless progress.

As I have already mentioned, I have no real remembrance of this time. I was still in something of a daze and Azarias easily led me as I stumbled around with no mental or physical coordination. I remember little of this time for two reasons. Firstly, I was still in something of a daze that I put down to delayed shock over the loss of Evie; a realisation that I believed had been triggered by the death of Simeon. The second reason for my haze of memory was due to my developing a fever shortly after my arrival on the island. Azarias later informed me that he was concerned that I had developed the same illness as Simeon. It would have been very easy for me to contract this illness having spent so much time with him during his own illness. Looking back, I was very lucky that I hadn't contracted such an illness, I had certainly run the risk of doing so. It may well have been that I was suffering from a much milder form of the same illness as Simeon, although it cannot be denied that I would have gladly changed places with either Simeon or Evie. Fate, however, had other plans and further torments in mind for me.

I apparently suffered from the fever for about three days. I was mostly unaware of what was going on around me. I lay in a daze for the majority of the time in a very blissful unconsciousness, only occasionally having to suffer the harshness of reality. I seemed to be free of my body and drifting in a light void. My thoughts flitted between one random subject and the next, most of which I now have no recollection. I remember briefly mulling over the certainty that I would never love another person again. This depressed me for a while, but I reminded myself that some people never got to love anybody in the first place. I drifted about in this void for a great while, sometimes comforted by pleasant visions and sometimes distressed by evil apparitions.

***

At the end of the three days, my fever broke and I regained my consciousness. I was, however, extremely fatigued and could do nothing but lay in bed. Azarias regularly brought me helpings of thick soup that he claimed was a local speciality. Gradually, I began to be nourished back to health. Although my physical state was becoming better, my mental condition showed no sign of improvement. I still lingered in a deep state of depression. For hours on end, I would do nothing but sit on the end of my bunk and smoke an endless stream of tobaccos until eventually my head was dizzy, my stomach turned and my fingers smelt only of smoke.

I was aware of the deep pit that I had slipped into and a voice at the back of my mind fired instructions at me, ordering me to pull myself together, but the voice of my conscious seemed too distant to me. It all seemed as if I was a member of an audience watching a performance that I was both a part of and yet distanced from.

Although I was recovering, I did have a terrible state of delirium that resulted in me actually cursing the day that I had ever met Evie. My thoughts at the time were unreasonable, but I could not help the fact that I considered the involvement of any kind of relationship something to generate pain. I completely dismissed my happy memories as being minor to the pain and heartache that I now experienced. I came to the firm conviction that I would never allow myself to become close to another person again. There was simply too much at risk, too much to lose from gaining any kind of intimacy.

As I gradually began to regain a state of normality, I began to see things more clearly. I couldn't place any blame on Evie — we had loved each other and that was something to be treasured. There are so many people that must have to struggle through their lives without the emotion of love — or having to live each day in the knowledge that they were either incapable of love or that despite loving their partner, their partner did not, and never could love them in return. I have come to believe that unrequited love is one of the worst and most tormenting states to live in. I would rather have died. There are those unfortunate souls who feel that they don't need to experience love and that they are better off without it.

I am lucky in the sense that I had Evie, even if she was taken away from me far too early. I never really experienced too much unrequited love or some of the pangs and suffering that so many poets seem to go on about.

At this time, I also became aware of the fact that I would never really reach a state of true normality again. Too much had taken place for things to ever be the same again. I was a different person now and it would take me some time to come to terms with exactly who I was; however, does anybody truly know who they are? I'm not sure that I do, and looking back, I don't think that I ever did.

It was at this point that the real pain hit me. Pain like I have never dreamed could exist. I suffocated in pain. I tore my hair out and ripped my clothing in anguish. I would imagine that if you have not known a similar situation, reader, you would think me a pitiful creature. You would no doubt tell me to pull myself together and get a grip. Well, such things are always easily said by those that have no understanding of the matter.

I became selfish. Why had this happened to me? What evil had I done to deserve it? What justice is there in life? What right does anybody else have to ever be happy again when through no fault of my own I have been made to suffer, when I have committed no real crime? If I had been capable, I would have destroyed the entire world at this moment. So intense was my heartache. My pain became an obsession. It consumed me and I willingly allowed it to. I welcomed it and I fed on it.

I tortured myself. Mentally and physically. I burnt my arm in an almost insane belief that this intense physical pain would dull the agony of my mental pain. I was narrowly prevented from gouging my eyes out because I could not bear to look upon the world again. It meant nothing to me. I was closely watched after that. I imagine, looking back now, that I must have been a pitiful sight and I am amazed that those around me had such patience to put up with my ravings. This state could not last forever. That is the way of insanity, but this was the first time that I realised how thin the line is between sanity and insanity. There is no difference to those that are closest to this line and it is the work of only seconds to cross it.

My inactivity at this time became the biggest burden around my neck. My mind raced in different directions, but my physical inactivity permitted me to dwell too much on the events that had taken place. My dark thoughts haunted me. I needed to occupy myself. If I didn't, I would just set myself to thinking and this would lead to further depression and self-pity that I had already fallen foul to. I realised that at all costs, I must keep busy. I had to occupy every waking hour, at whatever cost I never wanted the time to think again. With this in mind I finally ventured out to investigate my new home.

My new prison.

***

I was taken by surprise by what was waiting for me in the outside world. I had been conditioned to believe that this island was a damnable place and that exile amongst the Pariah would have been a fate almost as bad as death. Instead, what greeted me outside my sick room was a bustling community the like of which I had never seen before.

This was my first indication that I would be unable to trust the majority of things that I had been conditioned to believe all of my life. It is quite a shock to suddenly come to the realisation that everything you had been led to believe was true, is actually false. I can only really describe it as living your life and then suddenly waking up one morning to discover that what you had thought was your life and reality were, in fact, no more than a dream. Suddenly, you have to come to terms with a whole new reality. I think that is the best way to describe it — having to come to terms with an entirely new reality that was practically contrary to all that had previously been reality. I jump ahead of myself slightly, however.

The realisation that the island was not a prison, but a harmonious community was merely the first step on a path that would expose much of the lies that had been force-fed to us all since birth. Where had the lies all started? Where had the corruption first begun? Where do these things start? Perhaps it had all gone back so far that it was now impossible to tell truth from lie. Perhaps those spreading the lies had been so corrupted by their own lies, that they themselves believed the lies to be truth.

My new home was a community that was made up of people that for one reason or another, had rejected the society that I had been born into. I had been conditioned, by rumour, to believe that the Pariah were a group of people that had been rejected and exiled by their Sphere, because of the fact that they were below the required level of intellect needed to contribute to society. I quickly discovered that this is a total lie. It is true that some members of the community had been exiled from the landmass for various reasons. Others, like myself, had been forced into a self-imposed exile to escape from the injustice of society. Others had voluntarily left the landmass of their own free will, as they believed a better life could be created elsewhere.

I could hardly believe that it was possible that there were those that had left of their own free will without being exiled or forced out. Such a thing had never occurred to me before and it was truly staggering that there was so much that had been kept from us.

The Pariah had rejected the social contract and had established a new society. There were no Spheres on this island. The Pariah believed that it is not possible to so easily force people into groups, that are entirely governed by the fortune of their birth. There were no leaders, as the Illuminati would recognise. The Pariah had established a system that I can only describe as direct democracy. Decisions were taken and executed directly by the people.

First of all, yes, there was a structure. There have been those who have ridiculed the fact that the Pariahs have broken away from a rigid society only to create their own rigid society. Yes, there is structure within the society. I do not believe that it would be possible to function without some degree of structure to a society. A society cannot function on chaos.

The Pariahan system of government was far more complex compared to what I had been used to. Back on the landmass, it was the Illuminati that ruled in what I now realised was nothing short of a dictatorship. I was amazed at the system the Pariah had set up. I shall attempt to explain it to you.

The system was made up of three different groups. The most senior were called Administrators, followed by the Convocation and the Aggregation. The Administrators are a group of twenty people that were on call all the time, to deal with any emergencies that might arise. They dealt with the day-to-day running of the state. They have the authority to act for the state, but they are obligated to summon a meeting of the Convocation on matters of policy.

The Convocation is a group of three hundred people over the age of twenty-five. They serve for one year at a time and cannot serve for more than two years in a row. The chairman of the Convocation is elected weekly by lot. No chairman can serve more than once in a two-year period. They primarily act as a steering committee for the Aggregation. The Convocation cannot initiate policy, but they do draw up the agenda that is presented to the Aggregation for discussion. One of their other tasks is to ensure that policy discussions voted upon by the Aggregation are executed and upheld.

The Aggregation is quite simply the populous of the Pariah. All adults form the Aggregation. Anyone can address the Aggregation, but all matters to be discussed, must first be submitted to the Convocation to be discussed and voted on the agenda. The Aggregation has the right to amend any proposal put forward by the Convocation and can demand that certain subjects are put forward to be on the agenda for the next meeting. Every adult by right is entitled to be part of the Aggregation, whether or not you attend the meetings and take part in the discussions is entirely up to the individual.

That is a description, therefore, of the structure of the democracy. Tomorrow I shall explain how this complicated structure actually works in practice.

***

As my description of the democracy of this state clearly shows, the Pariah did not lack in intelligence. It is my intention now to describe how the system actually worked. Very simply, matters for discussion were raised for the attention of the Administrators. If the subject could be resolved by existing legislation then the Administrators would enforce the matter. Otherwise, they would summon a meeting of the

Convocation. The topic would be presented to the Convocation and the matter would be voted onto the agenda. At the next meeting of the Aggregation — which met monthly — the complete agenda would be presented. The Aggregation would then vote as to whether or not to discuss the subject. If the matter was voted for discussion, then everybody within the Aggregation would have the chance to speak on the matter under the direction of the current chairman of the Convocation. After the debate was concluded, the subject was put to the vote. If the vote was carried, then the matter became policy. If it was not carried then the Aggregation had the right to submit the matter for further discussion.

There are numerous other regulations that the Aggregation are governed by. For instance, it may seem to you that this democratic system I have described is all talk and no action. This is not entirely the case. Regulations state that when the Aggregation meet to discuss a topic, no individual speaker may speak more than once on any one subject and the maximum amount of time permitted for a speech is ten minutes. If the chairman feels that the debate is going on for too long, he may call the Aggregation to vote whenever he likes. There is no place for professional orators, or simply those that like to hear the sound of their own voice all the time.

It does seem like a lot of talk, but you have to remember that this is a society that has grown from the iron heel of dictatorship and if anything, they have gone in the opposite direction, to ensure that there is no oppression and that each voice is heard. Some might argue it is a swing too far the other way.

Although the Aggregation meets monthly it can be called to discuss and vote as many times a month as are needed, should there be matters of importance that need to be discussed urgently before the next month. In cases of extreme, life-threatening emergency the Administrators can make the emergency decisions without waiting for the Convocation to be called and the Aggregation to give its approval. However, as soon as possible after such an event, the Aggregation will meet and if it is decided that the Administrators had acted unjustly or in a manner not complying with the state, then the entire lot of them risk being banned from ever holding such positions again. They may, in extreme circumstances, even find themselves being put on trial for an abuse of power.

The Convocation are selected by lots from members of the Aggregation. As I have already stated, members must be over twenty-five years and may not serve for more than two years consecutively. Members can stand down whenever they like should they desire to leave before their term of office is over. The Administrators are elected by the Aggregation. Each member of the Administrators may serve for no longer than three years; after which time, they may never serve as one of the Administrators again. The only other main condition in order to become an Administrator is that you must have served for at least one year on the Convocation before you are eligible to be elected.

The restrictions on the amount of time that an individual may spend in office may seem harsh to some of you, but the intention is to lessen the possibility, of one person seizing power for too long a time. It is hoped that by adopting this system, there will be less chance for corruption to fester; or for the democracy to become stale within the grip of one group for too long. It is also a fair system that strives to ensure that the same people are not always in power, but that everybody gets to vote on decisions of policy and that all that wish to have the opportunity to serve on the Convocation or as an Administrator, should they wish to do so. From my observations it appears to be a system of government that worked.

Do not be mistaken into thinking that the Pariah can only act after they have voted on something. As I have already stated, the Administrators dealt with the day-to-day running of the state and between them and the Convocation, they dealt with many issues that simply did not need to be raised in the Aggregation. The Aggregation only really debated and voted on issues that were of importance in that they may affect the state or the individuals within it. I should point out that in matters of justice, the chairman of the Convocation acted as a Senior Lawman in Judgement whilst the Aggregation as a whole, acted as Jury.

12

As I sit here now, all these years later, the events of which I now write seem to me to be so distant. I have come so far from these events and life has changed so much for me that I look back on the events I describe within these pages and I feel as if they are events that happened to someone else. I have no personal link to them any longer. Does that seem strange?

Yet there are things that still seem recent in my memory. My journey had been one of tragedy, but it was far from over. I had lost a loyal friend; I had become separated from everything that I had once known. I had left behind the society I had lived in and all that I had once believed in had also been left behind. Most important of all, however, I had left behind the only woman I had ever loved. I had left her alone in the cold earth.

Everything I had ever known and everyone I had ever loved had been taken from me. My life was now completely desolate. During the period when I was recovering from my illness, I was plagued with the most restless sleeplessness that I have ever known. My brain, which I had always considered to be my greatest asset, now betrayed me. All night, and each night, I was tortured by my own memories. My demons of the night would come to plague me with remembrances of roads that I would never again walk down. I remembered in detail, every minor thing about Evie and everything that I associated with her.

I was caught in an impossible situation. Some nights my insomnia took a hold of me and kept me from falling into sleep. I would lay awake all night plagued by my demons from the past. On other nights, I would eventually combat the insomnia and due to intense fatigue fall into a sleep which would then cause me nightmares as I relived the events that had brought me to my current position. I couldn't win. Either I was plagued with insomnia, or I was rewarded with sleep, but plagued with haunting visions. I am not sure which of the conditions I would have preferred.

People would say such things as time being a healer. Before the death of Evie, I believed this as well, but it is only partly true. The pain I felt then still exists within my heart today. There are some things that time cannot heal for I still lie awake at night, thinking of the most beautiful woman in the world. The one true companion that I loved with all my heart and soul. The most perfect person you could ever hope to meet. The person I helped to kill. Time will never change that fact. Time can never make that fact any easier to deal with.

I don't think I would be lying if I said that I do not regret a single day that I spent with Evie. I do not wish those days away or undone. I do not wish that they had never happened. There were times, however, in these most dark days following Evie's death, when I must admit that my thoughts were unworthy. I debated with myself the fact that there seemed to be no sense in loving when losing caused so much pain. I cursed my pain that continued. Evie was dead and her pain was over. I had no doubt that she was at peace now, but my sad and useless life continued to stumble its painful way through its existence. When would my pain cease? I wondered, and in truth, it is a question that I still wonder even now.

Alpheus, my constant supplier of paper, talks to me regularly about Evie. What I mean by that, of course, is that he actually takes the time to listen whilst I talk about Evie. I remember it all. I talk about the time that we first met. That magical moment all those years ago when she took my breath away from across a crowded room. She looked so beautiful that night and was easily the most stunning woman in the entire place. I have often wondered what this fantastically beautiful and intelligent woman saw in someone like me. Why did she love me so much? It doesn't matter why she did, only that she did and that I loved her, I mean, that I love her. Time has certainly not stopped me loving her.

Alpheus listens to this foolish old man and his memories. I talk to him about everything. Alpheus likes the detail, not only of what I have done and about the events that have led me here, but about everything. I shared the memory of Evie and myself walking along a beach in the moonlight. I cannot remember where the beach was now, but I suppose that is not so very important. The memory of us walking barefoot in the sand and of holding her as we gazed at the stars, is as fresh in my mind as if it had happened yesterday. I know that I will never walk barefoot in the sand again, with or without Evie.

Whilst I was on the island of the Pariahs, I remembered all that we had said about the stars and I looked up at the stars and wondered if she was able to see me and was looking down on me at the same time. From where I am now, I cannot see the stars at all; and I suppose that means that she cannot see me either. It is one more thing that I have been robbed of.

I remember her smile and the way that she looked at me. As I write and remember now, I am filled with warmth and I smile at the memory of this woman that bewitched me. Yet even now, at the same time as these feelings overwhelm me there is a deep-rooted sadness that engulfs me. Sadness because as sweet as these memories may be, pain overtakes me because I know that there are no new ones to take their place. That is all Evie is now, a memory. So, I keep that memory alive as long as I live.

There are some memories, however, that I will not share with Alpheus. It is just for me to remember the first kiss that we shared and it is for me and me alone, the memory of the first night we made love. I remember so many things. The day we met; the way we danced together that first night; the manner in which we fell so deeply in love together; the days that we spent together; the nights we spent together; our marriage; our life together and most painfully of all, the memory of when I killed her.

***

I apologise if you feel that I am dwelling on the negativity in my life for too long, but let's be honest, have I not just cause for doing so? I know there are some people who are so strong that they can suffer such great loss and they can pick themselves up and carry on with their lives, always searching out the positive and finding reasons for getting up each day and moving forward; but I am not one of those people. Evie was my world and without her, there was no point in anything. There was no point in getting up each day; and yet paradoxically, I did get up each day. I didn't roll over and allow events to engulf me. My survival instinct was too great, I suppose.

A sense of depression and desperation will usually come to us all at some point during our lives. Sadly, also for most of us, this is likely to be a state of mind that visits us more than once. For the most unfortunate among us it is a state that visits us once and then never goes away. I have had my fair share of feeling like this. For the most part, my conflicts with depression have been only temporary visitations that have lasted for brief periods of time. I cannot remember many times during my life with Evie when I can say that I was inflicted with depression. As you will no doubt be able to guess, there have been a number of times since her death when I have been unable to say the same thing. I have tried very hard not to give in to this affliction, as I am sure that this is not how Evie would like to see me. There are moments when this is a losing battle. The depression is just bigger than I am at times.

I comment on all of this now as I have just recently been inflicted with a further attack of this terrible affliction. I tried to remember why it was that I was motivated to write these words in the first place. What was it that made me want to record on these pages the story of my life? I know that it was Alpheus that approached me and asked me to write my account, but I could easily have said no. What was it that compelled me to accept? What is it that drives me forward to continue to write? To start with I was convinced that it was for myself and myself alone. Perhaps as some form of penance for the life that I have led.

Then I began to consider that maybe I was writing for the history of the events. My sense of vanity allowed me to believe that perhaps it was for the sake of future generations that I was recording my account. This is, I suppose, the ultimate vanity. The belief that future generations, or even the same generation as now, will be remotely interested in your life. Why would anyone be that interested in reading about my life and the things that have happened to me? It is pure vanity to expect that other people will be interested in reading about our lives and the things that have happened to us. Maybe people will be interested. Maybe in one hundred years, they will finally get around to reading this. Maybe in one thousand years it will finally come to light, from wherever this document is being taken and stored by Alpheus. Or perhaps these words will never be read again. Who can say what the future might hold? It certainly is true that I could never have predicted the path that the future held for me.

So why am I writing this? If you are reading this then I may be speaking to you from the distant past of hundreds or thousands of years ago, just like the voices of the Ancients speak to us today from their long dead words. Perhaps my voice will not last so long and perhaps it has already started to fade, even as I write these words now. I imagine that I will never entirely know what will happen to these words that I write. That is certainly one of the chief lessons that I have learnt during my life. We can never be completely aware of the consequences of our actions. Life is a domino effect. We make a decision and we push it into effect and that one decision starts the dominos falling. One knocks into another and one thing leads to another. Before we know it, the first domino that we pushed over has led to who knows what.

I don't suppose it really matters what is going to happen to these notes that I write. It doesn't matter if nobody reads these words. I am writing this for myself. In order to purge myself of the events of my life. I still lie awake at night with my memories running through my head. It hasn't become any easier over the years. Perhaps for some people the pain does become less and the memories do become easier. That may be the case for some people, but it certainly isn't the case for me. I hate to depress or worry anybody that may have recently lost a loved one. Perhaps it will get easier for you. I do not know. I am not the ultimate authority on loss. We are all different and we all react differently to the situations that are presented to us. If you have lost someone then you may react differently to me. You have my sympathy either way. I know something of what it is that you are going through. I wish that there were some words of comfort that I could offer you, but there is nothing that can be said.

***

Over the most recent years of my life, I have had much time for reflection. I have reached the conclusion that too long a period of time for reflection is not a good thing. I have had more than enough time just recently to reflect over just about everything. I have reflected upon my life, but reached no comforting satisfactory conclusions. Perhaps there are none to be made. I have also spent much time reflecting on deeper issues, issues that I only really started to take an interest in when I was on the island of the Pariahs — but more of that later.

As you can probably imagine, I have spent a lot of my time recently reflecting upon the nature of freedom. So very many of us take our freedom for granted. It isn't until it is taken away from us that we realise what we have lost. I suppose that is true of so many things in life. If only we realised what we had whilst we still have it. We should learn to enjoy those moments because they are so often taken from us and it is not until they have gone, that we realise that we have lost something great. It seems to me that this life has only one or two very special, precious moments set aside for each individual, some of us may not even get those moments.

If we are fortunate enough to get our special, precious moment though, then we should seize it with both hands and make the most of it; for tomorrow it may be taken away from us once again and we will be left with nothing but a distant, fading memory. Did I really make the most of the time I had with Evie? I look back now and think of all the time we did spend together and I am happy; but I agonise over all the moments that I know that I wasted. All the times when we could have been together, but weren't. All the times when I had the opportunity to hold or kiss her, but for one reason or another didn't. All the wasted moments in our lives. I would give anything to hold her now. I would give anything possible for one last kiss. Perhaps one day I will go back to her. Perhaps if life does continue after death, I will meet her again. It is a belief that, true or not, is all I have got to hang on to.

Seize the moment. Before I ended up in my final destination here, I used to see people all of the time wasting the moments that they could have had together. Arguing about petty things that didn't make the slightest bit of difference, not taking the opportunity to be together when they had the chance. It used to infuriate me.

But I was talking about freedom and the loss of freedom. I used to think that if my freedom was ever taken away from me, then I wouldn't mind so very much so long as I was able to retain freedom of thought. For surely, we are only ever really free within the confines of our own mind. It is in our own minds that we must be true. We may be able to lie to everyone else; but at the end of the day, it is in our own minds that we must live and we cannot lie to ourselves, no matter how much we may try to do so. It is in our own minds where freedom of thought exists. It is within this fragile, complex structure that we can think what we like, do what we like and feel what we like. That is what I believed freedom to be. Despite any attempts that they may like to make, the Illuminati have no control over what individuals think. They may be able to control every other aspect of our lives, but they have yet to uncover a method for getting into our heads and controlling what we think. I have no doubt that if they ever developed such a method, however, that they would have no hesitation in putting it into immediate use.

Since my physical freedom has been taken away from me, I have had more time to reflect upon the theory that in our own minds we are only truly free. I think that it is still a very sound theory. Obviously, there are bound to be people that don't agree with me on this, but debate keeps a subject alive. If we all agree on everything then there will be no debate about it and before too long, we will forget the reasons behind what we are doing. By debating, we keep the topic alive and fresh, so feel free to debate anything I say — although I will obviously not be able to answer you, but perhaps somebody will.

Over the last few years, I have come to realise that there is another important fact about freedom that I had not previously fully considered. My situation over these years has enabled me to realise that freedom is really the opportunity to act, not the action itself. It is no good me having the freedom to kiss Evie when I desire (as I used to be able to do) if I no longer have the opportunity to do so, because I am confined and she is dead; but were she not dead, for arguments sake, I would still not have the freedom to act because of my confinement. Freedom is the ability to kiss her, not the actual act of kissing her.

It doesn't really matter whether or not I choose to take the opportunity up that is presented to me; that is my freedom of choice. I am still free to the extent that I could choose to take advantage of the opportunity if I so wish. I am no longer free should I not have the opportunity in the first place. I can certainly tell you that in my present circumstances, opportunity is not something that exists in a great deal of abundance. Freedom is the opportunity to act, not the action in itself. During my time on the island of the Pariahs I was to learn a great deal about freedom. I hardly knew it at the time but I was to learn many things on the island of the Pariahs.

Talk of the Pariahs reminds me that I have strayed from my story. I have allowed myself some indulgence of slipping into the present. I must now return to the past and relate the events that took place on the island of the Pariahs. It is then, and only after I have spoken of that island, that I can relate the events that led me to come to the current moment.

13

I have stated that I have had something of an opportunity to briefly explore my surroundings. I was, however, to a certain extent under guard. The Pariahs value their society highly and live in a certain amount of fear that one day they will be infiltrated by those intent on causing them harm. There is a real fear that the Illuminati may decide that the true nature of the island of the Pariahs is a threat to government and society on the landmass. If this were to happen, then the existence of the Pariah colony would be in danger. With all of this in mind it is to be understood if the Pariahs are cautious when it comes to dealing with newcomers. Being cautious is a state of existence that will enable you to live a lot longer.

Caution is something that is passed on from generation to generation. They have every reason to be cautious, of course, their existence is a huge threat to the Illuminati and the oppression that exists from where I had come. If the true nature of what life was like as a Pariah were to get out, then there would almost certainly be a revolution. Obviously, that is not something that the Illuminati want on their side and nor do the Pariahs want an influx of people fleeing oppression. Each person that is admitted to society from the outside has the ability to change that society to some degree. Not always for the best. It is an inevitability.

Newcomers to the island are hardly a regular occurrence at any rate, but from time to time, people do arrive on the island and seek sanctuary for whatever reason. People like myself driven by necessity; people who hear rumours of the island and go in search of it; people that leave the landmass for moral reasons; and then there are those that are banished by the Illuminati because they are believed to be outcasts of some description or another. Clearly, the Illuminati have no idea of what life is really like amongst the Pariahs, or they would hardly send people here. They appear to be as brainwashed and conditioned as the rest of us.

With all of this in mind, it is amazing how much of a secret the true nature of this place really is. One can hardly blame the Pariahs if they wish to keep it that way. They have all learnt to be cautious by necessity. Strangers arriving on the island are therefore treated with a degree of suspicion until they are able to prove their worth. When you arrive on the island there is nothing to suggest the true nature of the secrets of the society that are in existence. The outskirts of the island are inhospitable, and conform to the generally held belief that those on the landmass have, regarding the Pariahs. It is only when you get further into the island that the true state of the affairs reveals itself. It is a well-kept secret.

Those, like myself, who wish to make an application to stay and ultimately join the society are initially kept in segregation from the rest of the island whilst their claim is investigated and their case looked into. During this time the applicant is appointed with a contact from within the Pariahs. This contact investigates the applicant's claim and judges the individual's character to determine whether they have a justification in their claim. After some time of this, the case for the individual is put before the Aggregation. After a debate on the matter, it is put to the vote whether the applicant should be allowed to join the society or not. If the vote is in their favour, then they are allowed to join the society on a kind of probationary period.

Nobody would answer my question as to what happens to the applicant should the vote go against them. Logic rather suggests to me that if an individual fails in their application to join the Pariahs, then at the very least, they must surely never be allowed to leave the island again; otherwise, they would be able to tell of what they have seen. Obviously, they cannot allow this to happen. You do not have to be too intelligent or creative to work out that if you cannot leave the island, but are not allowed to stay on the island then the most obvious course of action is not very pleasant.

My point of contact within the Pariah community was a man by the name of Aaron. Aaron was a man in his thirties who had been born on the island. That is something that I should mention, that I have not. Obviously, there were some people who lived on the island who had been born and raised there. The society could not exist if it relied completely on those that joined from the outside. Naturally, families existed amongst the Pariahs.

Aaron was sent to explore my story and to find out what kind of person I am. The reader of this story well knows by now, the background of events that led me to arrive on the island. It may also be possible that by now you will have formed a judgement on my character. I hope that you look back through the years and look favourably upon me. Whilst Aaron was gaining information about me, it goes without saying that I was gaining information about him.

***

The Pariahs were as hospitable to me as I could have asked for and perhaps further than I could have expected. Until your case is debated by the Aggregation, you are allowed a certain degree of liberty although a very tight rein is kept upon you. I was conscious of a constant watch upon my movements. Sometimes the watch was obvious, sometimes more discreet, but I came to know they were always there.

Gradually with an amazing degree of patience, Aaron began to piece together my story a little at a time. Obviously, a great deal of my story he had managed to obtain from Azarias, but it was important for him to hear my story in my own words. Retelling my story kept open wounds that had so far had no time to heal. Aaron was, however, a skilful interrogator and never pushed his questions to me too far or too many at one time. He showed a level of patience that I have seen in few others. It would perhaps have been easy to have allowed my retelling to have dropped me once again into my darkness, but Aaron had a firm hold of me and controlled me like the expert that he was.

For many weeks, Aaron delved into my past and asked question after question about what had happened to me. Many times, I found that we were going over the same ground again. I soon worked out that the reason for this was because Aaron was looking for any small inconsistency, that might point the way to saying that I was not telling the truth. By spending so much time talking to me, Aaron was also beginning to judge my character and my beliefs. To this end we talked of many subjects — not just in reference to the reasons why I had been bought here.

By talking to Aaron, I learnt that to seek admittance to the Pariah society it was necessary to be of a like character. I don't think that anyone can really blame the Pariahs for wanting to control their society. The island was a paradise; a society of equality and morality which did not exist on the landmass. It is important to preserve those standards and not allow admittance to those who are likely to contaminate matters. It would be a travesty if this haven were to be twisted and turned into a society like that of the landmass.

Aaron's patience with me extended to the numerous questions that I was always asking him. It was understood between us that there were certain questions that I might wish to ask him that he would be unable to answer. The reason for this being that there were some respects of the island that were not made known to people until such time as they had been elected members. There was, however, a great deal that I was able to discover and much of what I have already told you is a combination of what Aaron told me and what I was to later learn.

There were several precepts that were essential to the Pariah society. It was essential that those who were making an application to join would agree with those precepts and be prepared to live by them and enforce them. I shall explain in a moment what these precepts are, but I should first of all make it clear, that there are not that many applicants to the island. I was informed that at the most, the island might have to deal with one outside applicant a year. Sometimes years would go by and there would be no applicants at all. Obviously, there are those that are born on the island who are automatically members. They do not have to undergo the rigorous induction process that I and other applicants from the outside have to go through. They are considered to be like-minded people by virtue of the fact that their parents are both already members of the community. It is generally accepted that from birth, these people will be raised with the precepts and ideals of the island and will presumably not present too much of a problem to the society. To those of us from the outside, however, it is an entirely different matter.

Children are raised on the beliefs that we give them and it is easy for children to inherit their beliefs from their parents and from those that surround them and who are instrumental in their growth. It is the same anywhere. The children born on the island are raised with the same ideologies as their parents, in the same way that my parents on the landmass raised me. We accept those beliefs that we are raised with. We accept them with little or no argument. They must be right because our parents tell us so and because we are dependent on our parents, we have faith in what they tell us. Is this wrong? If it is wrong on the landmass then is it wrong on the island? In a logical argument, we have to say that if it is wrong for the landmass then it must be wrong for the island.

I am now very tired and my light is fading. I have had a burst of energy of writing recently and it has now worn me out considerably. I must remember that I am now no longer as young as I used to be and I am not as capable now of some tasks as I once was. Age creeps up on us and the body ages although the mind does not. The mind believes we are still capable of doing that which our body is no longer capable of doing.

Now I am tired and I must rest. Tomorrow we will continue.

***

Yesterday, I talked very briefly about the fact that the Pariahs have various precepts that they live by. I mentioned this, but my tired mind and rough pencil were unable to progress far enough to be able to give you an indication of what these might be. Your patience in bearing with me for as long as you have is something that I appreciate beyond measure.

The precepts that the Pariahs live by are amazing in their simplicity. In no particular order these precepts are such as equality. In Pariah society all people are equal regardless of any circumstances such as gender, situation, belief, original Sphere or whether they were born on the island or whether they arrived here as refugees. All are equal, and I think this can be seen, in the relatively democratic system of government that they have, that allows all people an equal voice.

With that in mind, they also have a policy of free speech. All on the island are allowed to speak their minds and voice their opinions on any matters at all. That is why the entire populace make up the Aggregation and they are all allowed to speak if they so wish to do so. The only restriction that is placed on freedom of speech is that it must not cause harm to anybody or in any way be an incitement to stir up hatred or violence against another. Nor should it lead to any action that would be a breach of any of the other precepts.

The Pariahs believe in peace and have never had anything like a conflict or war that might take place on the landmass. If a dispute arises between people, then the matter is addressed before the Aggregation. Once the matter is addressed and debated upon, the vote is taken and the decision stands. All parties accept this and will not hold a grudge because of it. If someone were to decide to harbour a grudge and continue with the dispute, then one of the parties would be exiled away from the Pariah community. This perhaps sounds a little similar to activities upon the landmass, but the harmony of the community cannot be disrupted. Aaron informed me though that this drastic course of action has never been taken in his lifetime.

There is a prison system that exists for want of a better phrase. I asked Aaron about this.

'Crime is something that is very rare here,' he had explained to me. 'All of us have agreed to the social contract, for want of a better phrase. We agree it by living here. You agree it by the fact that you are willing to stay here.'

'So, just by being here I have signed up to it?'

'Yes. In return for obeying the rules of the social contract you are given the necessities that you require in life. Shelter, food, warmth, the right to justice and protection and so on.'

'And if you breached the contract?'

'If you breach the contract then you are no longer subject to the protection and rights of the contract. Break the contract, you forfeit your rights. You are no longer entitled to the protection of law. One of those things that you potentially give up the right to is freedom.'

I could see the logic of this.

The Pariah's have a high moral standard and a sense of morality or ethical belief is essential if you are to live on the island. They believe in a system of universal help. There is nobody amongst the Pariah movement who would not help another if that other needed help. Mutual assistance is an established way of life. There is no room on the island for anybody who is only out for themselves and for their own gain. Universal help and charity rule-out any selfish activities that exist on the landmass.

There is a promotion of unity that exists on the island that I have not found anywhere else. It is made clear from the very start that everyone is in this together and that we must all stand together and work together to promote the aims and the well-being of the mass. This does not mean to say that the individual is suppressed by the state. It may sound like a contradiction, but there is no problem with promoting individual creativity whilst preserving society's aims and principles. It is the selfish qualities that exist in some people that have no place here.

Last of all, I wish to mention two qualities that the Pariahs promote and praise highly. The first is truth. The pursuit of truth is considered to be a noble activity. I honestly believe that there is not a member of this community that would give any serious thought to lying about a matter. They would no more consider lying than an individual would consider impaling themselves on spikes. They really just cannot see the point of it.

Another virtue that is praised most highly by the Pariahs is that of the pursuit of knowledge. It is firmly believed that by following the course of knowledge, truth will be discovered. Knowledge is that which is all-important. Knowledge is betterment. From young children, the Pariahs are conditioned in the pursuit of knowledge. They are expected to ask questions and to take a keen interest in the world around them. By asking questions and developing one's own knowledge we can come to an understanding of who we are. These are the driving passions of the Pariah.

During the time that Aaron and myself spent together and he was obtaining my past history, he was also attempting to find out more about my character to discover if I was the kind of person that would be likely to uphold and support these same qualities and precepts that I have mentioned. Only like-minded people would be allowed to join the community that I was making an application to join. Where else could I go, in all honesty?

***

Pariahs spend a fair amount of time trying to uncover a meaning to it all. They are not content to allow life to pass them by unexamined. Many people have become confused upon the landmass and forget what life is all about. They become entangled in false values and unimportant ideals. On the landmass things like thought, expression and examination of life is an activity that is not encouraged. The powers that be are well aware that such activities are likely to encourage dissent and rebellion. Such things are obviously a threat to the established authority. I had seen the suppression of certain freedoms and groups of people on the landmass, but to my infinite shame, I never challenged these views and attitudes.

Why would I? From birth I had been conditioned that this was the way that things were meant to be. Besides, let us be brutally honest, it did not concern me. What were the Residuum to me? It did not touch upon me directly. These immoral attitudes — as I now see them — were things that I could very easily push to one side and place out of mind. It is easy to ignore such things and our minds become conditioned to doing just that. It was not until Evie was under threat that the immorality of it all was brought home to me. I admit all of this to my shame. If something is wrong, then it is wrong, whether or not it touches us directly or not and yet how many people on the landmass think like this?

Such attitudes do not exist amongst the Pariahs. They are conditioned to examine life because there is no established authority that would be under threat. Everybody rules and has a say in how things are done. There is no threat here by examining life.

Aaron was my point of contact on all of this. He was my guide and my teacher. He showed me what he could of the island and introduced me to many of the people that live here. Aaron spent an amazing amount of time with me listening to my story, my life, my history and my views and beliefs. During this period, I was able to learn much from Aaron about his own life. Having lived on the island all his life, he was very curious about where I came from and what life was like for me. I began to see my shame of compliance more clearly, every minute I spent with him. I began to wonder how it was possible that I spent more than forty years of my life there before I began to question things.

It was at the back of my mind, of course, that Aaron was not there talking to me because he was genuinely interested in me; he was talking to me purely because of the fact that he was required to report his findings to the Aggregation. As time went by, I became aware that it was fast approaching the time when my case would be put before the

Aggregation. Naturally, I was apprehensive in case my application would be rejected. Who knew what would happen to me if I were rejected? My apprehension was grounded in reality because Aaron had informed me that there was one hurdle to overcome if I was to be accepted.

I have explained how moral this new society was. I would have to stand up therefore, and explain how it was that I killed my wife.

14

Time is an illusion.

I can vouch for that, as I sit here in this meaningless room, where they have seen fit to place me, where I can write these words. How long have I been here? Years? Decades, perhaps? I don't know. One day is very much like another day. The events that I write about so distant and yet so vivid in my mind still. How can I truly qualify them by putting them into the man-made measurements that make up time? All is one, and that is an end of it.

I am so tired. It is the only fact that I am certain of at the moment. I do not sleep all that well and often spend most of the night lying awake, fixed on a single spot and thinking over the past. There is no point giving any thought to the future for it is always the same and as mundane as the day before. A never-ending cycle that will only be broken by my eventual eternal release, when I shall be free of the physical and mental bondage that I have been placed in.

I welcome the release that death would bring. What comes afterwards? Will I continue to exist in a manner that can only be dreamt of in this life? Will I see Evie again in that existence on a different plain? I don't know. I used to be certain of the fact that I would see her again but as the years have passed and my memory plays tricks on me, I am less sure. Yes, my memory plays tricks. As I have said there are times when all of these events are so vivid and yet there are other times when the memory is there but it is something that is hazy and although I reach for it, I am unable to grasp it and it remains elusive. Why does my memory play this cruel trick on me at times? Allowing me on the one hand to remember how life was with Evie and myself and then on another occasion, making it impossible for me to remember what her face looked like with any degree of clarity?

I do not know the answers to all of these questions despite my long, cold nights of trying to find the answers. I do not believe that I am any wiser now than when I began this journey despite the fact that I have learnt and seen so much. That is another contradiction. I find that life is full of contradictions. Just when you think that there is something that is a certainty, it seems that there will be something else that will pop up which will give a contrary view. The only thing that I can be certain of is that one day this journey will end. There can be no debate or contradiction about that.

Although I welcome the inevitable release that will one day come, I know that I must finish what I have now begun before that day will come. I cannot help but feel how glorious that day will be when it does come. They do their best to keep me alive here for they will not allow me to die, but it is a battle that one day they must lose and I will have the final victory over them.

***

Aaron was teaching me a great deal and I was like a child that had an empty mind that needed to be filled. I was someone that everything that I had believed in and thought was how the world was, turned out to be incorrect. Being on the island of the Pariahs was like waking up after a long dream in which I had dreamt a reality only to wake and find that the world was an entirely different place to the one that I had dreamt about.

I remember sitting in Aaron's garden talking to him about many things during my stay on this island whilst I waited to find out what was to be done with me. I remember one particularly hot summer's day when we sat in the shade of his tree and talked about society as I hungered for more of this new knowledge that I was being exposed to. There were no limits to what I wanted to know about this place that if I was fortunate enough, I might be able to call my home.

'How did this society come to exist?' I asked, as I gazed around the garden which seemed to be so peaceful. I do not think that I had known such a peace, either before or after this occasion.

'That is not an easy question to answer,' replied Aaron with a smile. 'How does any society come into existence? Over time and with mistakes along the way would be one possible answer. Any society, any law, is a work in progress. Nothing can ever be final and set in stone, there always has to be some room for improvement. Things were not always as they are now, but it is a process of evolution and implementation of law which has led us to where we are now.'

'You have no real rank structure that I can determine as they have on the landmass.'

'Yes, that is true. I have heard of your Illuminati and your Median and Residuum, is it?'

'Yes.'

'Pointless. Slavery is absurd and meaningless.'

I frowned at this.

'I'm not sure that slavery is something that we actually had.'

Aaron looked at me with a surprised look on his face. 'Is that what the Residuum would say if I were to ask them? Are they not a race of slaves, raised for the sole purpose of doing that which the rest of you do not want to do? That sounds like slavery to me.'

Not for the first time, I was having all of my assumptions questioned and being forced to look at life as I had known it from a very different perspective. I tried to change track.

'I'm fascinated to learn more of how this system that you have described to me actually works in practice. So many people all have a say in what takes place. It sounds like it could be a recipe for total chaos.'

Aaron nodded his head at this observation and thought for a moment before he replied.

'How does it work and stop itself from debasing into chaos? Each person in the community gives themselves completely to the community. Their conditions are the same for all. None has any interest in making things burdensome for the others.'

'Seems almost implausible to me.'

'That's not an unusual reaction given the circumstances in which you have been brought up and the way that you have lived your life up until this point.'

This troubled me and I felt more like a child than I had ever done at any point in my life so far. I certainly felt like I was being talked to in the same way that a parent might explain a simple arithmetic problem to a child that was lacking in understanding. Patiently going over the same ground over and over again until the child was able to grasp the simplest of problems. Despite my feeling of ignorance, or maybe because of it, I nevertheless felt compelled to ask more questions.

'What happens if someone disagrees with the majority?'

'In order that the social pact should work and not be meaningless,' Aaron sighed with what appeared to be infinite patience. 'It contains an obligation that alone can force anyone who refuses to obey the general rule that they should be compelled to do so.'

I wasn't sure that I liked the sound of this and I began to have my first doubts that despite everything that I had seen and heard, perhaps there was not such a thing as a perfect society after all.

'So, you could, in theory force someone to be free?' I asked, testing the water.

'Yes, I suppose you could look at it from that point of view,' nodded Aaron thoughtfully as he watched some insects flying around some of the plants in the garden as if his mind were really on higher matters than what we were talking about. 'It isn't really something that happens though as each individual, as I have said, would not do such a thing that would be deliberately burdensome to his fellow. It is all hypothetical possibilities.'

'Must the general will be so important in this society?'

Aaron looked at me as if I was a particularly thick child that was failing to grasp the simplest of ideas.

'Only the general will can direct the powers of the state in accordance with the purpose for which it was founded.'

'Which was?' I asked wondering how far Aaron's indulgence of me was likely to go.

'The common good for the establishment of a society was made necessary because initially individuals and their interests were in opposition. It is only made possible because those interests concur. It is really on the basis of common interest that society must be governed.'

The heat of the garden was making me lose track of a lot of what he was saying, but then, having grown up in the way that I had, political philosophy was hardly my strong point. I decided to change the direction once again and introduce something that was particularly important to me in my current situation.

'And what of law?'

'What of it?'

'How did you develop laws? For a society that prides itself so much on freedom, why have laws?'

He smiled at this. 'It would be very naïve, my friend, to have any society that did not have laws. A society without laws would be back to that level of chaos that you were talking about earlier.'

'Are all your laws fixed or do they change with circumstances and are new laws introduced?' He nodded at this question as if I was finally doing a little better than I had been so far.

'No law can be fixed as an absolute; as I said earlier there is nothing that is set in stone. Laws must be allowed to grow and change as necessity requires. If they do not, then they are stale and unworthy. Any proposal can be put forward to become a law, but without the general consent, they cannot be passed from proposal to law. We must ourselves authorise the laws that will ensure the happiness of all. That is what matters to us.'

'You seem to place a great deal of emphasis on the happiness of everyone.'

'Of course.'

'Is that how this society was founded?'

'In a manner of speaking. In order that a society and a people in the process of formation should understand the importance of sound policy and then follow the fundamental rules of the reasoned society that we have then it was necessary for the effect to become the cause.'

'I'm afraid you have lost me on that one.'

'It's somewhat of a paradox, I suppose. The spirit of the society which should be the result of the society and the laws will have to have guided those laws itself. Men would have to be what the laws made them.'

I was still not entirely sure that I was following this argument and it must have shown on my face.

'When a builder is constructing some great building,' he continued. 'it is necessary for him to examine the ground that he is to build on, yes?'

'Yes, I can see that.'

'If he does not and the ground is not stable then the entire edifice is likely to collapse at the smallest gush of wind or tremor. The builder makes sure that the ground is stable, which in turn will make his building stable. He does not build his building in the hope that the ground will become stable because he has built a straight and stable construction upon it.'

'I understand.'

'In the same way a wise man building a society will not begin by drafting the laws but will first consider whether the people for which they are intended are capable of receiving them.'

'So, there is no sense in creating a law that nobody would be able to obey?'

'Indeed, that would not make for a very happy society.'

We sat in silence for a short while, absorbed in our own thoughts and enjoying the sunshine. This culture was so alien to me that it was almost impossible for me to be able to comprehend it.

'This is all a very good intellectual exercise,' I said, breaking the silence, 'but it does not help my own particular situation at the moment.'

'No, that is true. The biggest problem facing you is the reaction to the knowledge that you killed your wife.' Aaron held up his hand to stop me from saying anything or making any protest at this. 'I know the circumstances surrounding the death of your wife as I have learnt from you and as my investigation has revealed. The exceptional circumstances of her death may be argued as mitigation in your favour, in order for you to be accepted into this society, but the biggest problem, will be convincing the general populace that this one death is not the start of others.'

'You mean you have to make sure that I have not developed a taste for it.' I replied with a slight hint of scorn in my voice which was ignored by Aaron, if he noticed it.

'That's a blunt way of putting it, but you are essentially correct.' We lapsed into silence again for a while whilst we pondered this problem. 'The issue is that taking someone's life, even in the circumstances that you describe is a concept that is entirely alien to us.'

'I can understand that. In truth, it's something that I have struggled with a great deal.'

'How so?'

'I have had a lot of time to think since Evie died; well, since she first told me that she was ill. I always believed that nobody, not even the state, had the right to take someone else's life. However, given the circumstances that she was in, and given the fact that I loved her a great deal, what else could I do?'

'I don't know.'

'Could I leave her to a life of suffering and exile because that's what the law says I should do? The law is not always right, and when it comes to things like this, I don't believe that the law will ever come above someone that you truly love.'

'I cannot imagine the situation that you were in.'

'Despite it all though, I know that there are those who would take the argument that no matter how much you may think you are in the right, there are no moral circumstances in which you can justify taking someone's life.'

'That is likely to be the view of many people here.'

'I don't doubt it. The thing is, that when I look back on it now, I can't say for certain that I wouldn't do the same thing if I had to live through it again.'

'I have had the opportunity to get to know you over these last few weeks,' he continued. 'I have learnt as much as I probably will be able to learn from you and the motivations that have led you to this island.'

'Does that mean that the time is approaching when a decision will be made?' I asked anxiously. Whilst we had been able to meet and talk as we had done over the last few weeks, it had almost been possible for me to forget the reason for why Aaron was talking to me and the judgement that I would eventually be under.

'It is.'

'When?'

'Your case for inclusion will be made next week at the next general meeting.'

'Will I be allowed to be present?'

'I'm afraid not. The debate will only take place between the citizens and you are not a citizen, at least not yet, so you will not be permitted to take part in the debate.'

This seemed a little unfair but I had learnt that there was nothing that I would gain by arguing the point. I looked around me at this island which I could only really describe as a paradise. I basked in the sun with my eyes closed for a while whilst I reflected that there was such a difference between the peaceful idyll of this land and the turmoil that I was going through in my own mind.

'Will someone argue my case in my absence?'

'Yes, your case will be presented.'

'Who will present the case?'

'That would be me. I have been the one allocated to learn as much of your story as I can and having achieved that task, it is my responsibility to relay the facts of your case to the Aggregation.'

'What do you think they will do?'

Aaron laughed which took me by surprise as despite all of his talk of happiness, I had not actually heard him laugh all that much in the time that we had spent together. Perhaps it was because we had so many serious things to talk about that laughing had not been appropriate. It hardly seemed all that appropriate to me now.

'It is impossible to say at this stage. The vote could most certainly go either way. It is not something that you should worry about.'

'That's easy for you to say.'

'I agree. However, the matter is out of your hands and there is nothing that you can do to influence the decision that will finally be made so it would be illogical of you to get stressed and worked up about it. You must resign yourself to accepting the situation and allowing the matter to take the natural course that it will take.'

I nodded, but I did not feel particularly easy, as we parted company on that day. Once more, events were out of my hands and I was nothing more than a spectator to everything that was going on around me, despite the fact that it involved me deeply.

15

'With regards to your situation,' Aaron continued to tell me, 'there are two basic schools of thought.'

'Which are?'

'There are those who consider the morality situation and the value of those morals derive from the motivation for the action that was performed.'

'You may have to expand that a little further,' once again I was feeling more like a child than ever before. It amazed me that given the reputation that the Pariahs had, they clearly were very different in reality to the way that the Landmass represented them.

'These groups of people feel that the morality of law, for example, is not something that is set in stone and is something that can be changed depending on the consequences of the situation. So, in your case, whereas they may view murder as wrong, they will acknowledge that your motivation for it was right. You see?'

'Yes, I suppose so. And the other group of people?'

'These are an altogether trickier bunch, as far as you are concerned. These are the people who believe in the absolute morality of the law. If it is wrong to do something, such as murder, then it is wrong to do it, no matter what the motivation was or the consequence or benefits that might come from it.'

'And which group are you in?'

'Oh, my dear friend, what I think hardly matters at all.'

I wasn't feeling at this particular point that I was having much luck, and I doubted that the upcoming debate would carry in my favour all that much either. I had become settled into my new life on the island of Pariahs. To realise that things were not fully settled and in theory, I could be back to the beginning again was not something that I cherished. I could have done with a friend, and whereas Aaron seemed to be in my corner, I felt that he was there because he had to be rather than because he wanted to be. I suppose you could say that about myself as well.

Law is a funny concept when you think about it. How many people obey the law because on its own basis it is the right and moral thing to do and how many obey the law because the threat of punishment is something that is more fearful? I suspect that there is a fair amount of the latter. Take the situation with Evie; Aaron and myself debated it.

'I can't believe that there are those,' I stated, 'who would find it moral to enact such a barbaric law as making it illegal to have an illness.'

'On the surface of it that would appear to be a justified position. However, there are those that would argue that it is necessary to uphold that law for the benefit of the rest of society. They will argue that when you are acting for the benefit of society, everything and anything is justifiable.'

'I don't think you can blanket-belief something like that.'

'But it is done. It even exists here. We have our rules the same as you and many of them may seem irrational to an outsider such as yourself. However, as I have mentioned we have an obligation to obey the rules if we want to live under the contract that exists in this land.'

'So, in a sense, the argument should have been that the moment Evie became ill, we should have left the Landmass and gone elsewhere rather than break the rules of that society.'

'I suppose you could say that, although the contract is something that you have already signed up to by being there. The moment she has contracted this illness and concealed it, she has broken the law. You can't really break the law and then leave.'

'It all seems a bit of a hopeless situation to be in really.'

'Perhaps, but there is always hope. You should never give up on that.'

***

There is no hope now, of course. For so many years I have been kept in this dark place, estranged from the rest of the world as they go about their daily lives, taking the smallest of liberties for granted. You never realise the freedoms that you have until they are broken, and taken away from you. It is the nature of things.

This is the only home that I know now. I have been here so long and I know that there really won't be any other place that I will be allowed to go and live out the remainder of my days. To be honest, I have been here so long now, that I doubt I would know how to function in the free world that is on the outside.

If the truth be told, it is something that I am afraid of. Does that sound silly? You that are free to do what you like have so many choices ahead of you. Do you turn right or do you turn left? Do you do this or do you do that? You decide when to get up and when to go to bed. How many choices do you make during the day? So many choices that it makes my head spin just thinking about it; how do you even begin to cope with it all? Where I am now, everything is regulated and there is no real choice in what takes place. There are small freedoms, but nearly everything that I do is led by the decisions of other people. After all these years, I have become used to it and I doubt that I could cope in the existence that I had before.

Before I was here, I was conditioned to the life that I led without asking too many questions and accepting as the norm, the structure of the Spheres. I then had to throw all that over and accept the fact that society was not as I had thought it was. I then went to the Pariahs and had to condition myself into realising that everything that I had once thought about these people was wrong. I learnt an entirely new system here. Now, look where I am.

I have now become conditioned to this life and it has been the only existence that I have known for a long time now, so I can't imagine that there will be anything that will change over it. If the truth is told, I don't want it to change. I have become accustomed now to this life and I know that I am too old and it is too late for things to change for me now. I just couldn't cope with it.

The routine of Alpheus bringing me paper each day and taking the scribbled sheets away has become a comfort to me now. It has become something that I depend upon. It is something that has become necessary for me to get through the day. It worries me what will happen when this story is told and there is no longer any need for me to write these words each day. It has become a life line for me that I fear to be without. Perhaps, when this story is concluded, I will have the final glory of death,

127

at last. It is something that I have longed for, for so many years. I would welcome its sweet embrace when it finally comes for me.

Sometimes I wonder how it is that I ended here. The short answer is because I murdered my wife. I can see that and I fully support that, if the truth is known. My question is though, how did I come to murder her? I had always tried to live my life a certain way that was law-abiding and unimportant, I suppose. I went about my daily routine and never wanted to be anything other than that which I was. I loved my wife and tried my best just to get through life without making any waves, and then all of a sudden, I found myself in a situation where I was an outlaw, a criminal.

My wife was dead and it was something that was done with my assistance and support. I should point out that there was no coercion in this matter. I did what I did because of the fact that she asked me and because it was the right thing to do. It was an entirely voluntary act on my part; be not deceived in that. I can argue about the circumstances and the situation that society had forced us into but the action was mine at the end of the day.

When he can, Alpheus sits with me and he encourages me to talk about the life that I used to lead and the experiences that I had with the Pariahs. He seems to find the entire situation fascinating and never tires of trying to find out as much as he can about me. I have to confess that it is nice to have someone to talk to. For so many years, I had no one to talk to at all and would spend so many days, weeks, maybe even longer without speaking; so much so that when I did finally speak, it was hard for me to recognise my own voice.

How much longer is there left for me to stay here?

***

It was not that long before the Aggregation was due to meet to discuss my case. It was something that I was not looking forward to as Aaron had left me in no doubt that my chances were not entirely brilliant.

I was not disappointed in this outcome. The debate took longer than I thought it would, but it didn't change the outcome any. It was probably the longest period of my life, waiting whilst the debate took place which seemed to be an eternity. There was nothing that I could do but pace up and down whilst my fate was in the hands of others. It wouldn't be the last time.

'They just can't get round the fact that regardless of the circumstances you were complicit in the murder of your wife.' I suppose he was being polite by saying complicit rather than saying I was more directly involved, which is the truth of the matter.

'I did what I felt I had to do.'

'Yes, I know that.'

'I am sorry that your people cannot understand what it is like to love someone so much that you are prepared to go to such extraordinary lengths to prevent them from suffering.'

'Well, as I said before, it is a hurdle to get over, the fact that there are a majority who feel that the law is the law; even if it is an unjust law and there really is no grounds for breaking it.'

'No law should be absolute.'

'Perhaps not.'

It was the outcome that I had expected. I knew that I would be rejected, but knowing that rejection is going to happen does not soften the blow when it finally comes. I would like to say I was resigned to my fate, but it hurt, like the death of Evie all over again.

'So, what happens to me now?' I asked, with some degree of concern. I was getting tired of having everything in the balance and wanted to get my fate sorted one way or another.

'There is the possibility of an appeal.'

'You people seem to like to talk a lot.'

'We don't rush things that are as important as this. In previous times there have been decisions that have been made rashly that later have been proven to have been wrong decisions. In some cases, it is impossible to reverse a decision and we must live with the guilt of what we have done. These days, we prefer to take our time over important decisions to ensure that the conclusion that we reach is the right one.'

'I suppose that is reasonable. So, tell me about this appeal process. I thought that the decision was final with no grounds for an appeal.'

'That is true, and that would normally be the case. I have, however, managed to bring about a temporary stay for the time being at least. Although appeals are normally not permitted, I believe that your case is sufficiently unique to be allowed a second chance.'

'So, what do we do?'

'We have the opportunity to present your argument again.'

'Is there any point?'

'What do you mean?'

'If we have already lost the debate, and the appeal will be the debate with the same people, what are we likely to gain from it?'

'We must develop better arguments.'

'I don't see how we can. The basis of it all is that if a law is unjust then it should not be followed. If your people have already rejected that, then there is little to be gained by reiterating it, surely?'

'Possibly not; but even if you believe that you are against all the odds and your chances are slim, is that any reason not to try?'

'I admire your optimism; but then you have less to lose than I do.'

He did not reply to this but merely inclined his head slightly which I took to be an agreement.

'What exactly is it that I do stand to lose?' We had never directly spoken about this as Aaron had always found some way to avoid talking about it. He seemed to avoid talking about it this time as well.

***

I suppose to an extent I had lost my sense of enthusiasm by this point. I know that I have lost it now, but I guess by this point, I was feeling pretty lethargic towards things and it was pretty impossible for me to summon up the necessary requirement to continue the fight.

I had come through a lot by this stage, both emotionally and physically. I had hoped that I would be able to sort out a life among the Pariahs where I might have been finally happy; but it was inevitable that my case would be rejected. Now Aaron was offering me the chance to appeal the decision. My most immediate response was to query what the point was. It would only result in a great deal more energy having to be spent on my part followed by pinning all my hopes on a reprieve and the appeal actually working, when in all honesty, it was highly unlikely that it would be a success. I was resigned to my fate in that regard.

Aaron had carefully avoided telling me what would happen if the appeal was rejected but it did not take a genius to work out that there was likely to be a rather unpleasant outcome for me at the end of it all. This is where the paradox came in for me. I imagined that the result was that I was going to be killed to prevent me from revealing the secrets of the Pariahs; or at the very least, they would have some place where I could be imprisoned for the rest of my life and remain under their control. Neither option particularly appealed to me, although I did consider the possibility that an imprisonment at their hands would in some way be something of a relief; which is ironic when I look back on it. I couldn't be certain that imprisonment was a possibility and execution was just as likely to be an outcome, despite, or maybe, because of their moral code.

Although in many regards, I would have welcomed death a great deal as being a release from the suffering that I had already gone through, there was still an element of resistance about me which made me fight death. I suppose I could have killed myself at any point, but regardless of how I felt about Evie and the situation that I was in, I just could not bring myself to make the ultimate self-sacrifice. It was one of those weird situations where I was aware that death would bring me the release that I felt that I wanted, but at the same time, there was some survival instinct within me that made me resist the idea of actually dying. I don't know if this makes any sense to you? It doesn't make a hell of a lot of sense to me if I am entirely honest. I just felt very messed up and it is a state that has continued. I would love to say that I have finally, after all my years of confinement, achieved some kind of inner peace and found a degree of rest within myself; but the simple fact of the matter is that I haven't.

Whilst I was on the Island of the Pariahs, I was fast coming to the conclusion that I was receiving some degree of mental torment for killing my wife. It probably sounds strange, but that was what I began to think. To take the life of another person is something that is considered to be horrendous in most cultures, past and present that I have ever heard of or could imagine existing. To kill your wife, to kill the person you love with all your heart is an abomination. How is that to be handled? When I killed her, I cut from me my very reason for existence and my very ability to survive, as surely as if I had cut out my own heart.

It sounds melodramatic, but that is simply the way that I felt. None of it made all that much sense to me though, as to why it was that I would not willingly embrace death. Perhaps there are those of us who cling to life too much.

I had some difficult decisions ahead of me though. With Aaron not making any clear exclamation to me as to what would happen to me after the appeal, my suspicions started to grow more and I started to think deeply about the path that I had decided to walk down and the future that lay before me, such as it might be. It was at this point that I realised that it was time that I took my fate away from others, whilst I waited around for them to make decisions as to what would happen to me and it was time for me to take matters into my own hands and control my own destiny. Something that I had not really done since that terrible night when I killed her.

16

Aaron worked on my appeal whilst I worked on my own thoughts. Aaron remained optimistic about whatever chances at my appeal he thought I had. I had already reached my own conclusions on what my chances were. A prisoner on the Island of Pariahs might be something of a luxury compared to other places, but it doesn't take away from the fact, that it is still a prisoner. A prisoner in the most splendid and well-treated of positions, is no match for freedom in squalor and the most deprived of conditions.

I continued to enjoy the limited amount of freedom that I had been granted on the island. I walked along the beach each day, basking in the sun and watching the waves break against the shore. Everything seemed so peaceful and so right. It was hard to believe the turbulent nature that my life had changed to in recent times. Walking along the coastline like this, I could almost forget my troubles and feel that I could spend the rest of my life here in reasonable happiness without anything else to worry about.

I walked long and chiefly my thoughts were towards Evie. There was nothing unusual about this; my thoughts were nearly always on Evie. Some memories of her are so distant now that I can hardly place them; they are like patches of fog that it is impossible to get a grip of. I clutch hopelessly at it but it continues to escape me. Walking along the beach reminds me of a similar time when Evie and myself were on the beach. We didn't go to the beach all that often as it was too far away from where we were placed and travel was not the easiest of things to do.

It must have been winter; I don't remember the sun being like this upon me. I seem to remember us being wrapped up in overcoats and the wind was bitter as it howled in from the sea. I remember us stumbling along the beach which I seem to remember as being stonier and rockier compared to the smooth, warm sand of the Pariahs. Due to the nature of the beach that we were on, we had to cling to each other. We held onto each other partially to prevent one or the other of us from stumbling on the uneven surface. We also held onto each other because we were in love and it is what we most wanted to do.

We stumbled along the beach, laughing at some long-forgotten joke whilst the wind continued to whip around us making the tails on our coats flap like flags. Eventually, I remember us finding a small café on the seafront. It was nothing special. The place was rather run-down as I don't think all that many people came here. We sat at one of the tables and examined the menu. I seem to remember the table cloth was of some horrible plastic material which was no doubt economical as it could be used to wipe spillage up rather than having to wash a linen cloth each time. I suppose it was a rather sensible idea, although its attractiveness was lacking somewhat.

We drank bitter coffee which under normal circumstances would have been absolutely vile, but which we didn't mind, because we were together and you can suffer all manner of things when you are together. It is amazing, the level of bitterness that you don't even notice when you have someone to share it with. Sometimes you can be so happy together that you don't even realise how unhappy you are.

There is no order to memories. At times you can be thinking about something like the beach which is something that happened a fair distance into our relationship and then you will be assaulted by a very early memory, only to be followed by a later one. It is a form of time travel with no means of control. The later memories are the ones that I like the least.

I remember our first real date after we had met at the dinner. I remember we had agreed to meet in a park and I arrived there early but spent ages waiting out of sight for her to arrive, so it didn't look like I was too keen when she did turn up. Silly, the things that you do when you are so interested in someone, that you try to act as if you are not interested at all. I carried a single red rose in my hands which had been staggeringly difficult to get hold of and had cost me a fair amount of credit, but was something that I felt I had to do.

She arrived looking more beautiful and radiant than I had remembered and more so than I would have thought possible for anyone to look. From that moment on, everyone else who was in the park ceased to exist. Once again, it must have been winter as I remember that there was a rosy glow to her cheeks which made her look all the more beautiful. I am sure I remember seeing her breath in the cold air as well. She was the most beautiful woman that I had ever seen in my entire life.

In those days, we were still unsure of each other and we lacked the familiarity that would come with time. This memory is pushed to one side with a memory of her wearing a grey, long-sleeved, roll-neck sweater which clung to her and showed off all her curves. She was sitting on my lap and we were kissing passionately whilst I cupped her breast with one hand whilst the other surrounded her and pulled her close to me.

All of these memories show me how lucky I am to have been with Evie. My relationship may have led me to the difficult position that I was in on the Island of Pariahs and the situation that I am in now as I write these words, but despite all of that, I would not replace one second of the time that we spent together.

Not one second.

***

Alpheus sits with me whilst I write these words. There has been another clamp-down on security, due to an inspection that is due to take place. We must be extra careful about not having these words captured by those who would do us harm. I must remind myself from time to time that the writing of this chronicle is something that is not a light-hearted task at a memoir, but is actually something that could have very serious consequences if it were ever to be discovered. Words are the most powerful of weapons that exist.

From time to time, Alpheus asks me questions and gets me to clarify some of the things that I have said. He acts like an editor of my life; forever pointing me in the right direction. I wonder if it is all worth it. I have convinced myself of the importance of recording all of this, but I wonder if these words are ever destined to be read by anyone else other than Alpheus and myself. It is impossible to say and I would imagine that I would be long dead before I ever got the chance to find out.

The one thing that I find most difficult to deal with at the present is my constant tiredness. The lack of activity all this time rather than giving me any form of rest actually makes me more lethargic and I struggle through the day doing the most basic of things. Sometimes, there is no difference between being awake and asleep, I feel so unrested. Going to sleep is a nightly occurrence that I absolutely dread. I can control my mind at most other times aside from when I must surrender to slumber and then I am betrayed by my inner demons, who will not allow me to rest because of the things that I have done. Will I never know peace?

I have talked before about death and the release it may bring but I have come to worry now that it will not bring me any peace at all and instead, I will have the torment that I have at night all of the time. I can imagine the suffering that would bring to my already tormented mind. The never-ending remembrance and suffering for my crime. At the moment, I can prevent myself from sleeping for as long as possible so that I do not have to surrender to the torments. I do everything I can to resist dying but I know that this is an impossible task and that one day, I will have to surrender to this and then my black demons will have won and they will have me to torment at their leisure and there will be no escape for me. It is not an attractive possibility for me, but perhaps it is no more than I deserve. I will resist for as long as I am able to though.

It gets harder with each day that passes.

***

All of this stems from walking along the beach on the Island of Pariahs. If I am unacceptable to be here amongst those that are already outcast, then what am I? Where will I ever find a home? I could see a long future stretching out in front of me which would mean being hounded from place to place with no one wanting me to stay and nowhere that I would again be able to settle. A life of perpetual torment and misery. Either that or I would be incarcerated somewhere that may prove just as insufferable. The choices were not good for me.

Those of you who are reading this I cannot begin to imagine what your circumstances are like and I would not presume to pretend to understand your own conditions. I can only hope that you find yourself in a situation that is far happier than mine. That includes both my individual circumstances to which I must accept my own part of blame as well as the circumstances where I was born and in the unjust society that I have lived in. I say all of this because I hope with improved circumstances you may look more favourable upon me. It might be that you need that level of understanding to fully appreciate why I did what I did next.

***

Aaron continued with his plans whilst I began to work on my own ones. After I had been told that my application had been rejected, I became even more introspective than I had been before, and I had been pretty withdrawn in my own thoughts since the death of Evie. As I was walking along the beach, filling my mind with my memories of Evie, I had what I can only describe as an epiphany.

Ever since Evie had died, I had become depressed and sunken in my own thoughts about her. Not only the obvious depression that would come with the loss of a loved one, but also the depression that came about because I knew that I had been the instrumental cause in that loss. True, she would have eventually died if I had not intervened, but I had nevertheless, intervened. Our plan for her to have a peaceful death had backfired and she had suffered. No matter how I put it, she had suffered and she had suffered at my hands.

I came to the realisation that this was why I was suffering the torments that I was inflicted with. There seemed to me that there was only one way to get round this and that was to admit to what I had done and accept the punishment that was my due. I could have surrendered myself to the Pariahs and allowed them to do whatever they deemed necessary, but I did not think that this was a course of action that would ease my torment. It was not the Pariahs that I owed anything to. I would have to face the fact that the only way that I could achieve peace was to return to the Landmass and face the punishment that the legal system offered.

You may think that this is an insane course of action to take, but it seemed perfectly logical to me in my beleaguered state. There was a symmetry of justice to it all as far as I could see. I had committed a crime back home, so the only way to be at peace, was to return home and face the punishment for the crime that had been committed there.

Alpheus has been particularly interested to know the logic behind my decision to return and it has been a question that has been asked of me a number of times. I think it can be seen that I was in an impossible situation. I could not seek sanctuary with the Pariahs and there was nowhere else that I could be safe. If the Pariahs had accepted me into the fold, would I have been so keen to return and give up my haven? In all honesty, I don't know the answer to that, but I would guess, that if I had been offered safety there, then I might have stayed. It was the rejection that prompted me to have the thoughts that I did about returning. I may have come to the conclusion that I did in time without necessity making it quicker. I don't know.

I can dress it up in as many ways as I like, but the simple bottom line of the matter is, that I felt returning to face whatever was decided for me, was the right thing to do. I had killed my wife and now was the time to pay for it.

The only issue that remained was as to how I was going to get home. I had to keep my intention secret from Aaron and the rest of the Pariahs. I could understand their desire for secrecy about the society that they had created. If word got back to the Landmass about how things really were here, then there was every chance that their society would have been in danger, as such a way of living was not something that I imagined the Illuminati would tolerate. I did not want to be the instrument in bringing invasion and death to this peaceful island, even if they had rejected me, I had no grudge against them and I already had more than enough blood on my hands as it was. Whatever I decided, it would have to be done in secret for they would surely not let me escape and run the risk that I would spread the word. Of course, I would do my best to keep their secret, but who knows what might be revealed when the pressure is on?

I could hardly blame them for this, I am sure if the situation was reversed, I would have done the same to protect the society that I lived in and had worked so hard to make a paradise; but it was no paradise for me. I would not find a paradise, for I had destroyed the last hope I had at happiness. Moaning about it was not going to do me any good though, it was time for action.

The problem was just how I was going to get back home. There is a big gulf between thought and action. Having made up my mind as to what I wanted to do, there now remained the task of how I was to do it. After all I was stuck on an island some distance from the Landmass with no means of getting home. It was not an easy problem to come up with a solution for. I knew that I nevertheless had to find a solution because regardless of what else happened, I was going home.

17

Now that I had made my decision I felt as if a great weight had been lifted from me. I had no idea why I had not made the decision before; it was a perfectly logical thing to do. I had some thinking to do to try and come up with a way to carry out my plan and I wasn't sure of how much time I had left before Aaron returned and told me that the appeal was not upheld and therefore my freedom would be taken from me permanently. Time was running out fast for me.

Time was running out fast. How ironic a thing to say when today, time is the one thing that I have in abundance. Time is a disease for me now, which eats away at me on a daily basis. It drags and takes from me my very energy. When I was younger and happy with Evie, I wasted so much time, not taking the chance to do the things that we should have done and make the most of the situation. I wasted time on pointless things when I should have dedicated every moment to Evie and spending time with her. When I think of all the time I wasted in those days, when now, time hangs on me like a mocking chain around my neck pulling me down. Time has had its revenge on me for wasting so much of it.

Time always wins in the end.

***

There was obviously only one way off the island and that would be to go by ship, the way that I came. Ships did come to the island from time to time and were not an unknown occurrence. The problem would be getting on one of them and off the island without the Pariahs knowing about it or without the sailors giving me up to them. It was something that I only really had one shot at. If I were to mess it up, then there was no chance that I would be able to try again. It was a tricky situation.

If I were able to secure passage back to the Landmass by one means or another then I would be fine. Once there, then everything should be straightforward. It was just a matter of being able to get there. The most obvious thing to do would be to ask directly one of the captains, if they could give me passage back to the Landmass, but a little thought made me realise that they were hardly likely to do this. If the Pariahs were concerned that I might reveal their secrets to the Illuminati and thus endanger their whole society, then the sea captains must also be concerned that they would be in a precarious position if I should reveal the assistance that they also provided the Pariahs. Naturally, everyone was out for their own interests, and I can't really blame them for that.

The only logical conclusion was to stowaway on the next available vessel and hope that I would not be discovered before we reached the Landmass. I was certain that if I were discovered then there would be no issue with me being thrown overboard or disposed of in some manner. There was an element of risk about it all, but where in life is there not risk? All I had to do was have the courage to follow through with my plan.

As secretly and as discreetly as I could, I would expand my walk to gradually take in the port area of the beach. I tried to do this slowly so as not to draw too much attention to myself as I was certain that I was still being observed no matter how covertly it might be. As I walked, I examined as carefully as I could, each of the vessels that appeared in the port. Smaller vessels were of no use to me as there was no place that I would be able to successfully hide in them and not be discovered for the long trip back to the Landmass. It was around this time that I began to realise the enormity and the difficulty of the task that I had set myself. In my thoughts, it had appeared to be the easiest thing in the world to do to return to the Landmass. It was noble and the moral thing to do and yet here I was, stumbling at the very first hurdle. How could I possibly hope to succeed with the rest of the plan?

***

I remember candlelight most of all. It's a strange thing to say, but this cell in which I spend all of my time now is dimly lit by a candle and I spend a great deal of my time looking into the flame. Imagining the past and seeing the figures that the flame seems to produce. It reminds me of the times when Evie and myself would have dinner with soft candlelight illuminating the mood. What was so romantic in those days is now changed to a symbol of confinement these days. Funny how these things change.

Evie and myself had a lot of dinners together. We would always prefer to dine out when we went to an Entertainment or to the Cinematograph. It was an expensive thing to do, but we enjoyed it a great deal. There were times when we would spend credit on expensive times together, but there were also times, when we would do the simplest of things, that required no credit at all.

Alpheus, my constant companion, sits with me whenever his duties allow. It is not as frequent as I would like, but ultimately, he has things that he must do, whereas I do not have all that much pressing upon my time. I am grateful for what he can give me and he has certainly given me a lease of life with the detailing of this chronicle. I must continue with it for I am often in pain these days and there is only so long that I fear I will be able to continue to write before I must either conclude my story or give it up entirely.

Because I had not been able to ask anyone directly about travel plans, I had no idea when the vessel was going to leave. I had to judge my time very carefully. Over the time that I had spent on the island, I had watched the movements of the sailors carefully and I think I had reached a point where I was able to judge when I felt that a vessel was about to leave within the space of a few hours. If I misjudged it and got on too early, then I would have run the risk of my disappearance being noticed by Aaron or one of the other Pariahs. This would have necessitated a search and I am sure it would not have taken too long before they had realised that I was on one of the vessels.

I also had to consider the fact that I was being watched. It was necessary for me to use some degree of subterfuge in order to escape from my observers. I had been on the island for some time by this stage, so had reached a point where I was able to observe a lot without making it look too obvious that I was observing. After some time of this, I believe that I had identified those among the Pariahs who were most likely to be the ones that had been set the task of keeping me under observation. Having identified these familiar faces, I was able to avoid them. I led them into thinking that I was in one place when I had secretly slipped the noose and was heading in a different direction entirely.

I had, after some time, found a vessel that I believed would be sufficient for my needs. Under the cover of darkness, I crept on board the vessel and worked my way as silently as I could down into the bottom of the vessel amongst the creaking wood of the beams. Even though the vessel was in the port, it still swayed and rocked with the waves that knocked against its sides. I hated sea travel. My previous voyage, being the first that I had ever undertaken had not left me in any way keen on the voyage that I was about to undertake, but necessity left me with little choice. I tried to draw some kind of morbid comfort from the fact that this would be the last voyage that I would undertake, probably of any description.

I found what I hoped would be a quiet area where no one else would go and I settled down to wait in the hope that it would not be too much longer before we set sail.

***

As you can imagine, I am hardly all that active these days and yet despite not being all that busy during the day, I still struggle to sleep at night. The dreaded insomnia descends upon me and I am left tossing and turning on my bunk, too desperate for sleep to actually be able to sleep.

I can cope with all manner of things in my life; I have had to; but I struggle a great deal with this inability to sleep. If you are fortunate enough to have never had this problem then you will not understand how much of a torture it is, to not be able to sleep. It seems like such a small thing, but in reality, it is one of the worst things that I think can happen. You may think that is an exaggeration, but if you were to spend some time with me in my situation, you would understand.

My eyes hurt due to the lack of the sleep that I have suffered already and in my fragile situation, I must be careful that I do not end up in the Infirmary once again, for if I do, I shall struggle with this chronicle. Sometimes I feel that the writing of this chronicle is an insurmountable task. I don't always feel that I have the will to be able to continue with it, there is so much that I have left to say, but with each word that I write, the tiredness just seems to hit me and drag me down. The pain that I have in my hands makes the movement of the pencil across the paper sluggish.

I know that I must continue though, as I know that justice must be done and I must record all of my thoughts about the events that I have lived through. How else will future generations understand the injustice of the society that we created for ourselves? How else can they better themselves and do what we have been unable to do? We must learn from the past if there is to be any hope for the future. The future is the only hope that we have.

I am too tired.

***

I have had a very strange relationship with time over the years. I have made comment already about how time plays tricks on me in this small room of mine. It played tricks on me again as I waited in the bottom of the vessel in the hope that I would not be discovered and that we would soon set sail. I have no idea how much time passed as I sat there, cramped in the darkness. Unable to stand up and unable to lie down so tight was the chosen place of imprisonment that I had picked for myself.

I have no idea how long I was there when I was suddenly jolted awake. It amazed me that in such cramped positions, I was able to fall asleep in the first place, but I had been able to do so, when I suddenly woke with a panic. My limbs were aching a great deal from the position that I had forced myself into. I diverted from my mind from the pain that was shooting through my body and tried to bring my mind round to the reason why I had been jolted awake.

I listened to the creaking of the beams and realised that this was probably the reason for why I had been awoken. The creaking was louder and the roll of the vessel was more pronounced. We were at sea! So far things were actually working. Secretly, I had never believed that they would and I had felt certain that I would have been captured, but we were now at sea. All I had to do now was stay undetected for as long as the voyage and then slip ashore when we docked. If I could do that then I would be back home.

I felt a degree of guilt over the betrayal of Aaron, who had shown me nothing but kindness. I could not allow sentiment to get in the way of the plan that I had formulated though. I had to return and face my penance for the crime that I had committed and I knew that Aaron and his fellows would have done all that they could in order to prevent me from leaving the island and returning to the Landmass.

I cannot tell you how long I remained in the dark, cramped place that I had chosen. I had the smallest amount of food with me which I tried to ration as best I could. I would have given anything to be able to get out and stretch my limbs, but I could not run the risk of being seen by anyone. It was a great moment to practice mental discipline and rise above the pain and discomfort that I was feeling and place my mind on higher things. It was also something that I entirely failed to achieve.

Each time I heard the voices of the sailors I swear my heart stopped beating for fear that I was about to be discovered at any second. Fate must have been on my side, for once, as I was able to get through the entire voyage without being discovered or being too ill. The next tricky thing for me to do was to be able to get off the vessel without being discovered. This was less of a problem than it was the other way around. Now that I had reached the Landmass I was in less of a need for secrecy as I had been when I had begun the voyage.

Nevertheless, I waited until such a time as the activity on the vessel had died down from the hustle and bustle of arriving at the dock and then I slowly exited from my prison. One thing that I had not factored in was that I was not able to make a quick run for it, as my legs were still so numb from being cramped up for such a long time that for a moment they would barely work and I could hardly stand. After a few moments of massaging them though, I was able to make the move and I crept silently from the vessel and made my way onto the shoreline.

Once there, I realised that although my plan was to face justice for what I had done I didn't actually have any practical plan as to what I was going to do next.

18

I would love to say that it felt good to be home, but I doubt that it would have felt all that good for me to be anywhere. I was a man with a mission. It had occurred to me that I could surrender myself immediately to the authorities and get the matter over and done with. This was a possibility, but I was not really ready to throw myself upon their mercy, or lack of mercy, just yet. I wanted to see what had been going on in my absence. Being with the Pariahs, I had not been able to hear the latest news from the Landmass and I was keen to know how Doctor Asa was getting on.

I felt that I had been away for a very long time, but in reality, it couldn't have been as long as I had imagined it was. Fortunately for me, I was able to arrive back at the Landmass under the cover of darkness. I couldn't have timed it better if I had tried. I waited until the vessel had settled and then as I have stated I made my way, with my aching limbs, back to the shore where I tried to blend in with the others who were going about their business. I felt that at any minute, hands might be laid upon me and I would be arrested before I had the chance to do the things that I wanted to do.

It is a strange feeling being a fugitive. You get into the mind set of thinking that everyone knows that you are on the run and that everyone knows that you have this big secret to hide. With every sound that is made you look in terror, with every movement you think that this is the moment when someone is going to come and get you. If you happen to see a member of the authorities, you suspect that this is the moment when your time is up. Of course, it is all rather in your own head. Being a fugitive makes you paranoid about what is going on. In reality, it is your imagination and no one cares less. It doesn't stop you from being on edge, because at any moment you might come across that one person who does know that you are a fugitive. The important thing is not to run if you see a member of the authorities. If you do, they will run after you because it is their instinct to do so, even though they don't know why they are running after you. You just have to maintain your cool and act as naturally as possible. This is harder to do than it might seem.

Everyone has their own secrets and their own business. As I walked through the crowds of people, I took the luxury of thinking about the people that were around me and what secrets they had. What was the business that they were engaged in? I didn't think that anyone would have secrets as deep as mine, but you never entirely know and there is always the possibility that there was someone that I was brushing shoulders with who had even deeper secrets and things to hide than I did. Was I the only murderer amongst them? Who could tell? You can never tell the secrets and the inner most thoughts of the person who is next to you.

I worked my way through the crowds and tried to blend in as best I could without drawing attention to myself. It surprised me that even at night, this place was still so busy. I dreaded to think what it would be like during the day when all the work was going on, but it seemed to me that this was the kind of place that remained as active as this for all the hours of the day. The Residuum were the ones that were mostly at work here as this was brutal manual labour that required no thought. Here and there I saw the odd Overseer. I tried to blend in as best as possible, but I had no idea whether it would be best to pretend to be a member of the Residuum or an Overseer. In the end, I opted for bland insignificance in the hope that I would be camouflaged against the others. If I had tried to disguise myself as an Overseer amongst all of this work going on, then it would potentially have drawn suspicion from the real Overseers who did not recognise me as one of their own. It is tricky the path that we tread once we have started on our way. I could not have imagined before all this had started that I would end up as I now was. As I have said before, we can never be fully aware of the consequences of our actions. Perhaps if we were, we would not do anything at all; but then we would still not be aware of the consequences of our inactions.

***

It seems so cold these days. I don't remember it always being so cold, but perhaps the lack of physical activity that I have these days adds to the

147

coldness getting into my bones. I swear that I never used to feel this cold. Old men suffer from the lives that we have led and my life has been one that has resulted in me suffering more than most perhaps. It is no better than I deserve.

Other than the candle we are allowed no heat here. I have blankets, of course, which are mainly threadbare now and provide me with little comfort, but they are better than nothing, I suppose. The candle gives off hardly enough light, it is almost impossible to get heat from it and we are also strictly rationed on how many candles we are permitted to have. Therefore, I have to be very careful on the amount of use that it has. The consequence of this, therefore, is that not only is it cold here most of the time, but I also spend a fair amount of time in darkness.

There is a window, if you can call it that. It is really a hole in the wall, which hardly amounts to the same thing. It is set high up so it is impossible to look through. It isn't very big and it does allow a small amount of light to come through during daylight. There is no glass or covering of any kind so during the winter season the cold gets in, as well as the other elements. It is a misery really. I suppose when they designed these places, they were not thinking that the comfort of the inmates was the highest priority though. If that is the case, then they really were very successful about this. I can vouch for that.

Once the dampness seeps into the walls it never seems to go away. It radiates dampness from them and from there, seeps into every nook and cranny, it gets into the blankets and then there is nothing that can be done to protect you from the dampness and cold. The blankets never seem to dry out and there is no means to assist this happening. It is no wonder that the coldness and the damp gets into my bones and makes me suffer and ache so much. It is an intolerable situation to be in but this is my day-to-day life now. The stone walls retain the dampness even in the height of summer and so there is really very little relief all year round.

I say that but it is perhaps not entirely true or maybe fair to say it is misleading. The damp does remain in the walls, even during the summer, but that doesn't prevent the place becoming like an oven during the hottest periods. I am not sure what is worse, the intolerable heat or the insufferable cold. Either way, it is difficult to cope with. The only break that comes in the summer is the odd thunderstorm which for a moment breaks the infernal heat and mugginess, bringing with it the sweet smell that comes with wet grass. It is the most wonderful feeling of all and I try my best to stand as close to the window as I can so that if it is coming in the right direction, I might feel some of the rain upon my face and smell the freshness as if the very world has been swept clean and fresh.

I suspect that you will have very little sympathy for this. After all, I did murder my wife. No matter how you look at it and dress it up in morality and the decisions that I made for the best of intentions, you cannot take away from the fact that I killed Evie. In many ways, I deserve all that I got for that act. There is nothing else I can say about it. Justice bringing deserved punishment. I only tell you about it so that you can understand fully the conditions of my life, not because I want any pity from you.

I know I am beyond that.

***

It took me some time to fully realise where I was and to get my bearings. Having come ashore during the night, I had no idea where I was and how far I had to go to get back to the district that I used to call my home. So many things have changed since those days.

After some time, I eventually realised that I was no more than a few hours away from where I wanted to be which I thought of as extremely lucky, as I could easily have been days away from where I had to go. It is funny how things work out.

I will not bother to relay my trek across country to my destination as it was uneventful and there really is nothing that is worth mentioning about it. With time, I arrived outside Doctor Asa's house and was distressed to see that the house that I had been welcomed in so many times, had spent so many happy moments in was now boarded up and gave the appearance of being entirely desolate. I was rather shocked by this as I had not been expecting it at all. For a moment, I stood there in shock with my mouth open looking like some kind of idiot.

'They came for him.' The voice seemed to come out of nowhere, so engrossed I was in trying to work out what had happened. I turned round and saw an old man standing behind me with a slightly sinister smile on his face, that made me feel rather uncertain.

'Came for who?'

'Yonder Asa,' he said, pointing a dirty finger at the house. 'The one who used to live there, before they came for him.'

'Who came for him?'

'The authorities, of course. Who else?' It seemed a fair answer and question and was uttered with the confidence of someone who seemed to know a lot about the authorities rounding up people all of the time and carting them off. I wondered how much of this sort of thing he had seen before.

'What did they do with him?' I asked apprehensively.

The old man gave no answer to this but just shrugged and pulled a pipe out of his pocket, which he began to stuff with tobacco mechanically with his hands whilst looking off into the distance as if there was something more important to be seen in the grey sky elsewhere and that my question was of no importance to him whatsoever. It probably wasn't. I noticed that his hands were dirty and stained with tobacco. I decided to try a different question as I suspected that there would be little that I would get out of this man if he was not prepared to give it up.

'Do you know where he is now?'

The man turned his attention towards me and stuffed the pipe between his teeth, or between what little of his teeth I could actually see. Most of them seeming to be missing or those that remained were cracked and tainted yellow and black.

'I might,' he consented, after a while of searching me with his eyes.

'Could you take me to him?'

'I could.'

'Would you take me to him?'

'No.'

'Why not?' This was a little annoying.

'I don't reckon there is anything in it for me,' he replied, grinning around his pipe which he had still not lit. He might have had something in this observation as I had started to learn that there were very few people in this world who were prepared to do something for nothing.

'Would this help?' I said, as I showed him a credit that I had been keeping among the few that I had managed to keep hold of for essentials like food. I was reluctant to offer him credit to take me to where Asa was, but I had no idea how much time I had before the authorities found me, so I reasoned that I did not really have all that much time to waste. If this strange, old man could save me time by taking me to Asa, then it would have to be worth the credit which would not be of any use to me once the authorities laid hands on me.

I swear that the old man's eyes glinted when he saw the credit and he shuffled forward slightly to get a closer look at it. I handed it over to him so that he could inspect it more closely. I ran the risk that he might steal it, but I was reasonably confident that given his age and ancient look, he would not be able to out-run me no matter how my body had suffered in the cramped vessel. He took the credit in his dirty hands and rolled it over his fingers as if checking to see if it was real. I half expected him to put it in his mouth and bite it, but he stopped short of this.

'I reckon I could show you where he is then,' the old man said, as he pocketed the credit so swiftly that I could only imagine that he was long practised at it. He must be one of the Residuum, surely, but he seemed to be more articulate (in his way) and also more confident in his approach to me, than any member of the Residuum that I had so far met. He was almost outside of the Spheres — in a Sphere of his own. It was all very confusing. His age didn't make sense either as I couldn't imagine that there was a member of the Residuum that would live to as old as he appeared to be.

'Is it far?' I enquired, wondering how much time I would have to spend in this man's company, as I had started to notice, now that we were closer, that he really did smell appallingly.

'Not so far,' he replied and smiled with a grin that proved my suspicion that he did not have all that many teeth and also overwhelmed me with a smell of rotting flesh from his own mouth, that I struggled to not show my revulsion at. This seemed to only make him smile all the more.

And now I am too tired to continue and my pains in my chest have returned that have plagued me lately. Enough for today.

***

My chest pains are one of many pains that I have these days and I regret that these discomforts along with my general tiredness, so often make me stop my flow of writing. I must remember my age and my condition though, (as if I could really forget it) and remember that I am not that which I once was, and can no longer act the same way that I once did. Sometimes the mind plays tricks on us though, convincing us that we are capable of things that our body gave up many years since.

We can all be betrayed in this way. There are those who are betrayed by their body which is no longer capable of doing what the brain insists upon and there are those who are betrayed by their brain which declines in health, whilst their body is more or less capable of what it always was. I have long debated with myself which would be the best course of action. Would I be better losing control over my body and yet remaining sharp in the brain; or would it be better to lose control over the brain and have no idea what was going on with anything else? It is a difficult one. An active brain, healthy in a body that cannot survive must be like a prisoner who is unable to escape. On the other hand, the oblivion that a diseased brain might bring would be fine, so long as you were not aware of the fact that your brain was going and you were losing so much. True, when the end came you would be oblivious, but there was still the slope to travel down before that time came.

My brain has not yet brought me the oblivion that I could hope for, and perhaps it never will. I shudder with the memories that it makes me remember. I grieve for my wife every day that I continue to live. I feel sorrow for my gallant, trustworthy, fallen friend Simeon; and I shrink back in shame when I remember the short journey that the old man took me on and the discovery that it would lead me to find.

19

After a short while in the company of this old man, I learnt that his name was Avi. He seemed very reluctant to tell me what his name was initially.

'I don't see how knowing my name will make any difference to anything that is happening,' he muttered between his clenched gums, as we made our way through grubby streets towards wherever it was that he was leading me. Begrudgingly, he told me his name, but due to the intense reluctance, I have my suspicions as to whether Avi was his real name. I suppose at the end of the day it really didn't matter if he was telling me the truth or not. I did not tell him my name as he showed no interest in knowing what it was, which saved me from having to tell him a lie.

As we walked through the streets, what struck me the most was how dirty everything was compared to the cleanliness of the Pariah state. I suppose this was because the Pariahs did not have the level of industry that was on the Landmass, so therefore had a more natural environment compared to this polluted waste. We walked through streets that were in sore need of repair with broken flagstones and houses that overhung the streets and were too crowded. Such crowding was rife for disease and I tried to cover my mouth as we worked our way through the narrow lanes and thoroughfares. Everything was in a bad state and there was nothing green or fresh as far as the eye could see. I am amazed that I had not seen what things were like before.

Not for the first time I wondered how it was that people could live like this. I suppose the answer is that if you know no better, then you accept the circumstances that you are presented with, or lumbered with. This was assuming that there was an ambition to be better than they were and the Residuum were hardly renowned for their ambition and desire to better themselves. They probably accepted this life as the norm; assuming of course, that they actually gave it any thought at all.

Avi interested me as I could still not place which Sphere he came from. He seemed to know his way around the Residuum areas well and walked with a familiarity that seemed to suggest that if he were not actually part of the Residuum, then he certainly felt at home amongst them. There were two reasons that did make me doubt that this is where he was from. The first was that he had approached me in the first place to speak. Most members of the Residuum, if indeed not all of them, would not have dared to speak to someone out of their Sphere in the approach that Avi had made to me.

The other aspect that told against him was his advanced age. Granted that due to the harshness of the life in the Residuum he may have looked older beyond his years, but even taking that into as a factor, he nevertheless still looked much older than I would have expected someone in the Residuum to be. As I have stated before, the life expectancy in the Residuum was not a lengthy one. I pondered all these thoughts as we walked through the streets and decided to just come out and ask him.

'Don't hold with no Spheres,' he muttered in response to my question. 'Reckon they are designed to try and keep people in their place and there is no doing that if you are determined enough.'

It was an answer that added more questions than it answered, but I was coming to expect nothing less from this strange old man. As I was clearly not going to get any sensible intelligence from him, I decided to remain silent for the rest of the journey and turned my thoughts back to the Pariahs. I wondered how Aaron was and if he was angry or in trouble because of my disappearance which would have long since been discovered by now. I couldn't imagine that he would get angry as it was not something that struck me to be in his character, but I hoped that there would be no retribution for what had happened. I meant him no ill will. I didn't mean any harm to the Pariahs at all. It is true that they rejected me, but I cannot blame them for that. I understand fully the position that they were in and the difficulty that they faced and I cannot say that I would not have done the same thing had I been in their position. Despite my rejection, I respected their society and the things that they were trying to do. I pledged that I would keep their secrets for as long as I was able to and that they would not suffer any harm from anything that I might say or do. I may have betrayed many things in my life but I was not about to betray them.

***

We had been walking for longer than Avi had led me to believe that it would take us to arrive where Asa was. I began to suspect that the old man did not really know where Asa was and that he was leading me round in circles through streets which were so similar, that I would end up being lost; and then he would abandon me having taken the credit from me and would leave me to the mercy of the rouges that I felt sure were lurking in every doorway.

Perhaps it was my imagination playing tricks on me, or perhaps there was someone waiting around every corner, prepared to jump out and rob me of my meagre belongings. Being wanted by the authorities is likely to make you feel a little bit paranoid. However, there is a big gap between thinking that people are out to get you and knowing that they really are out to get you.

After a while, we began to leave the shanty, little houses behind and the path opened up into fields of the surrounding countryside. It was at this stage that I began to really worry as to where it was that Avi was leading me. Perhaps his intention was to lead me out of the populated area into a quiet place, where it would be easier for his friends to rob me without any witnesses. It was only a short walk into the countryside when we stopped.

'Here he be,' said Avi with a smug look on his face. I didn't understand what he meant, there was nothing out here. There were no houses, this was not a populated area and there were no people standing around or sign of life at all. The only thing that was visible was the gallows that are erected on the edge of each populated area where the wrongdoers are hung, for whatever punishment that they have inflicted on the society. It is a place that I fully expected to end up in myself at some stage in the not-too-distant future once the authorities had finally caught up with me.

'I don't understand,' I said, looking around me confused.

'There,' Avi said with impatience, pointing a dirty finger at the gallows. I would swear at this point that my heart actually sank in my chest, if I had imagined that such a thing was possible. I dragged my eyes to the gallows and looked at them properly for the first time and as I did, I saw Asa. That wonderful man who had been our doctor, our friend, our confident for so many years. There he was hanging from the gallows in front of me.

'I told you they came for him,' continued Avi, with a smirk in his voice once again.

I was speechless at this point, looking at the body that swung gently in the breeze that had caught it. If Avi had not pointed him out to me then I very much doubt that I would have recognised him at all. For one, I hardly paid any attention to the corpses that hung from these places, they always made me feel rather uncomfortable, which I suppose was the reason for it. Secondly, I would not have recognised him without prompting because so much of him was eaten away. I have no idea how long he had been hanging there; his body had not only started to decompose, but had also been eaten away by the carrion birds that flocked to the area for a free meal. His eyes were gone, and I had no way of knowing if this was something that had happened to him before he had been brought to this place as a torture, or whether it was the work of the birds. Large sections of his cheeks had definitely been eaten away and it was clear that the birds had pecked away at the fleshier parts that were exposed to them.

I felt sick. Sick because of the physical sight that was in front of me, the kind of thing that I admit to never having the stomach for; sick because of the noble man that I had once known who had now been brought so low before me; and sick, because I saw in his sightless face my own future before me.

I heard Avi chuckling behind me as if he sensed my thoughts. He clearly found the entire thing very amusing and was laughing at the little trick that he had played on me, by telling me that he knew where Asa was when all along, he could just as easily have told me that he was dead, without subjecting me to the hope that I would soon be meeting my friend once again, the only friend that I had left in the world; and now I was robbed even of him. I became aware that the tears were streaming down my face as I stood there, looking at the pitiful sight that was before me.

I turned in order to admonish Avi for the cruel trick that I felt that he had played on me, but he was gone and was nowhere to be seen. He had left me alone with nothing but my grief and my guilt.

***

It was sometime later that I discovered what had actually happened. Asa had been arrested soon after I had left the Landmass for the Island of the Pariahs. Somehow, the authorities had uncovered the truth of what had happened with Evie and from the discovery of her illness and the true nature of her death, it had not taken all that long for them to put the pieces together and work out the involvement of each person in our little deception.

Asa had been arrested as soon as his part in the cover up had been discovered. I later learned that he was interrogated at some vigorous length with the kind of malice that only our own authorities can muster. Apparently, he had refused to co-operate and confirm anything that the authorities already knew. Nevertheless, convinced of his guilt they pressed on. After a while, he was unable to take the pressure of the interrogation any longer and his heart gave way before they could get anything from him. His nobility amazed me and I could not hope to get even the smallest amount of courage myself, if I were to find myself in the same situation as he was.

Obviously in this particular case, the authorities were correct in their assumption of the guilt of the person that they were interrogating, but it made me wonder if there had been people in the past that they were not so sure of and had tortured into confessing things that were not true. Torture has never been reliable in gaining accurate information about anything, but that doesn't seem to stop those that are sadistic enough into going through with it. They get some perverse pleasure from it, I suppose, to make up for their own inadequacies in some other aspect from their lives.

The perverse nature of the society that I live in is easily shown in the fact that despite Asa dying of a heart attack whilst being interrogated, they nevertheless continued with a trial in his absence without any confession from him and obviously without him being able to raise any defence and found him guilty of his part in Evie's death. They then had him taken to the spot where I found him, and hung him from the gallows despite having been dead for some time already. The law is the law and justice is justice, I suppose they would say. Merely because someone is dead does not mean that they should be allowed to escape the punishment that the authorities deem they should be subjected to.

I will leave you to make your own mind up about these things. My view might be considered to be fairly tainted.

***

From the morbid sight of the ending of the noble Doctor Asa, I turned my direction away and headed for the home that used to be so happy for us. Nevertheless, although I had turned my attention away from the ignoble end of my friend, his image continued to haunt me for some time afterwards; in truth, I suppose that it still haunts me to this day.

I wanted to visit the grave of Evie, but it occurred to me that if the plot to cover up her illness had been discovered, as it clearly had, then the authorities would have wasted no time with their vindictiveness and she would have been exhumed by now and probably had her bones abandoned somewhere. The very thought of this filled me with dread. I tried my best not to think about it, but I couldn't stop myself. It was bad enough to remember that my wonderful wife was dead and that I had played an active hand in bringing her death about. What was worse was to think about the fact that she had been denied her final resting place and the peace that she so deserved. What a cruel world it is that we live in, where people who think themselves superior to the rest of us can make such decisions that impact upon us all.

I knew that there was no chance of visiting her final resting place as it almost certainly wasn't her final resting place now and I dreaded to think where they might have dumped her. I wondered how much more I could take of it, to be honest. It is bad enough to know that the person you have loved all of your life is dead, but to know that they have been persecuted into death is too much to be able to take.

In the absence of a grave to visit, I decided that I would visit our old home, where we'd lived together. I knew that there was a risk that this would be as emotionally damaging as everything else that was going on, but I could not resist the possibility of returning to my old home that had seen so many happy hours. I suppose there was an element of self-torture that I was trying to inflict. My friends and loved ones had suffered and died on my behalf and yet I was still here and still living and breathing, when I surely did not deserve to be. I knew that once I was handed over to the authorities then my life would be as forfeit as everyone else's, but in the meantime, I suppose there was no reason why I should not suffer a little on my way to the end. You might think it is an irrational view, but I felt justified in it somehow.

It took me some time to make my way across to where we used to live. I was a fugitive after all, and although I had come back with the purpose of handing myself in, there were things that I wanted to do first of all and I did not want to be captured too soon. Therefore, I was furtive about how I made my way across to my old home, rather than walking openly in the streets without a care in the world. I was far from not having a care in the world.

I arrived at my old home after an uneventful journey and discovered that like Asa's house it was boarded up. I am not sure why these houses were not full of new people. Perhaps it was too soon and the notoriety that lingered with the places meant that nobody was prepared to live there yet; it might even be possible that the places would have to be demolished before they could be lived in again. Some people did not like the idea of living where something like that had taken place.

I approached the back of the house and was able to prise apart some of the wood that had been nailed across the rear door. Once I had managed to get one of the planks out, it was relatively easy to get the rest out so that I could get inside. My nails and fingers were broken and bleeding, but I couldn't have cared less. Inside the house, everything smelt stale and damp as if the very life had been sucked out of the place and there was nothing left inside aside from decay. It amazed me how quickly this sense of decay can move into somewhere which until relatively recently, had been so full of life.

There was hardly any furnishing left inside the house, all of our belongings were gone. I am not sure if they had been stolen or perhaps confiscated and auctioned off. Either way, the place was empty and echoed with every step that I took. How is it possible for something to fall into decay so quickly? I asked myself again, as I stood in the middle of the place and heard slow, dripping water, coming from somewhere. I don't know what I had expected to find when I came here, but if I were in any way, expecting to find any of the warmth that there had once been in these walls then I was going to be sorely disappointed. All that was left here now, was an empty shell of a place that had once been so important to me, but now was nothing.

I looked around me at the desolation that was the home that I had once been so happy in. The broken glass of the windows, the dampness in the air and the pools of water that had formed on the floor of almost every room. Every now and then there might be a scattered remnant of what this place used to be like. An old book in the corner warped by dampness and rain. A piece of something that no one had found any value in, so had left behind to be abandoned to nature.

It made me realise that there is a lack of permanence about so many things. We build our lives and we think that we are on solid ground, but eventually, all things must come to this. We build homes around us that seem so solid, but they are illusions. One day, even the sturdiest of buildings will crumble and fall. Nothing is permanent that we are vain enough to construct and imagine will last forever. The same can be said for ourselves, of course. We seem in our own minds as if we are likely to be here forever, but we too must one day crumble into dust as sure as anything else in life. One day, we will end up as Asa and our homes will end up as this one had. I suppose the lesson is that we should really make the most of it all whilst we have the chance.

It was at this point, as I was standing in the ruins of what had once been my life, that the authorities found me.

20

The authorities found me in the ruin of what had once been my home. I imagined that they probably were tipped off to my return by Avi. Avi probably didn't know who I actually was, but perhaps he had gone to speak to the authorities, and told them that someone had arrived, who was interested in knowing the whereabouts of Doctor Asa. From there it would not have taken them all that much of an effort to work out that it was I that had returned and was asking the questions. I later learned that this was pretty much exactly what had happened. When Avi had left me at the scaffold, he had scuttled off straight to the authorities and told them what he suspected. I hope they paid him a good price for the intelligence.

My detention was not very subtle and I was treated roughly as I was carted from my final home, the last place that I ever truly felt happy. My protestations that I would come quietly, indeed that this was the reason that I had returned to the Landmass, fell on deaf ears and battered and bruised, I was dragged from my old home and taken to a cell where I was thrown in and left. For all I know, I could have been left here to rot for the rest of my life, perhaps that was their intention. It did mildly amuse me that they had not even bothered to find out if they had the right person when they took me into custody; they merely assumed that I was the one they were looking for; or perhaps they reasoned that if I were not guilty of the crime that I was actually guilty of, then I must have been guilty of something else for being where they had found me. I don't suppose they really cared all that much if the truth were known.

I remained in my very small cell for some time with no word from the outside as to what had happened. I expected that I would either be left here to rot or I would be dragged from this dingy little place at some point in the near future and strung up on the same gallows as Doctor Asa. It was difficult to say which I most looked forward to. Neither was particularly attractive, but I had to remember that this is why I had come back. After being in the cell for some time, I was dragged out and taken to a place that was slightly bigger but no better in its aesthetic appeal. In the centre of this room was a small, wooden table which had taken on the same grey colour of the walls. The entire place looked like someone had taken the colour and drained it out of the surroundings, so that it might depress the occupants even more so than they undoubtedly already were.

Shackled to my wrists and my legs were long chains which had been placed on me as soon as I had been taken from my cell. There was not much movement in them and the leg shackles were so close together that it was impossible to walk in anything other than a shuffle. They clinked and rattled against each other with every movement that I made. The inability to walk very fast seemed to cause endless amounts of amusement to the guards, who would push me in the back with wooden clubs to make me walk faster, which was something that I could not do and something that they clearly knew that I could not do. As I had been taken to this new room, I caught glimpses of my fellow inmates who were also shackled in the same way and were also similarly encouraged by the guards to walk a little faster to wherever it was that they were going. From time to time, there would be a loud laugh that would break the silence that was only otherwise broken by the rattling of the chains and the cursing of the guards; the laughter came from the guards who laughed when their individual charge had fallen over which was the inevitably result of trying to walk fast in the shackles. I determined that I would not suffer the indignity of falling over on top of everything else that I had already suffered. It was something that I was unable to keep and before long, my knees and my hands were cut, bloodied and bruised.

Upon arriving in the new room that I had been taken to, my shackles were locked into metal rings that had been embedded in the floor near the table and I was allowed to sit in a chair that had been provided for me. I suspect that the guards were not very happy about this and would have had me stand, as they gave me the chair begrudgingly and then pushed me into it which caused me a sharp pain that shot straight up my back.

Once I was settled into reasonable discomfort, I was able to turn my attention to the other side of the rickety table where sat a thin man who looked in more need of a decent meal than I was. He wore eye glasses on the end of his nose. I don't think this is where they were meant to be as he had a habit of continuously pushing them back up his nose so that they were actually in front of his eyes, which was presumably where they were of most use. However, they would slip back down again to the end of his nose. It became a deep fascination to me to watch over the weeks that were yet to come as I was convinced that one day, they would slide off his nose completely.

'Leave us,' he said. For a moment I didn't realise who he was talking to or what he was referring to and obviously neither did the guard who was standing behind me, as it took the instruction to be repeated in a slightly higher tone before it was reluctantly obeyed.

'My name is Nogah,' the man said, when we were eventually left alone and he had returned his eye glasses to an appropriate place. I thought it was nice that he had told me his name, as nobody had seemed remotely interested in mine for some time. It turned out that he already knew my name.

'Why did you come back?'

I decided not to answer this as I was not prepared to give anything away that might result in anyone else having the same fate as Asa; therefore, I would be doing my best to keep Azarias, the sea captain and Aaron out of anything that I did eventually say. Simeon was beyond any attack that they could have launched on him, but I was still conscious that it might cause issues for his family were I to confess his involvement. I was also aware of the fact that they were probably playing games with me already, they must know what had happened by now. I could not imagine that Asa would have been able to hold out for all that long. I wondered how long I would be able to hold out against the torture before I eventually cracked and told them whatever it was that they had wanted to hear.

I had never moved in the kind of circles before, where I got to meet anyone who had undergone what they referred to, as the Interrogation with a capital I. This was a euphemistic way of saying torture as it amounted to the same thing. Although I had never met anyone who had undergone the Interrogation there were always rumours about it. Rumour stated that there was no one who could survive it. No matter how determined you were to withhold information, they would eventually break you down to a point where they could get you to admit to anything

163

at all, no matter what it was. This is why it was an unreliable means of finding out information. If you were eventually so broken that you would admit that up was down and black was white just to stop the pain from carrying on then your testimony is meaningless as you are clearly just admitting to anything in order to get a release. On the other hand, the authorities would probably point out that the evidence proved that nobody who underwent the Interrogation, was proven to be innocent by the time that it had finished.

Nogah seemed to sense that I was thinking some of this as he looked at me quizzically with his head on one side.

'I am only curious for my own reasons,' he eventually said. 'This is not an interrogation to find out what you will confess to.'

I was not sure what to make of this so I decided that the best policy was to say nothing at all and wait to see how things developed. To an extent, it is a philosophy that I have frequently adopted in life. I would like to say that it is a philosophy that has stood me well over the years, but then I am writing this from my crowded little room with paper that is smuggled in and out to me by Alpheus, so it probably has not been all that good for me when I now think about it.

'I am on your side,' Nogah continued, when it was clear that I was not going to say anything. I found this statement hard to believe. After the murder of my wife and all the grief that had followed it, I found it hard to believe that anyone would take my side willingly. Nogah sat back in his chair and looked at me with a degree of disappointment for a while, as if I had somehow managed to upset him; perhaps I had. He must have been younger than me, but I suddenly felt like a child that had disappointed an ambitious parent.

'How am I going to offer a defence for your trial if you will not talk to me?' He took the eye glasses off his nose when he couldn't keep them on and then threw them down on the table in a gesture of frustration.

There were a couple of things that took me by surprise in this statement. The first was that there was a possibility of raising any kind of defence to what I had done and the second was that judgement had not been passed on me automatically, but that I was apparently going to have a trial.

***

I wrote too much yesterday and now it has left me with hardly the energy to lift a pencil for some days. Alpheus feared that I was going to be so weak that I would be taken back to the Infirmary. There are only so many trips that I can have left to go there now. I am getting older with each second that passes and my health has become worse over the last years, to the point where my eventual permanent rest cannot be so very far away from me now. I will welcome it when it comes if I am honest. That will sound morbid and maybe even defeatist, but I have lived a long life now with a lot of it spent in pain, both physical pain and pain of the mind. I long for the idea that I will be able to rest from it all at some point. I acknowledge that this is only speculation on my behalf. None of us knows, what, if anything, happens to us after we have died. For all I know my torments may begin afresh and with more vigour than I have known so far. Alpheus will do his best to keep me alive until this chronicle has been completed and then, who knows what will happen next?

I long for rest. I know that there is a possibility that I will not get it, but I long for the rest that has escaped me so much in the last few years. The final peace where I will not ache so much any longer. The peace that will come when my eyes no longer hurt because of the tiredness that I feel. When I can move without my limbs, muscles and bones crying out in protest and pain at the smallest of movements. I long for the time when I can sleep without dampness or suffocating heat.

Sometimes, I wonder if I am just longing for too much that will never actually come true. I suppose we all must have a degree of longing though; it is what gets us up each morning and drives us forward. Although in my case, failure to get up in the morning would no doubt result in someone coming in and dragging me off the bunk and kicking me until I got up. I suppose in its own way this is also a longing, a longing not to be motivated by the guards to do anything.

My tiredness is something that I have lived with for some time now so to an extent, you might be forgiven for thinking that it might be something that I have grown to terms with. I have not. I believe that I can hardly sleep because I am plagued by the events of my life. Yes, I know that I did what I did out of love because I could not continue to see Evie

165

suffer so much, but whichever way I look at it, I still cannot get away from the truth of what I did. It has plagued me ever since.

***

'A trial?'

It was the first words that I had spoken to Nogah, which annoyed me greatly, because as I was being dragged to see him, I had pledged that I would not open my mouth and say a thing so that I would not be tempted to betray anyone else. I was determined to take the blame for my own decisions.

'Yes, a trial,' said Nogah, looking as pleased as if I was a simpleton who had suddenly solved an equation that had been puzzling me for some time. I was surprised by the idea of a trial as in all honesty, I had not expected that I would have one. I had expected to be locked up whilst someone else decided my fate and then I would be taken away and executed on public display somewhere, as a lesson to anyone else who might think about defying the authorities the way that I had. Failing that, I expected to be left in the cell to rot for the rest of my life. A trial smacked of something that was verging on fairness.

'You did not expect a trial?' asked Nogah again, with the uncanny ability to seem like he was reading my mind.

'No.'

'Everyone has the right to a trial.'

'Did Doctor Asa?' He looked a little sheepish at this question.

'Yes, he did.'

It obviously had not been something that had gone in his favour, but then, I held a suspicion that these trials were for show anyway. Nor did Nogah inform me that it was a trial that had taken place after he was already dead. Yes, we did have trials. Our society may have been heavily flawed but there was still a resemblance of process left. I just held the belief that the decision had been made as to the outcome of the trial before the first word had been spoken. It was a pretence to make it look like it was something that was fair. Asa's verdict was something that had probably been a forgone conclusion and I suspected that the same could be said of me. I wondered why we had to go through the process to ultimately just delay the inevitable.

'Why did you come back?' he asked me again. I was confused by Nogah, as I had no idea what it was that he was here to do. If this was the beginning of the Interrogation, it was certainly being handled in a way that was different to how I imagined that it would progress. He had also said that he was there to help me, if I were having a trial. I began to wonder if it was true that he was there to help me. I debated this for so long that he assumed that I was refusing to talk to him again.

'Look, I can't help you if you won't talk to me.'

'Who are you?' I asked, looking up at him with all my confusion probably obvious on my face. This was just not taking the turn that I had expected that it would.

'I told you my name is Nogah.'

I nodded and then leaned forward as far as the chains would allow me to do and looked at him directly in the eye.

'Yes, I know that, you said. But who are you?'

'I'm your advocate,' he replied, when he finally seemed to understand what it was that I was asking. 'I'm here to defend you in your trial.'

21

The idea of a defence for my case was something of a novelty for me. I had not expected to have to defend my position; I merely had expected to be punished for it. I was rather taken aback because I had not really thought that I would have to go through this.

I had many meetings with Nogah over the coming weeks. He came to see me almost every day and eventually a kind of trust began to form and before too much longer, he had managed to get the entire story out of me as to what had happened. It came in fits and starts and was not a story that I was able to tell in one go. When I eventually finished, Nogah sat back on the old chair in the room where our meetings always took place. He looked very thoughtful for a moment and then he returned once again to the first question that he had greeted me with.

'Why did you come back?'

'It seemed the right thing to do,' I replied, with no intention of going into the fact that I felt I deserved punishment for what I had done. I felt that he might think that this would undermine any case and defence that he might think we had.

'Plus, you were out of options, I suppose?' I looked a little blank at this, so he continued. 'You were rejected by the Pariahs, you had nowhere else to go and faced imprisonment or death with them.'

There was truth in this and I regretted that I had told him my full story. I left out the names of the people that were involved so that there would be no comeback on them, but I began to think that I should probably have kept the Pariahs entirely out of the story and pretended that I had merely hid somewhere on the Landmass. The problem with this of course, is that they would probably have put me to the Interrogation to find out the names of the people who had hidden me on the Landmass for all those months. Names that I could not provide them with, of course. I did wonder if it would have been better to have edited my story slightly though. It was too late now. There are times when excessive honesty can be rather damaging.

'It's an incredible story,' Nogah stated, as he sat with his fingers overlapping each other and staring into the middle distance. I gained the sense that he either didn't believe me or that there were elements of the story that he did not believe. I found this rather frustrating, as aside from actual names, I pretty much told him the truth. I remained quiet, looking at him, leaving him to his own thoughts about what I had said.

There is a survival instinct that exists in all of us. Unless we are suffering from serious medical or mental deficiencies, most of us will continue to want to keep a grip on life no matter how desperate our situation may seem to us. I had resigned myself to the fact that I would return, be captured, imprisoned and then either executed or given a lifelong imprisonment, that would kill me slowly but just as surely as a trip to the gallows would have done.

However, now the subject of a trial had been raised and not only that, but here was a man who was prepared to offer up a defence for me. Obviously, I had no idea how good an advocate he was but there was a possibility that I might be able to live on. I was not resigned and my story was not necessarily completely over. Granted, it did occur to me that if Nogah managed to argue for imprisonment, it might not be all that long before I wished that he had not bothered, but I would still be alive and whilst alive, there would always be hope and a chance that one day I might be free again. I say he could argue for imprisonment because in all honesty, I had no hope at all that he would be able to argue a defence so good that I would not receive some kind of punishment and would be allowed to walk free. I had to be realistic about these things.

'Is it your intention,' Nogah continued after some thought, 'to argue that the love you felt for your wife and the pain of separation by adhering to the law and so on, are the mitigating circumstances for why you murdered her?' It was rather a blunt question I felt.

'I would prefer not to use the word murder.'

'I'm sure you would,' he said, coming forward again in his chair. 'However, it is a word that the prosecution will mix no bones in using and dress it up how we will, you do not deny killing her, which ultimately comes down to murder in the eyes of the law.'

I was silent at this. I began to wonder how good he was going to be at arguing my case after all. He didn't seem to have all that much hope and after listening to him, I began to feel that I didn't have all that much hope either.

***

Murder is an emotive word. There is less emotion in the phrase 'mercy killing' or 'euthanasia' but ultimately, I suppose when you do get to the nitty-gritty of the matter it comes down to murder. For a brief period of time, I argued with Nogah the definition of the word murder. Very often, I had discovered that the legal system seemed to hang on technicalities and nuances of certain words and phrases.

'Murder would seem to suggest that I did not have the consent of the other person to act in the way that I did,' I argued, having by this time become far more vocal with him.

'True, but then there is nobody that you can call to provide evidence of that is there?'

I remained silent. This was a fair point. Simeon was dead from a virus contracted at sea, Asa had been executed and any testimony that he may or may not have provided at his own trial would only be turned against me, and of course, the prime witness was Evie, who was dead at my own hand.

'I would argue,' he continued, 'that the simplest definition of murder is the unlawful, premeditated killing of one person by another. That is the legal definition that the prosecution will most likely be working from, and when we examine that, we have to come to the conclusion that it was murder.'

He had a fair point. Killing Evie in whatever capacity you prefer to frame it was something that was illegal as far as the State was concerned. It was, therefore, without a shadow of a doubt unlawful. Premeditated? The evidence of my own mouth that I had taken great lengths to obtain the opiate told against me on the point of premeditation. Finally, it was I that killed her. It was difficult to see how we would be able to get away with not using the term 'murder'.

'There is little hope then?' I finally said.

'There is always some hope,' he countered, but he didn't sound all that convinced. I began to wonder how much of my defence was just going to be for show. The more I thought about it and the longer I spoke to Nogah, the more hopeless the situation appeared to be. I cursed the day that I had first set eyes on him. Before I had met him, I had been resigned to my fate, upon meeting him I had been allowed to grow the seed of hope within my soul and now that my story was told, I was back to where I had started again; only now I was to go through a trial that must have its outcome secured before we even started. Not for the first time in my life, I felt that I was facing insurmountable odds and had to fight the desire to crawl off to a dark corner somewhere and give up.

***

I am trying to write quicker these days than I did when I first started this chronicle. It is a slow progress and I have been writing for a great number of years now. In fact, Alpheus tells me that I have been writing this chronicle for what is now approaching fifteen years.

Fifteen years! It hardly seems possible. For you, future reader, who glances across these words it has probably taken you so little time to read what has taken me a virtual lifetime to write. It occurs to me that Alpheus will probably edit this document and rearrange it into something of a more orderly fashion. There will be bits that are placed in the correct order, as I am aware of the fact that my writing and my mind is often all over the place. I am also aware of the fact, that I have, from time to time, written on these sheets words that are nonsensical and I feel sure that Alpheus will have destroyed these, as they do nothing to advance the actual account of my life. Alpheus was originally keen for me to only tell the story of how it was that I ended up where I am now, so that future generations could see that it was possible to fight against the system, although it is possible to argue that ending where I now am it is a fight that I lost. I have decided to include reference to my daily life in present times so that a more overall picture can be obtained of my life and what has been as well as what is and what inevitably will be.

It amazes me that I have lasted for as long as I have if I am entirely honest with you. This is probably something of an amazement to my captors as well and they probably resent the fact that they have had to keep me for as long as they have when I failed to do the decent thing and die years ago. I suppose there is always a chance that they might become ultimately bored with me and decide to have me executed after all. So long as I can finish this chronicle, I think I could cope with that. I strongly believe that this is the only thing that is really keeping me going at the moment. I suspect that when I do not have to write each day, then there will be no reason for me to continue with anything else. It is certainly the only thing that keeps me going at the moment.

You may wonder why it is that I have taken so long over this. Well, there have been frequent bouts of ill-health where I have either been confined to the Infirmary and thus unable to write anything for practical reasons; or I might have been in a frequent bout of depression where despite having the opportunity to write, I did not have the inclination to do so. Thus, there have been periods of many weeks that have passed without a word being written in this manner, much to the annoyance of Alpheus, I am sure.

When all the circumstances have been right for me to be able to write this chronicle, I have had to do so in long-hand with a stumpy pencil; scratching away at the rough paper. I have had to stop sometimes because I have run out of paper or I have needed to have my pencil sharpened; or maybe there were just too many other people around so that it was not safe to write these words. At the end of each day, whether I have written little or I have written a great deal in tiny handwriting covering both sides of the page, it is taken from me so that it can be secured somewhere safe, in case my cell or my person are searched and this highly illegal document should come to light.

In this manner, so much time has passed me by.

***

So, the initial feeling of hope that I had experienced at the thought of a trial and a defence was beginning to fade away and I was back to thinking that it was a hopeless situation once again. This annoyed me a great deal. When I had made the decision to return to the Landmass, I had expected that I would be punished for the actions that I had taken with regards to my wife; I was resigned to this and was more than prepared to go along with it. Then along came Nogah and changed everything by giving me hope that things were not completely done with.

It is a very cruel thing to give someone who is clinging to a plank after a shipwreck, hope that they are about to be rescued, only to take it away from them once again; and that is how I had felt. I was tired and could not hold onto my plank any longer and was expecting to be washed off with the next tide and then all of a sudden, there had been a glimmer of hope on the horizon, and just when my survival instincts kicked back in again, my hope sailed by without me.

Nogah was offering me a defence, not because he believed in my case and felt that I deserved one, but because it was something that had to be kept up if the farce of the trial were to have any semblance of fairness. In my more meditative moments, I felt incredibly sorry for the man. He had not asked to be in this position and he was really trying his best to make something out of nothing. It couldn't have been all that easy and I can't say that it was something that I would like to have done. Part of the reason for this is that it was still in the back of my mind that I didn't really deserve a defence and what I did most clearly deserve, was the punishment that the court decided upon for killing my wife. It is rather difficult to raise all that much of a defence when you think that you are guilty yourself. Nogah didn't have the easiest of tasks in the world.

'You will obviously remain here until your trial date is decided upon,' he told me at the end of one of our sessions.

I nodded at this. I had expected nothing less. I certainly had not imagined that they were going to allow me to wander around the Landmass, free until they were ready for me.

'Do you know when that might be?' I asked instead. He shrugged at this, as if to say that no one could understand the logic of these things and it was really something that could be announced at any time. The frustrating thing now was the waiting around. Waiting for the inevitable to happen. I suppose there were two ways of looking at this. Firstly, the longer the wait the further off the ultimate decision was that would be made about me and my future, or possible lack of it. On the other hand, all the waiting and uncertainty was tedious. If the case were to come before the court soon, then I would at the least be doing something to take away from the monotony plus I would then know the answers.

I have never really been all that good at waiting around. I decided to take the bull by the horns and ask Nogah directly what my chances were.

'They're not good, I will not lie to you,' he said, with a look of depression on his face as if to say that his answer had been the most positive thing that he could say about my case. For all I knew it was the most positive thing that he could say. I think we would be fooling ourselves if either of us thought that there was an abundance of hope for the situation that I was in.

'We can but do what we can do,' concluded Nogah, as he gathered his papers together.

It was a sensible philosophy that I could not fault all that much at the fundamental level, but I could not help but wish, as I was taken back to my cell, that he had decided to conclude our conference with something a little more encouraging for the days that were ahead.

I did not see Nogah again for the next few weeks. We had discussed everything that we could about my case and there was nothing else that we could go over. I hoped that he was still doing some work on it though, even if I were not seeing him, although I wondered if he had put it to one side as a forlorn cause and was concentrating on other things.

After a couple of weeks, I received word that my case was about to be heard. The time had finally come.

22

The first thing that happened was a most blessed relief for me. I was given a wash. It may sound like the simplest of things to you, but I had not been allowed to have access to soap and water, since I had been thrown into the cell where I had languished for some time now. To be taken into the shower area and allowed to have the dirt washed from my body made me feel as if I had been reborn. Despite the roughness with which I was hosed down and the shabby area where I showered, it was blissful.

I was then shaved which was the first time that I fully realised how much my beard had grown in the last weeks of confinement. Obviously, I was not allowed to shave myself but had it done for me so that I might not have control over the razor which I might have used it to harm myself or another. I could have hoped that the person who was charged with shaving me had been a little more diligent and gentler in his administrations.

When I was returned to my cell, I was pleased to find that a new set of clothing had been placed there for me. I had not realised how quickly clothing can become dirty and turn to rags when you are wearing them all of the time. I had become used to what I was wearing and what I looked like and I suddenly felt strange in my new appearance. It amused me how quickly I had become used to my poor state and how unusual it felt to be back to normality again.

I was then ushered in to see Nogah, who was dressed in very formal court clothing. He told me that my case would be prosecuted by a man called Ziv and the case would be judged by senior lawman, Abiel. These names meant nothing to me although clearly Nogah had stated them as if he had expected some kind of reaction or impression from me. I gathered later that they were both very important people and their allocation to my case gave it a degree of importance, that it would not normally have attracted to a simple murder case. I would have preferred it if they had been a little less competent and respected in their jobs.

Nogah shuffled from foot to foot when he had finished telling me this little piece of information and I was very disconcerted about how ill-at-ease he seemed. For the first time, I began to really think that he thought there was no hope for this at all. I wondered, if that were the case, why we were being made to go through with the sham of a pretence of a trial. In all of our discussions, I had never seen him look so nervous before. It was without a shadow of a doubt very disturbing. In contrast, I must confess to feeling very calm and unflustered by any of it. Eventually, Nogah realised how uneasy he appeared to be and the somewhat comical, quizzical look that I was giving him and he shuffled off, muttering that he would see me in the court when the time came. I believe that he was very annoyed that he had allowed his façade to fall for a moment in front of me and it irritated him.

Left alone with my thoughts, I could not allow my mind to dwell and worry on whether Nogah had hurt pride at being found out to be human. I suppose that this was a difficult case for him. I had no idea where he stood in the profession that he practiced, but if he managed to argue for anything other than execution, it must stand him in good stead; whereas he must also have realised that he had been given a case to argue which was virtually unwinnable. For the briefest of moments, I felt sorry for him, but this quickly passed when I saw my wrists that had been rubbed raw with metal.

***

Eventually, I entered the court room for the first time. Never before in my life, had I entered such a place, and despite the seriousness that hung upon me, being there now, I felt a deep interest in my surroundings. Indeed, in much of what was to follow I was in many regards strangely dispassionate and distanced from the entire affair, as if it was something that was mildly interesting, but happening to someone else.

The first thing that struck me when I walked into the court was the smell. Almost everything had been made out of wood, but it was wood that had blackened with age and looked decayed. The entire room appeared to be suffering from neglect. There were also numerous leather-bound tomes that were scattered along the desks and I wondered how much of it was a show of intimidation rather than of any practical use.

If the intention was intimidation, it was not working with me. Despite the interest that I had in my surroundings, my prevailing emotion was one of tiredness, both physical and mental. I was tired of everything by this stage and I just wished that I would be allowed to sleep and forget about everything; but I was not allowed any respite as even my dreams were haunted with memories of Evie, some of comfort, but more often than not, ones that left me feeling very disturbed. I had no idea of how tired I would eventually become and how these dreams would haunt me for years yet. It is probably a good idea that we do not know what the future may bring.

Nogah was sitting at one of the highly-polished tables looking even more uncomfortable and out of place than he had seemed in the prison. I began to wonder if there was a place where he was comfortable and relaxed, able to be himself; but then I reasoned that perhaps this worried state was him being himself. This was who he was.

On a table opposite him sat someone who was similarly dressed and I assumed that this was the fabled Ziv, that I was expected to know about, but had never actually heard of. I examined him with interest and noticed with a sinking feeling that he appeared to be far more confident in his appearance than Nogah was. I grant you it would not have been hard to do this, as I believed that I currently appeared more confident than my own advocate did.

I was ushered towards Nogah who did not appear to acknowledge me and I stood waiting. I presumed that we were waiting for the senior lawman to arrive who would preside over the case. As I waited for this momentous event, I became aware that there was a gallery behind me and that there were numerous people crammed into it. I was surprised to see that so many people should want to turn out to see my case being heard. It seemed that my incident which had been conducted in such privacy for the love between two people, had become so public and exposed to everyone. I tried to look behind me to see if there was anyone that I recognised amongst the crowd; perhaps some friends or neighbours had turned out to see the strange conclusion to a story, that I began to realise had caused a degree of scandal.

Nogah coughed in an exaggerated manner and looking down at him, I realised that he did not approve of me seeking out people in the gallery and rather saw my interest in the courtroom to be something in bad taste. By this stage, I had reached a point where I could not really have cared less what he thought. I began to think that Nogah was not likely to be doing me any favours and was more likely to be putting his own career above my life. I suppose it had always been so. I might have felt a pang of sympathy for him having to defend so hopeless a case, but none of this was about him.

Suddenly, Nogah and Ziv joined me in standing which I found curious as I was unaware of any signal or indication that this ceremonial courtesy was needed. As they stood by their almost telepathic means, a door that I had not previously noticed opened and in walked a man that I assumed was Abiel, the senior lawman. He walked in a majestic fashion to a bench that was raised above all of us and sat down without saying a word. He was richly dressed in robes that I would imagine would have cost more than most normal people earned in a year. Upon him sitting, Ziv and Nogah also sat down. I was about to join them when another cough from Nogah gave me the direction that I was not expected to sit down. It turned out that I was not expected to sit down through any of this procedure. Clearly, it was not intended that anyone should enjoy their trial in any form of comfort.

It was then that the preliminaries started, such as my name, age, address etc, establishing all of the things that were necessary so that they could be certain that they were putting the right person on trial. I could not help but marvel how nobody had bothered to check any of this to see if they had imprisoned the right person over the last few months. I allowed my mind to wander through most of this legal jargon and paid little attention to what was going on around me. I felt curiously detached from all of it.

Eventually, Ziv stood up and faced the court, and I refocused myself, as it seemed that this is when things were about to start to happen.

***

'It is my intention to show the court,' Ziv said, addressing Abiel in what

I can only describe as a very pompous tone, 'that the defendant wilfully murdered his wife and in doing so, also conspired with others to cover up the fact that she was a sufferer of the Virus.'

I watched him with a degree of interest and it felt strangely to me as if he were talking about someone else. I felt very detached from it all. Nogah was probably very annoyed that my lack of interest and frank boredom was clearly showing, so for his sake if not my own, I tried to turn my attention back to the focus of the conversation. I became aware that I had tuned out for some of the conversation.

'In this case,' Ziv continued with a look of almost pure hatred on his face, as he took in my countenance, 'I intend to prove the defendant's lack of respect for authority, for justice, for the safety of his fellow citizens as well as for the total lack of regard that he has for human life — including that of his own wife who he brutally, premeditatedly murdered.'

Ziv sat down with a look of mild satisfaction on his face. I thought his opening statement was a little harsh as I doubt that it could be argued that the murder of Evie could be classed as brutal, even if we accepted that it was murder, which I was not really denying. Clearly, this opening speech gave me a clue that Ziv was intending to make this a personal matter.

Abiel continued to scribble something down on some papers in front of him and then looked up and nodded at Nogah who stood up. I could not help but feel that he seemed insignificant and almost minute next to the powerful Ziv, who had rolled out his case with thunder in his voice and fire in his eyes.

'There are elements of this case that we shall not seek to deny,' Nogah said in a nervous voice, which seemed to bring a smile to Ziv's lips although he tried his best to conceal it. 'Whereas we will not deny these elements of the case, we argue that there is mitigation for the actions that the defendant took. There is injustice that must be addressed within the law. There is a greater love than love for the law or for fellow humans that can drive people, like the defendant, to step outside of the law and take the law into their own hands for the sake of a loved one. Be not deceived into thinking this a mere murder trial. This is a test case upon which the very right to love someone is being placed on trial; and that is the matter that I shall be addressing to this honourable court.'

Nogah sat down and I was slightly impressed. Although he had started weak and haltingly, he had warmed to his subject a great deal and by the end of the little speech, was verging on something that could almost be described as passion. I looked around the courtroom and began to see that I was probably the only one who seemed all that impressed by the events. Ziv sniffed as he sat at his desk as if something distasteful had just been placed under his nose; which I suppose in his eyes it had; and Abiel looked mildly bored as he scribbled something further on the papers that were in front of him.

I tuned my thoughts out for the following, which appeared to be a lot of legal jargon and challenges back and forth that I could neither understand nor really follow. I decided to place my thoughts elsewhere and if something important happened, then I would be sure to be told later.

***

A short while afterwards, I was led back to my cell where my nice, clean clothing was taken from me once again and I was reintroduced to the rags that I had come to know so well. Presumably, this was so that I could not make them dirty in my grubby, little home and therefore be able to present myself to the court as reasonably respectable still. Once re-attired, I was taken back to the meeting room where Nogah was waiting for me.

'Well, I think that went reasonably well,' he opened with. I was non-committal.

'What happens now?' I decided to ask instead.

'Well, that was the opening statements where we give everyone direction as to where we are going with the case.'

'No room for surprises then?'

'No.' He looked at me as if I was very stupid to suggest such a thing. It seemed rather pointless to me to open a case by telling them everything that you were going to do, as it tended to make the rest of it rather boring as you knew what was going to happen. 'I could not help but notice that you seemed to not be following everything that was said.'

'Well, some of it was far too legal in its jargon for me to follow.' He nodded at this as if he could really not expect anything else from someone such as me.

'May I remind you though that this is *your* trial. It is your life that hangs in the balance here, nobody else's.'

I nodded at this. I was more than aware of the fact that this drama could end with my death. He just didn't realise that I wasn't all that bothered by it.

'You seemed to be thinking of other things for great segments of the argument.'

'I was thinking of Evie.'

'You were thinking of Evie?'

'Yes. I can't quite place the memory. I remember dancing on a patio or something. I think it must have been before we were married. Perhaps it was her parent's house. I really can't remember. She was teaching me some dance or other that she had learned. She liked to dance. I'm not sure I ever told you that.'

'No.' To be honest, he looked at me as if it was no matter here nor there if I had told him this fact.

'It was summer and we were in each other's arms dancing. Maybe it was more of an excuse just to hold each other and be close, rather than because of any desire to teach or learn a new dance. I don't think there was any music.'

Nogah was looking at me rather strangely. He sighed and then continued with the court procedure as if I had not said anything at all.

'Now that the opening speeches are out of the way, Ziv will present his case to the court starting from tomorrow. When that concludes, it will be up to me to present the defence. Once that has been concluded, Abiel will retire from the court room and consider his verdict which he will then deliver. Does that all make sense?'

'It makes perfect sense,' I said, although for the life of me I couldn't see why he was getting so stressed about it and emphasising so much to me.

'Good,' he clapped me on the shoulder, a mark of familiarity that I rather imagined that he regretted doing the moment that he had done it; not least because of the clothes that I had changed back into. He stood up and made his way to the door. 'Try to show a little more interest in the future. If you don't seem that bothered by what is going on then you can't imagine anyone else to really.'

23

I suppose I could understand why it was that Nogah was frustrated with me. He was doing his best and my lack of interest in the proceedings could not have been doing much to boost his confidence, in what was already something of a difficult case for him. I vowed that I would try and show more of an interest for his sake if for no other reason.

The following day, I was redressed in my court clothes and taken back to the court room where things were exactly the same as they had been the day before. I was still not allowed to sit down, which I was starting to find as something of a strain. Obviously, comfort was not something that featured heavily in how they liked their defendants to feel.

'There are numerous matters that can be laid before the defendant which show his total disregard for the law, for society and for his fellows, as well as his wife,' Ziv opened his argument. 'This is not just a matter of murder, although it is the foremost of all the charges that can be brought before him. There are numerous other offences that have been committed that shall be shown to this court during the course of this trial. I have every confidence that by the end of the session, the court will have no doubt at all in their own mind that the defendant is guilty of all of them. We shall also see his total lack of regard or any degree of remorse for the heinous crimes that he has committed.'

Remembering what it was that Nogah had told me, I tried my best to look very interested in what it was that he was saying. It was a little easier to do this time due to the vicious personal attack that he seemed to be making on me. He seemed to be taking things so much more personally than any of the rest of us were, including myself.

'To begin with, I would like to address the matter of his wilful concealment of the Virus that was contracted by his wife. As the court is aware it is illegal to conceal this illness from the authorities. Why, we may ask ourselves? I am sure the defence, as has been indicated, will hold that his concealment was something that he did out of love; but is not the law something that has been created by the state for its greater love of its citizens?'

He paused here for a moment and looked around the room as if daring any of us to contradict him. I didn't have the energy and Nogah didn't seem to have the inclination to do so. He seemed to be riveted to what Ziv was saying as if it was more important to him than it was to me.

'Before we get into the details of the nature of this concealment,' continued Ziv, when nobody had risen to his challenge, 'let us consider why it is that this law is in place. Is it here to cause needless suffering and to drive wedges between man and wife, between parents and children and so on? No, it is not there for that reason. I concede it is there out of our fear. We fear this Virus. Why do we fear it? We fear it because there is no known cure for it. Despite all of the years that we have lived with it, we do not know how we can fight against it. We fear it because we do not know how it infects us. Is it a miasma that floats in the air? Is it a contagion that is passed on by touch? We simply don't know. Our best medical advisors are even unable to answer the question of why it is that some may be infected by it and why others are not affected at all. Indeed, the defendant is a case in point for this. We do not know why his wife should have been struck with this terrible Virus and yet he stands before us today, alive.'

He looked around the courtroom once again, and not for the first time, I was again struck at how like a drama this was. It was as if we were at the theatrical or cinematograph. I was truly impressed with the display that Ziv was putting on.

'Why is it illegal to conceal this Virus? The answer is simple. Because we fear it so much, we have no idea how it may spread. We passed the law that we did with regards to this contagion so that we might protect the people of our society, so that we might prevent this from growing to an epidemic and wiping us all out because we do not know how the disease is spread from one of us to another. Concealment of the Virus is a selfish act. It is not only selfish, it is irresponsible.'

At this stage, he pointed his finger directly at me. 'By concealing this illness, you helped to put everyone at risk. Who knows how many other people may have become infected because you allowed your wife to go around unchecked? Who knows how many she may have been responsible for murdering before she eventually died herself? This act of selfishness could easily have cost the lives of dozens more of us, if not even more than that. The spread of this disease is so unknown and viral, that one unchecked person with it could result in the infection of thousands.'

He had raised his voice a great deal towards the end of this speech and I could see that it was either something that he felt very passionate about or he was one of the best actors that I had ever seen in my life.

'You may think I exaggerate,' he said, almost quietly now so that people leaned forward to catch his words more easily. 'But I assure you there is nothing exaggerated about this. The defendant here is before us charged with the murder of his wife. I put it to this venerable court that due to his selfish actions in concealing the Virus, he has murdered countless others that we shall never hear of; and as such he is one of the most dangerous men that we have ever had stand before us.'

I felt that this might be going a little too far, and I expected that Nogah might object to it, but he just sat there as seemingly taken in by this performance, as the rest of us were. I began to see why there were so many people in the gallery. This was clearly a main attraction and Ziv was playing to them as much as he was prosecuting a case of law.

***

We had a short recess after this, whilst lunch was taking place. I wasn't really given as fine a meal as I suspected that my fellow courtroom participants were currently imbibing, but then I expected nothing less really.

I could not deny that the opening part of Ziv's attack on me had been impressive and forceful. I am sure that if I had been the senior lawman presiding over this case, I would have found me guilty of the offence without having to listen to another word. I hardly felt that my own advocate, Nogah, was going to be up to putting on a similar display, against someone who was clearly so practised in his art. The onslaught continued after the recess.

'We have seen how the defendant has a total disregard for the law and for the safety of his fellow citizens. We can see how he cares little for the society in which he lives and would willingly allow us all to die from this most horrible of illnesses rather than uphold the law and do the honourable thing. Indeed, the only reason why we even allow him to stand trial before us today is because we know that he is himself clear of carrying the Virus.'

This made clear to me why it was that they had taken the blood sample that they had from me when I first arrived at the prison.

'This conspiracy of silence was one that he was not a sole agent in. Indeed, he contrived to implicate two otherwise upstanding and respectful citizens who had previously been regarded highly within the community, but whose contact with this man, resulted in them being turned into base criminals. The first was a so-called friend of the defendant by the name of Simeon; I shall come to him later, for there is much that I would like to say about him.'

I wondered what it was that he had to say about Simeon that he was saving for later. I began to worry a little for the first real time since I had walked into this room.

'The second is Doctor Asa who until enrolled in this sordid little plot by the cunning and deceitful nature of the defendant, was a much respected and noble member of the community. It was this plot by the defendant to conceal against the law that turned this man into a criminal and robbed him of his good character. As the court will know, Doctor Asa has been tried in this very court room, of his part in the plot to conceal and murder, and he was found guilty of his role in that concealment. We do not make a case that this once respected man was guilty of the murder of this man's wife, but we made the case that he was just as guilty as the defendant, in concealing an illness so deadly, that so many others could have died as a result of it. We have here Asa's testimony.'

With this he held up a sheath of papers from the many that littered his desk. I was doing my best to keep calm at the moment as his tirade on Doctor Asa was something that was frankly starting to make me feel angry.

'This confession,' he said as he waved the papers about in the air. 'This confession of his crime has done much to help us in understanding the true depravity of the man who stands before us today. The man who is so clearly guilty of all of these matters. As the court will know, Asa was found guilty of his crime and was executed for his concealment of this serious, deadly disease in true accordance with the law and with the decision of this court. I put it to this court though that it was not this court that killed Asa. It was not the law that killed Asa, although it would not matter if it were the court and the law that killed him as we have righteousness on our side in doing so. No. I put it to the court that the person who is guilty of the death of Doctor Asa, is the defendant himself. It is this man who involved and induced the doctor into committing the offence. By doing so, he sealed the man's fate as surely as if he had signed the death warrant himself.'

Upon concluding this statement, Ziv stood still in the centre of the court, pausing for dramatic effect no doubt, with all eyes upon him. I was fuming inside but a warning glance from Nogah made me keep my tongue. I trusted that he had something equally as impressive to present to the court because my case, which had never looked good to begin with, was looking disastrous about now.

It was at this point that the case was adjourned to the following morning. There seemed to be a lot of this. Whenever things seemed to get into the swing of it, someone called a halt to it for some reason or another. I was taken back to the cell that had become my home, feeling glummer than I had done in a long time.

***

The following day, Ziv continued from where he had left off as if there had been no break at all in what he was saying.

'The death of Asa is not something that bothers this court all that much. He was a traitor and he betrayed his medical profession that he had so diligently followed throughout his life. All of his achievements in life wiped out by one act of treason at the end of his life. An act of treason that was instigated by the man who stands before you today.'

He was pointing at me again, as if he doubted that anyone else in the room was aware of who it was that he was talking about.

'But this man's crimes do not end there. His corruption of an innocent, respected doctor is but one of his crimes and the only one that we are interested in when we speak about Doctor Asa.'

He paused once more and I began to realise that these pauses for dramatic silences was a trademark of the way that Ziv operated in his profession.

'We see that there are two crimes of which the defendant stands accused. The wilful concealment of the Virus and the corruption of an otherwise law-abiding citizen that he coerced into concealing the Virus with him. We must now move on to the third of the crimes to which it is my painful duty to lay before the court, that of the acquirement and possession of illegal substances. The testimony of Doctor Asa, as well as the defendant's own statement that he has made to my colleague, Nogah, has shown that he plotted and planned to obtain an illegal opiate from the Residuum which he then used to assist in the murder of his wife. There are several points that must be raised here. Firstly, there is the fact that he conspired with his friend, Simeon, to obtain the opiate. As I have said before, Simeon is someone that I will touch upon later. He then journeyed some distance to meet with a man from the so-called Resistance who supplied him with the opiate. By doing so, he has linked himself to a known terrorist group and shown that he is a traitor to the state.'

'Do we know the name of this terrorist?' It was the first time that Abiel had spoken, although he had been making continuous notes throughout the entire matter.

'Alas not, Senior Lawman. Despite our best efforts it would appear that this man which the defendant calls Azarias, has concealed his true identity too well for us to discover who it was that he really was.'

I took some small comfort from the fact that Azarias, if nobody else, had escaped from this incident without punishment.

'That is disappointing,' concluded Abiel.

'Indeed, it is. However, what information that we have been able to glean from the testimonies of the condemned and the accused has been passed to the authorities and they have used this information to purge that area of the Residuum, where it is believed that this transaction of opiate has taken place.'

Abiel nodded his satisfaction at this and I felt rather sick. So many people had suffered and died because of what I had done as a personal act between my wife and myself.

'The deaths of these Residuum members are of no consequence to this court or these proceedings, we merely lay their deaths at the accused's feet, as another example of the moral irresponsibility that his actions have led to.'

Abiel nodded his head and made a notation with his pen upon the papers that were spread out in front of him.

'Proceed.'

'Thank you, Sir. The reference to the opiate is important on a number of different levels. The accused does not deny that he obtained this opiate so the charges against him must now include consorting with known terrorists as well as possession of an illegal substance of opiate without authority.'

Ziv paused once again and looked around the courtroom, taking in everyone before he resumed talking.

'However, the possession of the opiate proves something far more sinister, namely that the death of the defendant's wife was premeditated. The defence are unable to argue that the death of his wife was spontaneous or as a result of her uncontrollable illness as a sudden means to end the suffering that he saw before him. Rather, the acquisition of this opiate some time before the death of his wife can only be seen as what it is; a premeditated murder, carefully worked out in advance and executed with cold efficiency.'

He paused once again and I looked at him as he looked at me. I wondered how much was personal hatred in his gaze and how much was just another job to him.

'The defendant and his advocate will no doubt argue that it was a death that was carried out with the full cooperation of the deceased. There are a couple of issues that we would like to address with regards to that. Firstly, the fact that due to the nature of the crime there is nobody left alive who could provide witness to this fact. Secondly, we must take into account that even if there were witnesses, even if we accepted on face-value, the defendant's claim that this was a mercy killing, conducted with consent, it still remains that consent or no, it is an illegal act to kill another and still the defendant would be guilty.'

He sat down at this and I gathered from it that the day had concluded once again and it would have to wait until the next session for the case to continue.

24

It is difficult for me to remember everything that happened during the court case. I have no notes or transcript to work from and am only putting it together from my memory, which is all I have. It all happened so long ago now. I acknowledge that there may be aspects that I have forgotten or that I may get certain parts of it wrong and if that is the case, then I apologise. I can only record things the way that I remember them. The problem is that when it comes to the remembering any incident, all those involved will remember it a different way, even if asked to recollect it close to the event. You can imagine how distorted my memory could well be after all these years. I have tried my best to be faithful in my account, not only of the court case, but of everything that I have recorded within these pages. If there is anything that I have got wrong then I can only apologise and say that this is the way that I remember it.

I did not see Nogah before the court resumed the following day. It didn't surprise me that he was keeping to himself. Ziv was presenting a pretty good argument which I would not have hesitated to have found me guilty. Perhaps it was just as well. I had returned to the Landmass with the intention of being punished for the death of my wonderful wife and it seemed that my wish was certainly likely to come true, as I could not possibly imagine any defence that Nogah could raise, would in any way succeed.

'We now reach the most serious of charges that we lay before the defendant,' Ziv continued when we had resumed matters the next day. 'That is the charge of murder. I feel that I need not go into too much detail about this as it has already largely been covered in what I have said already. We have learned that the murder was premeditated and we have learned that it matters not whether there was consent for the murder or not. No citizen can consent to their own murder. We applaud the defendant for his honesty in admitting that he suffocated his wife when the opiate did not appear to work as he had intended. I ignore the consent angle of this case for it is irrelevant and I submit before this court that the murder of his wife was committed by the defendant with no thought to anything but the wilful murder. He obtained poison so that she might be killed in this manner and when the poison that he had illegally obtained, failed to bring about the result that he was looking for, he resorted to brute force. It is clearly guilt of this which brings him back to stand before us today.'

For someone who didn't think that there was all that much that could be said about the murder of Evie that had not already been said, he clearly still had a lot to say. I stood uncomfortable with all eyes upon me as he launched into his tirade against me for the murder of my wife.

'Murder is an abhorrent crime. It is perhaps the worst of all possible crimes. To rob someone of their life can be the stiffest of all cruelties. I would argue, however, that the murder of a loved one is the worst crime of all. To have placed your love and trust in someone who then turns on you and betrays that trust, is the most horrible of things possible. It is a betrayal of trust and of love. It is a crime against nature as well as against law. It is a crime that must carry with it the most severe of all penalties. I would ask that the court remember that, when giving consideration to sentence.'

Abiel shuffled some papers and made more notes. Nogah looked pretty sick, but then he always did so I was not sure if it was the case that was making him feel this way or whether it was something of his natural disposition. Ziv collected some papers together and then resumed his case. I gained the impression that he seemed to be enjoying himself somewhat, which hardly seemed as professional as I would have liked.

'After this most terrible of crimes had taken place, the defendant seems to have had a rare crisis of conscience as he fully realised the nature of what it was that he had done. In a panic, he decided to flea justice and escape. This act of escaping from justice is clear evidence that he knew that what he had done was wrong. It is evidence of his guilt. If he truly believed that he had acted in the best possible faith, then why did he run? Why not stay and allow matters to take their course? If nothing else, this escape and attempt to preserve his own life and freedom is clear evidence of the actions of one who is guilty.'

There was another one of the pauses that Ziv seemed to love so much and the silence in the courtroom hit me for the first time. The only sounds that could be heard was the scratching of pens across paper as Abiel, Nogah and the court recorder scribbled down what was being said or their own notation on it.

'This now then brings us to the last two charges that I will lay before the defendant. The first of these is a repetition that we have already had with regards to Asa; that is to say the coercion of another into the concealment of the Virus. In this instance, the other being that of the defendant's friend, Simeon. We have already seen how the forceful nature of the defendant coerced the vulnerable Doctor Asa into concealing the Virus and therefore becoming complicit in the crime. By the testimony of Asa and the admissions of the defendant, we also see that the same course of action was followed with regards to Simeon. The seventh charge before the court must, therefore, be the coercion of another into the concealment of the Virus. This is nothing short of a conspiracy. A conspiracy that could have resulted in the deaths of far more people than we know of. Yet, the true nature of how much damage this concealment has caused may never be known to us. There may be those out there that are infected and that have died because of the concealment of the Virus by this irresponsible man that stands before us today.'

The pause was lengthy this time and once Abiel had finished scribbling whatever it was that he was writing, he looked up at Ziv.

'And the last charge?'

'The last charge is relating to Simeon. If you will hold with me for a while, I wish to present a suggestion to the court for consideration towards upholding the final charge.'

'Proceed.'

'The defendant tells us that in the company of Simeon, he escaped from the Landmass in a vessel that went across the sea to an island where he resided, until he made the decision to return. He maintains that he went to the Island of the Pariahs.' At this, there was a stirring and muttering from the gallery, the first time that I had heard anything from them, so much so, that I had all but forgotten that they were still there.

'Silence,' stated Abiel with authority, that brought about immediate silence from the gallery. 'Continue.'

'We dispute that such an island exists and we submit to the court that the ravings about this island and the so-called idyllic life that exists there are nothing but a fantasy on behalf of the defendant, fabricated perhaps with the intention of sowing further subversion amongst society. It is well known that the Island of the Pariahs does not exist. It is a myth, a fairy tale that should never make it out of the nursery. We submit that any such reference to the Pariahs be struck from this case.'

'Advocate?' This was addressed to Nogah from Abiel.

'We have no objections,' Nogah said, rising from his seat to say this and then sitting immediately back down again. I looked at him in astonishment, and wondered whose side he was meant to be on, that he had so readily dismissed half of my story without so much as an argument. He had the decency to not return my gaze.

'So noted,' continued Abiel. 'That being the case, where is it your suggestion that the defendant went following the death of his wife?'

'It hardly matters. We maintain that the location of where he went is immaterial. It is possible that he did escape the Landmass for some time and hide on an island somewhere, but it is not the place that he describes in his statement to his advocate. It is also possible that he remained hidden on the Landmass somewhere. We may never know; however, we will accept for the present his premise that he left the Landmass. For it is the journey from the Landmass that is more important to this case than any possible destination that may exist or otherwise.'

'Very well.'

'It has already been accepted that he escaped from justice in the company of his friend, Simeon.' Here Ziv picked up some papers from his desk and examined them as he continued to speak. 'He states that during this sea crossing which was violent, Simeon grew ill with an unknown condition and that he ultimately died from this illness and his body was disposed of at sea. He does not know the name of any of the sailors that he crossed with and they are impossible to trace. How convenient that he does not remember this. How convenient that his friend should die and his body be buried at sea, where recovery is impossible. I put it to this court that what really happened on this voyage was that the defendant killed his friend Simeon. The final charge that we levy before this court is that of murder.'

This final comment had brought further mutterings from the gallery which were again silenced by Abiel.

'We submit,' continued Ziv when the court was silenced once again, 'that the death of Simeon is far too convenient, and his sudden illness nothing but a fiction from the delusional mind of the defendant. We submit that what in reality happened, was that during the sea voyage the defendant realised that Simeon was a liability to him. He was someone who knew too much about the true murder of Evie. He had to be silenced. We submit, that the defendant, upon the realisation of this, did murder Simeon and having placed fear in the minds of the sailors into thinking that there was sickness on board, had convinced them to dispose of his body with promptness before any examination could be determined to prove the true nature of his death. We have only the defendant's word as to what he said happened on that vessel and the defendant's word has already been proven to be untrustworthy. He is a most dangerous criminal. The final charge must be murder.'

***

During the short recess that followed, I was graced by a visit from Nogah who sat next to me.

'It must seem pretty bleak at the moment,' he said uneasily, as if he had believed everything that Ziv had stated and expected me to launch an attack on him at any minute. Perhaps he did believe this. I decided to say nothing in response to his question. 'The important thing to remember at the moment is that this is the prosecution side of the argument.'

'What next?' I sighed.

'This afternoon, the prosecution will sum up their argument so far and give their concluding statement. The court will then be adjourned for another period and then it will be time for me to present my case.'

'You didn't argue the point over the Pariahs.'

'There really was no point. It is accepted by the system that such a place as you described does not exist. We would not have gained anything by arguing against that. It would just have weakened our position even more than it already is.'

I had to admit that this didn't sound like I had much of a hope. I began to wonder why it was that we were bothering with this farce. I suspected that Abiel had already made up his mind as to what the verdict and the sentence was going to be and that he was merely going through the motions. It was a show at fairness. I nodded wearily and resigned myself to listening to the summing up.

'We have laid before this court eight charges,' Ziv continued when we resumed. I marvelled how he kept using the word 'we' when he was the only one that had been doing the talking. 'To recap these charges, we lay the charges of concealment of the Virus, coercion of another into concealment of the Virus times two, namely in the persons of Doctor Asa and Simeon; consorting with known terrorists; the possession of an illegal opiate; the murder of the defendant's wife, Evie; escape from lawful justice and finally, the murder of the defendant's so-called friend, Simeon. We submit these charges for your consideration.' With this he handed a paper up to the desk where Abiel sat.

'The charges are duly noted and entered into the record,' said Abiel taking the paper from Ziv. 'You may commence summing up.'

'I thank you, sir. There is little that needs to be said in the summing up of this case, that we have not already argued in the laying of the charges.' I was very pleased to hear this, but I suspected that it would, nevertheless, not prevent him from talking regardless. I was right.

'The list of crimes that I have laid before this court are a traumatic, appalling list of evils. I am sure that we look forward to seeing what my colleague, Nogah, has to say, for surely there is no defence that can be offered for such a blatant disregard for life and the law. The crimes committed by the defendant speak for themselves without any need for embroilment which could only serve to confuse the issues that are here presented. The crimes stand on their own as examples of the cruelty that man may steep to. You may ask why it is that the defendant decided to do what he did? He may maintain that it was because of love for his wife. Murder someone because of the love that you have for them? It sounds implausible that you should kill that which you love so much. Perhaps his intention in concealing the Virus was one of love, who knows? However, from that moment onwards, he started on a slippery slope that was out of control and had consequences that were diabolical. That is the crux of the matter. The consequences that happen as a result of our actions can hardly be determined. The concealment of the Virus that leads to the infection of countless other people that we will never know. The coercion of committing a crime to others which would lead to murder and to the execution of an otherwise respected citizen. Perhaps the opiate did not work as well on his wife as he would have liked because it was diluted due to the defendant taking some for his own drug addiction. How else could he have developed such outlandish illusions such as an island of perfection ruled by Pariahs? A nonsense that the court in its wisdom has seen fit to ignore.'

Ziv paused and took a sip of water.

'All of this is something that should be taken into consideration when it comes to the eventual verdict of this case. I am confident that there can be no other verdict other than guilty in this matter; and I am confident that having reached that verdict of guilt, there can be no other sentence but that of the sentence of death. The prosecution concludes at this point.'

And he sat down with folded arms and a look upon his face as if to say that it was a job well done. Which I suppose it was.

25

I had to admit that the prosecution had done its case well. I found myself at a dichotomy. On the one hand, I wanted to be punished for the death of my wife, the other charges that had been laid before me were immaterial as far as I was concerned; except perhaps, for the alleged murder of Simeon, which I found to be farcical and offensive at the same time. From this point of view though, things were going my way and I was likely to receive the punishment that I had deserved. On the other hand, though, I had not expected this trial, and had become caught up in and found myself wanting to fight against the inevitable, that Ziv had argued so well against me.

I found it difficult to know where to stand in all of this and what the best course of argument would be. In many regards, I still felt that I should resign myself to the torrent that was Ziv and allow the court to take its justice upon me. Nogah was still of the opinion that we should fight though and it seemed to upset him greatly that I should even think about not entering a defence. It seemed to go against what he held to be the basis of the legal system. I believed that it was all pointless as I am sure that the verdict of guilty had been decided beforehand. Nogah and myself argued greatly over this before the time finally came, when it was his turn to stand up and offer the almost impossible defence against the argument that Ziv had presented to us all.

'The case argued by my learned colleague has been most compelling,' Nogah began, in a faulting manner when his time at last came to speak. 'It is a most compelling argument that he puts forward for why it is that my client is guilty of the crimes that have been laid before him.'

I didn't think that this was the greatest of opening arguments and I could only hope that at some point in the very near future, Nogah was about to get spectacularly better at what it was that he was doing. I may have been a little too optimistic about this.

'If it pleases the court, I will take each of the charges individually.' Abiel nodded at this in a rather impatient manner which seemed to suggest that he wished Nogah would get on with it. I wished that he would get on with it; watching him was frankly rather painful and the sooner he got into it, the sooner it would conclude.

'The first charge that is laid before my client is that of concealment of the Virus.' I noticed with a degree of interest albeit in a slightly detached manner, that Ziv tended to refer to me as the 'defendant' whereas Nogah had started to call me his 'client' something that he had never done up until this point which I found rather amusing.

'It is true,' he continued, as I watched him with mild interest, 'that my client did conceal the fact that his wife, Evie, had contracted the Virus. The only defence that could be raised to this is one of mitigating circumstances.'

'And what might be the mitigation?' enquired Abiel, looking down his nose at Nogah as he continued his battle with his eye glasses.

'The mitigation is that he loved his wife dearly. The love that he had for his wife outweighed the love that he had for the state or for the law. Wrong, I know, misguided even, arguably even dangerously stupid; but which of us cannot say that we would not be prepared to do all that we could for someone that we truly love with a burning passion?'

I thought he might have gone for the wrong argument here as looking around the courtroom, I could not imagine any of them being consumed by a passionate love.

'Blind obedience to the law is as dangerous an activity, as the prosecutor would have you believe my client is for disobeying it. If the law works at all then it must be a living law. It must be a work in progress with always room for improvement. The reasoning, as outlined by my colleague for why the law regarding the Virus should be obeyed, has been clearly laid out; but it is a dispassionate law that treats the sufferers of this disease as outcasts as Pariahs, the very word tells us what we are to think of these people. It is a cruel and unjust law that expects husband to turn against wife; father against son; mother against daughter and so on; and all for the love of a society that gives little love back for what it demands of its citizens.'

Here he paused, but I suspect less for dramatic purposes as Ziv seemed to do and more to do with the fact that he had to control his eye glasses. 'I ask you to look upon this transgression of the law as a transgression of an unjust law that is outdated and badly in need of reform.' I was pleased to see that Abiel was scribbling away just as much as he had been during Ziv's comments. Ziv himself remained seated with his arms folded, looking singularly unimpressed by the argument that Nogah was advancing.

'The second charge that my colleague has laid before the court, is the coercion of another into the concealment of the Virus.'

'Times two,' interjected Abiel, which I didn't think was particularly helpful and made me think that he really had made up his mind about this case already and certainly didn't seem impartial.

'Indeed, times two. The defence to this is to refer you once again to the fact that this is an unjust law to conceal the Virus. My client did not coerce Asa and Simeon into helping him conceal the illness. They did so because of compassion and because of love. Love for Evie and love for my client. They did not want to see my client in pain for having to banish his wife and they did not want to see his wife suffering any more than nature and fate had already decided that she was going to suffer. They showed compassion and what they did was voluntary. It was of their own free will. Once my client disclosed the information to them, which he could have kept to himself, they could have turned both of them over to the authorities; but instead, they chose the correct route. The path of compassion and kindness rather than obeying an unjust law. They showed compassion and it is my hope that this court will show some of the same compassion in dealing with this case.'

I thought he might have been expecting rather too much on that front.

***

The trial had briefly stopped once again and after a short break, Nogah picked up from where he had left off.

'The next charge that is laid before us is that of consorting with terrorists. I dispute this. The word terrorist is an emotive term and the books of the Ancients show us that what one would describe as terrorists another might describe as heroic fighters against oppression. The Ancients have shown us that the fine line between these two is most often defined by whoever wins and ends up in power and decides to write the account of the struggles that they have experienced in the way that they chose. Let us not be so quick to condemn terrorists when my learned colleague cannot even tell us who these people are that my client is alleged to have contacted for the opiate. If we do not know who they are, then how can we say that they are terrorists? I move that this charge should be dismissed for lack of evidence that my client has had any contact with any such people that may be determined as terrorists, until such a time as this court produces such people here in this court to accuse my client directly.'

I was quite surprised by this. Nogah had actually spoken with a degree of passion here that I really did not think that he was capable of. He also surprised me as his words were very close to subversive and could be argued as direct criticism of the state. From the clicking noises that Ziv was making with his tongue, I could tell that he felt the same way, and probably now thought that Nogah was little better than I was.

'We then approach the charge of possession of an illegal opiate. We do not deny this. Desperate times are stated to call for desperate measures. I have established the love that my client had for his wife and he could not cope with the idea of her suffering. At her own request, my client obtained the illegal opiate. Think of it for a moment. My client who has previously upheld the law and been a model citizen, is forced into a situation where his most loved wife asks him to obtain this substance that will help ease her suffering and ultimately end it. Think of the emotions that must have been running through him at such a time. I cannot imagine it. Can any of us truly imagine it unless we happen to be in the situation ourselves? I think not. Yet, he summons the courage, and he goes into the most dangerous of places to obtain the substance at great personal risk. Risk that he might be captured by the authorities and risk that he might be set upon at any minute, by the savage Residuum, that so few of us would dare to have any contact with ourselves.'

He paused here again and looked around at the assembled multitude taking in the gallery, as he seemed to make eye contact with everyone, daring each to state that they would be as brave as I had been. Despite myself, I could not help but start to be impressed by Nogah's performance. Before he commenced, I had assumed that he was going to provide a token defence based on the fact that everyone is entitled to a defence no matter how hopelessly guilty they are. He seemed to be going a lot further than I would ever have imagined that he would. He also seemed to have a complete disregard for his own safety and I imagined if he were not careful, it would not be all that long before he ended up standing where I was.

'As to the murder of my client's wife, Evie. We do not deny the death of this wonderful woman and we do not deny that my client was involved in that death. The death was conducted at her request and with her consent. The question is all wrong. The question should not be should my client be tried for the murder of his wife, but rather, should someone who has no hope of living and who is in such pain that they have no quality of life, should they be allowed to die? Should someone be allowed to help them to die if they are unable to do so themselves? And should that person who has done what the last thing that any loved one can ask of another, should they be tried for murder?'

There were a few mumblings from the gallery again over this and it struck me that it was probably not an argument that had been raised in a court like this before. They were soon silenced by Abiel who did not seem inclined to want to start such a philosophical debate here and now in his courtroom.

'Is this murder?' Nogah continued, when things settled down. 'If we are to take the full definition of the law as my colleague would quote it to you then yes, I suppose it is. But I argue that the law must be malleable. The law must be able to judge each case on its own merits without the constraints of legal definitions that my learned colleague would use to smother it. The law is a living article and must be allowed to develop. This is not a case of a man who has killed a stranger for their purse or murdered someone in a drunken brawl. This is the case of a couple who loved each other, perhaps more than they should have done; certainly more than the law would allow them to do. This is the case of a man who killed for love. The case of a man who killed his love as the last act of love that he could give to prevent suffering. Is it our place to make that suffering worse?'

The question hung in the air unanswered and then Abiel closed the proceedings for the day and it would be up to Nogah to conclude his argument, when things resumed the following day.

***

I sat in my cell that night in the grubbiest of clothing once again and ran through the events that had taken place over the last few days. Despite myself, I found my interest in the case growing and I even felt that there was a possibility that there might even be some hope.

I still could not imagine that there would be a chance of me being found not guilty. That was something that would be far too much to ask for. I could see that with the arguments that Nogah was using, he was hoping that Abiel would find clemency in his guilty verdict. I imagined that this might mean life imprisonment; however, there was always hope whilst there was life.

It was then that my thoughts would dive down once again though and I would think that this was not right. So much suffering had been caused by my act of love towards my wife. So many people had died and been persecuted because of me. I lay there on my hard, infested bunk and thought about Doctor Asa and Simeon. I thought about the numberless members of the Residuum that had died whilst the authorities tried to find out who had given me the opiate. I wondered if the woman I had seen doing the washing in that stifling room was still doing her washing or whether she was amongst the nameless dead that must lay upon my conscience. Most of all, I thought about Evie.

The pain of missing her was unbearable. Of all the pain both mental and physical from my experience, I knew that it was nothing and could be nothing to the pain that I felt over the loss of my wife. I felt so tired and defeated. I know that there are people out there who cope with the loss of a loved one. I know that somehow, they find the strength to carry on and it amazes me that they are able to do this. Where does this strength of will to continue come from, when the very reason for living has gone forever?

I do not know how it is managed in others and I applaud people that seem to manage to do it. All I know is that it was becoming increasingly more difficult for me to go through life without the woman that I had loved so much; without the woman that I had killed. I just didn't know how much longer I could go on without her. I knew that the only solution to this problem was my own death. It is possible that this would be something that the state demanded, providing Nogah did not do too good a job.

26

I can probably be forgiven for the dark thoughts that invaded me from time to time. I hope you may forgive me for my thoughts flicking between one thing and another as well. I had always tried to lead a simple life, but fate had conspired against me and I had ended up with the life that I had. If I had been of a mind to seek out intrigue and danger, then I probably would have led a boring life. If there is nothing else that I have learnt, I have realised that you don't always get what you want. None of us can really pick the lives that we want. We are dealt the cards of fate and we have to play with what we are given. There is no sense in getting worked up about it. This is a philosophy that is all well and good, but it does not stop me from suffering with depression. I wish I knew the way to elevate that particularly malady.

Eventually, I managed to get to sleep that night, after Nogah had opened the defence, but it was a struggle. I believe I have already mentioned that I have suffered a great deal over the years with insomnia and it is a pitiful thing to have to cope with. You should never make decisions when you've not had enough sleep. It is a lesson that I know well, but one that I have never fully learned, which probably explains why it is that the day before me panned out the way that it did.

'The next charge that I draw attention to is that of escaping from lawful justice,' Nogah resumed, when the formalities were out of the way. 'Put yourself in my client's position. His wife has just died and whereas we accept that he provided a role in bringing about that death, it should not detract from the fact that there is still an incredible emotional upset that can be expected from the death of a spouse. Surely, we can accept that as a given fact. Having accepted the fact that my client was in a distraught emotional state following the death of his wife, how can we hold him to account for the actions — the well-intentioned actions — of his friends?'

Nogah looked around the room once again as if he expected an answer to this question which I assumed he didn't. He continued.

'His friends acted in a manner that they felt was best for their friend. It was their plan that he should leave, and it was they, that put the plan into action. My client did not play a single action of planning in this instance and was easily led by his friends who acted in what they assumed was in his best interests. Due to the emotional state of my client at that time, he was easily led. This was not the actions of a man who was consciously making the decision to flee justice. These were the actions of a man who in a moment of intense emotional strain and stress, was easily led and guided by his friends who believed — no matter how misguided we might think they were — were acting in good faith to protect their friend.'

I felt rather emotional as I stood there listening to the words that Nogah had chosen to say.

'There also remains one fundamental flaw of the prosecutions argument with regards to this particular charge. The charge is that my client has escaped from lawful justice and yet here is. He is not on the run or in hiding and he has come back of his own free will. A voluntary act on his own behalf to face the justice that the prosecution feels that my client has escaped. Presumably, he has escaped by submitting himself to the case that is now underway.

'The final charge that has been levied towards my client is that of the murder of my client's friend, Simeon.' He paused here and shook his head slightly at this before continuing. 'This is perhaps the most extraordinary of all the accusations that have been made against my client. My client maintains that Simeon contracted an illness whilst undertaking the sea voyage which proved to be fatal. We do not know what that illness was, after all, my client is not a doctor. Simeon died from this illness after a protracted period of suffering and was buried at sea in accordance with maritime procedure and protocols relating to potentially infectious diseases.'

There was a pause once again whilst Nogah looked around the courtroom once again.

'The prosecution maintains that there is no evidence to support what my client states happened. If we acknowledge that this is true then we must also acknowledge the fact that there is no evidence to support the murder the prosecution alleges happened. It is nothing more than a fantasy on behalf of the prosecution case and I am surprised that they have even had the audacity to bring it forward as a charge in this case.'

With that, Nogah nodded reverently to Abiel and sat down at this desk. Abiel continued to write for some seconds after Nogah had finished speaking and it seemed as if the entire court and the gallery were holding their breath. Not a sound could be heard from anywhere other than the scratching of that pen across the paper. After a while, he stopped and looked down at Nogah.

'You may begin your summing up, advocate.'

Nogah cleared his throat and then once again stood up.

'My summing up is not something that I need linger about for a long time. It is sufficient to say that the defence that I have raised for each of the charges before my client speak for themselves. We do not say that my client is innocent; he accepts his involvement in this situation. What we do say though, is that he acted under mitigating circumstances. Which of us can truly condemn a man who acts for love and what can we say about a man whose friends will break the law to assist him and to protect him? We have no illusions about this case nor are we unrealistic as to the learned judgement that will be made over it. All we ask is for clemency and compassion. We ask for the court to show the courage of acknowledging when something is wrong and then using this magnificent forum to do something about that unjust law and to truly stand up for justice and show the whole Landmass what can be done in the name of righteousness.'

With this, Nogah sat down and concluded his case. Abiel continued to write something for a brief moment and then looking up again addressed the court.

'I will now withdraw to consider the arguments that have been raised on both sides. When the court next convenes, I will issue my verdict.'

And for the time being, that was it.

***

'How long will this take?' I asked Nogah, when I was back in my imprisonment and he had come to visit me.

'It is difficult to say,' said Nogah, sitting next to me and polishing his eye glasses. 'I would not grade this as a particularly complicated case so it is unlikely to take days as some cases do when it comes to senior lawman deliberation. The fact that it is going to take any amount of time at all would seem to suggest that we have at least given Abiel something to think about.'

'I think you gave a compelling argument.'

'Let's hope that Abiel thinks so as well. Thank you though.'

'I didn't think we had much of an argument before you started talking. The prosecutor gave a very forceful case.'

'Ziv is very good at his job. He knows what he is doing and he is a compelling force to come up against.'

I nodded at this and we sat in silence for a short while.

'You should know,' continued Nogah, 'once the verdict of guilty or not guilty is delivered Abiel will offer you the chance to say something before he passes sentence.'

'It seems strange that I should only be allowed to speak in my own defence once sentenced has already been passed.'

'That's the law. However, my advice to you is that you should decline to say anything.'

'Why?'

'It can't do any good at that stage. You would be better leaving things as they are.'

'Do you have any thoughts on what might happen?'

'I really do not know. I think we have to resign ourselves to accepting that the verdict will be one of guilty. I really can't see how Abiel can decide anything else. The force of the argument that I have tried to use is to push Abiel in the direction of leniency, for when it comes to sentencing. It is all we can hope for really.'

'Life imprisonment?'

'Better than death.'

I still wasn't so very sure about that one.

***

The deliberation was concluded by the following morning. I don't know whether I should feel that this was too soon a time or be pleased that it took him as long as it did. I did know that I was getting tired of standing. Abiel shuffled his papers and then began to make his address.

'After careful consideration of all of the charges that have been placed before this court, I have now reached a conclusion upon each one. Upon the charge of wilful concealment of the virus. The prosecution makes a strong case for the reason why this is an unlawful act. The danger that is presented to fellow citizens leaves no room for selfishness. The defence admit to the crime but have put forward mitigation for why the accused did wilfully conceal knowledge of the Virus. The claim is that the concealment was done due to the love that he had for his wife above that of the state. I understand this argument, but it is my belief that the law remains the law. In the charge of wilful concealment of the Virus, I find the accused to be guilty.'

There was a pause here whilst a piece of paper was handed to someone else in the court who took it and filed it some place. All eyes were riveted on Abiel.

'The second charge is that of coercion of another into concealment of the Virus. This is a charge that is in reference to Doctor Asa and Simeon. The prosecution had laid claim to the coercion by the accused against these two people. I have read the testimony of Asa that has been submitted as evidence and I see nothing in his confession that accuses the defendant specifically of this crime. The defence have raised the issue of free will and that each party has acted on their own in this case with an argument for no coercion from the accused. I have weighed this matter up and based on the evidence that has been presented with regards to the charge that the accused did coerce Doctor Asa into concealing the Virus, I find the accused to be not guilty.'

Again, there was the same action of papers being passed.

'With regards to the charge listed as number seven in relation to the coercion by the accused of Simeon in the concealment of the Virus, I likewise find the accused to be not guilty.'

The paper was passed once again.

'This brings me to the charge that the accused did consort with known terrorists in relation to his obtaining the opiate. The prosecution argues that the unknown male from whom the accused obtained the opiate is a traitor to the state and a member of a terrorist resistance. The defence argue that this man cannot be classed as a terrorist because we do not know his name. The accused does not deny his trip into the Residuum or his meeting with the Resistance in order to obtain this opiate. Indeed, it is something that he has gone to quite extraordinary lengths to do. I do not buy into what the defence claim as his courage in doing this. The accused knew that he was consorting with terrorists when he obtained the opiate, he clearly and openly mentions the Resistance. Terrorism is a danger to all society, no matter how the defence wishes to dress it up. It is the responsibility of this court to send a clear message with regards to terrorism. With regards to the charge of consorting with known terrorists, I find the accused to be guilty.'

The same pantomime of papers being passed was once again enacted. The courtroom remained silent with everyone hanging on each word that Abiel was saying. My glances at both Ziv and Nogah showed that neither of them betrayed any form of emotion.

'The charge of possession of an illegal opiate is a case that is not denied by the defence. There is little that can be said about that other than the destructive, and in this case deadly, use that they have upon our citizens. There is an epidemic of opiate use within society and once again it is the responsibility of this court to send a clear message that this kind of substance abuse will not be tolerated. With regards to the charge of possession of an unlawful opiate, I find the accused to be guilty.'

I decided to opt out of watching the paper exchange this time and desperately wanted to crane my neck back and see what the reaction was in the gallery, but I felt that the best thing to do at the moment, was to be as passive as possible and really pretend that this was something that was happening to someone else.

'We come to the charge now of the wilful murder of the accused's wife, Evie. This is the most serious of crimes, as has been outlined by the prosecution's case. The defence raise the issue that this was a mercy killing and that it was carried out with the consent and the cooperation of the deceased. It may be that this is indeed the case. It may be that the accused was acting with the best of intentions in ending the pain and suffering that his wife was in. I can state that with regards to this I have nothing but the utmost of sympathy for the accused and what it was that he was going through. However, that does not change the fact that the law is very clear on this matter and it still remains an offence to kill or assist someone to kill themselves, regardless of any form of consent which is inadmissible in the eyes of the law. Therefore, with regards to the charge of the wilful murder of the accused's wife, Evie I find the accused guilty of murder.'

I don't suppose that this was all that much of a surprise really.

All that remained so far were two charges. By my reckoning I was running four guilty verdicts against two not guilty verdicts. I was not sure that it would make all that much of a difference when it came to it.

'The next charge that I wish to address is that of the accused's alleged escape from lawful justice. The prosecution makes the case that the accused had a crisis of conscience over what he had done and therefore escaped the justice that he surely knew was to follow. The defence argue that he was led by his friends in his distress at having been bereaved. Putting aside for one moment the fact that the bereavement was something that was brought about by the accused's own hand, I can't help but find the defence's argument compelling that he has returned and is here on trial today. At the very best it could be argued that the accused has *attempted* to escape lawful justice and then for whatever reason this attempt has been abandoned and the accused is with us today. Therefore, in regards to the charge of the accused escaping from lawful justice, I find the accused to be not guilty.'

And now there was only one final charge to go and then I would find out what the future had in store for me, and perhaps more importantly, how much of it I actually had.

'The final charge is that of the murder of the accused's friend, Simeon. The prosecution case seems to centre around the fact that we only have the accused's word for the events that happened on the sea voyage during which Simeon is alleged to have died. There are some issues that I feel that I must raise with this charge. Firstly, I am inclined to agree with the defence that there is no evidence to support that Simeon was murdered by the accused or indeed by anyone else for that matter. I am inclined to agree that the murder of Simeon by the accused is speculation on the part of the prosecution. I would also point out, and I am surprised that the defence has not raised this themselves, that as far as things stand at the present moment, we have no body of Simeon either. We, therefore, have only the accused's word that he is even dead. For all we know, he may be alive and perfectly well somewhere. Therefore, with regards to the offence of the murder of Simeon I find that there is insufficient evidence to substantiate that an offence has taken place at this time. The accused is therefore found not guilty of the murder of Simeon.'

He handed the last piece of paper with his verdict down from his bench and then faced the courtroom once again.

'The accused is found guilty of four of the offences that have been laid before the court and not guilty of four others. The accused is guilty of wilful concealment of the Virus, consorting with known terrorists, possession of an illegal opiate and the wilful murder of his wife, Evie. Does the accused have anything that he wishes to say before sentence is passed?'

I looked at Nogah who minutely shook his head so covertly that I doubt anyone else would have seen it. This was the stage when I would speak in this courtroom for the very first time.

'Yes, there is something that I wish to say.'

27

I suspect that this was the first time Nogah had been surprised by a client. It was certainly the first time that I had seen him surprised since we had met. He wasn't the only one. The entire courtroom seemed surprised and I surmised that the opportunity for an accused, or rather condemned as I was at this stage, to talk was something that was rarely, if ever, actually taken up. They were in a difficult position though as the law clearly stated that the condemned had the right to address the court before sentence was passed, despite the fact that etiquette probably dictated that this was a right that should never be taken up.

'Proceed then,' said Abiel, coughing slightly and looking rather bemused by the whole thing. It wasn't hard to imagine that he didn't have many accused persons take him up on the right to speak.

'Firstly, I feel that I should offer my thanks to my advocate, Nogah, for his well-argued and reasoned defence of my case. At the same time, I should also compliment the prosecution on their side of the debate as well. It pleases me a great deal that with four guilty verdicts and four not guilty verdicts it seems as if each of you have won half the case.'

This comment provoked a titter of laughter from the gallery which was immediately silenced by a glare from Abiel, who certainly didn't seem to find any of this amusing.

'I sense that it is unusual for the condemned to speak at this juncture of proceedings, however I do feel that there is something that I should say that I have not yet had a chance to say to this court.'

I paused for a moment to gather my thoughts as this was probably as spontaneous and as much of a shock for me as it was for the rest of the court. I had not anticipated that I would make use of this platform that had been left open to me.

'Most of what I would have said in this respected assembly has already been said, and perhaps, better said by my advocate. I wish only to reinforce certain issues. I loved my wife and indeed I still do love my wife; more than anything in the world. I love her more than I could ever love a state or a law; and I am pleased that when it came to the moment when I had to choose, I chose my wife rather than my Sphere or state. I believe that this is the way that things should be. My friends also chose me and Evie rather than their obligation to the law and state. I commend them for this and I grieve for their loss because of their assistance to me. It may seem alien to some of you here that someone would be prepared to put their loved ones before the law, before their state, before their own safety and continued existence. If this is the case, then I have nothing but pity for you for being so misguided in your beliefs. I can see that my senior lawman, Abiel bristles at this and would dearly love to stop me from talking; but he is too well trained in the law to interrupt. He is so manacled to the law that he knows that regardless of what I say here now, I have the right to say it, and that is a freedom that we lack on the Landmass. It is one of the many freedoms that we lack. Not all freedoms are to do with chains and cells, but are the constraints that are placed upon our own minds, by a state that wishes to control us rather than give us the most basic of rights.'

I paused here and looked at the mixture of faces that were looking at me. Some bewildered, some confused, some interested and some angry.

'I urge you to think about it for a moment. Think of all that is wrong with our society. Our status and our careers are an accident of birth depending upon which Sphere we are born into and hold nothing against individual merit. We are conditioned from birth that we will live where we are told to, associate with who we are told to and do what work it is that we are told to. None of us have the freedom to do what we want. Worst of all perhaps, is the fact that we — all of us, are guilty of slavery. Let us not mix our words about it for we have enslaved the Residuum as an inferior species and yet these are our fellows, who surely have just as many rights as we do. How many millions have we allowed to die because of our silence at believing them to be inferior to us? Shame on us.'

I began to see more anger in the faces of the people around me as they clearly didn't like to hear what I was saying.

'I am sorry if my words offend you, but if that is what it takes to force change, then it is offence that must be caused. We must stop this rot in our society before it is too late.' I paused again and regained my thoughts.

'I have strayed slightly from what I intended to say. My intention is this. I love my wife and it was my choice to help her die and when that attempt failed, it was I that chose to kill her, to prevent her from suffering any more than she already had. This deed has haunted me since the moment that I committed it. It has plagued me and been like a constant ache in my side, never allowing me rest or relief. Some comments have been made as to why it was that I decided to come back to the Landmass. The answer to this is simple. I am guilty of the death of my wife and I deserve to be punished for this. What I wish to say, Senior Lawman, is that when it comes to your sentencing, I wish you to take into account what I have said and that I feel that I deserve nothing less than the full penalty that the law can inflict, upon someone who has been found guilty as I have.'

***

There was nothing short of an eruption of noise when I concluded what I had to say and Abiel was banging loudly on his desk for some time before some degree of order was eventually restored to the courtroom.

'Does the accused—' began Abiel when the noise had ceased, only to stop himself before he went any further and then began again. 'Is it the accused's own recommendation that he be given the stiffest penalty that the law allows?'

'Yes, that is the accused's own recommendation.' I was happy to be able to confirm this for him.

'And are you aware of the fact that this means the death penalty?'

'I am so aware of that yes, thank you.'

Abiel sat back with a bemused and rather worried look on his face at the same time.

'Advocate?' he turned his attention towards Nogah, to see if there was any sense that might be had in that quarter. Nogah slowly rose to his feet.

'My earlier appeals for clemency and compassion still stand as far as I am concerned. However, this latest appeal from my client is something that my client has made of his own free will, against my advice and without consultation as to the nature of the content.' He then made a slight shrugging gesture, as if to say that he had done his best and the entire matter was out of his hands now. He sat down again with an entirely resigned look on his face. Ziv just sat there as if he had never seen the like before in his entire life, which to be honest he probably hadn't. Abiel sat back, pondering everything that had happened.

'Very well,' he eventually said. 'This court is in adjournment until summoned, when I will provide my final summing up and sentencing in this case. Take the condemned back to his cell.'

***

Now, you are probably wondering why it was that I had done what I had done. If you are then that is a bit of a shame because I think I had made my situation reasonably clear by this stage as to how I felt about everything. I will not deny that there are many at the time and since who thought that I had pretty much shot myself in the foot with the comments that I had made. Well, that may be the case, but if it is, then that is what happened and there is nothing that can be done to change any of it now. It would have been interesting to see if the sentence from Abiel was any different before my outburst than it was afterwards. We will never know now.

Several days went passed before I once again found myself standing in the courtroom for what I presumed would be the last time. Abiel came in, last as usual, and sat down, shooting me a glance as if I were some Pariah that had dared to defy existence and had wandered into his court. He sat down and shuffled his papers for a short while, which was something that I thought was unnecessary as he had only just walked in with them so presumably knew the order that they were in, or if not, he could have sorted them before coming into the court in the first place.

'I have spent much time deliberating over the last few days on the appropriate sentence for the guilty man who stands before us,' he said, whilst giving me another very suspicious look. 'During the course of this deliberation, I have consulted with both the prosecution and the defence as well as seeking external expert advice. I believe that the decision that I have reached is the most appropriate given the nature of this case.'

He paused here for some time whilst looking over his papers once again, as if he was trying to work out if the decision that he had made was the right one whilst probably wondering if it was too late for him to change his mind.

'The points made by the prosecution are well taken. Given the nature of the crimes that you have been found guilty of and the admissions that you have made yourself, it is clear to me that there is a subversive element to you that is dangerous and could be regarded as highly contagious and damaging if it were to be left unchecked. The comments that you chose to make in your address only add to the subversive nature of your character and confirms that you probably are as dangerous and criminally-minded as the prosecution would have this court believe that you are. It is a matter for academic debate whether this revolutionary streak that seems to exist in your character was there all along and you have taken advantage of the situation that presented itself to do the unthinkable, and murder another human being; or whether the situation that you found yourself in was the cause of your ill-advised thoughts. I do not know what the answer is to that question and I hardly think it really matters. The fact remains that you are a subversive, dangerous man who is clearly criminally-minded.'

He paused to allow all of this to sink in and I stood there trying not to be too offended by what I could not help but feel was something of a personal attack that he had launched on me. After all, I suppose he was only doing his job and he did have the gallery to play to; something that he appeared to be doing rather well.

'Nevertheless,' he continued with his serious tone that was compelling to listen to. 'I have also not been deaf to the words of the defence advocate and his plea for clemency and compassion. I firstly asked myself whether such a man as I have already described deserves any form of clemency from this justice system that he has so wrongfully abused. The answer to that is problematic. On the one hand, the law must be seen to be firm against such individuals as you. A message must be sent to all others who feel that they might be able to act in the same way as you have done and then not be punished for their transgressions. On the other hand, it shows great leniency and compassion in the law if it is able to show even the most unforgiven of its perpetrators, that the law is just.'

He looked around to see if there would be anyone that agreed with this or disagreed. I doubted that there would be anyone that had the courage to argue with this man in his own courtroom, possibly anywhere else either for that matter.

'Nor do I accept the argument that the sentence should be lenient because the law is unjust. The law is the law, whether it be unjust or no, it remains the law and until such a time — should there be such a time — that the law would be changed, then it shall be upheld in this courtroom. It is not the place of courts to change laws because of the fact that the defence believe that they are unjust — or anyone else believing it for that matter. Let us think no further on the matter of that.

'There then remains the matter of your own outburst to this court. Perhaps it would have been wise to listen to the counsel of your own advocate for this outburst of yours has caused much of the debate that has come to me about your sentence. You say that you wish to have the full penalty of the law exercised upon you. You say this knowing that the penalty, without clemency for your crimes that the law permits is death. To be taken from this place and executed, in full view of all citizens, and there your body left to rot, as an example to all others who may wish to follow in your misguided footsteps.

'This is the penalty of the law that you ask for; and this is what causes me the issues that I have been searching over during the last few days. It is a generally accepted fact, that the manner of the death that you would be subjected to is so horrific that it is not something that anyone in their right mind would voluntarily undergo. I have, after much counsel and debate, reached the conclusion that due to this, you are not in your right mind.'

There was murmuring in the court once again which was silenced by Abiel slapping the palm of his hand down on the desk hard, which rang out like a gunshot throughout the room. I could not help but think that such an action must have caused him a degree of pain but it did not show on his face to any degree.

'You have been found guilty of four offences which include the murder of your wife and you have asked for the strongest penalty that the law allows. In passing sentence on you, it has been decreed by this court that you are suffering from either temporary or permanent insanity. The sentence of this court is that you therefore be committed to an asylum for the criminally insane, where you shall remain until your death or until such time as it is deemed that you are sufficiently mentally fit to have judgement passed upon you. This case is now closed.' He slammed his hand down once again.

28

So, there it is. There we have it.

The last part of my life spent not in prison, but in an institution for the criminally insane. A sane man amongst lunatics with no hope of reprieve. I cannot begin to tell you what it has been like. I have spoken much about my little cell during the course of this narrative and how terrible it is, but there is one thing about it that I have not told you; I love it. It is my sanctuary, for within these walls I am able to be myself and escape the dangerous people that are my fellow inmates. It is the only place that I feel safe; for who can feel safe amongst the insane that have no account of responsibility for their actions? I shudder at the things that I have seen whilst I have been here and each night, I am lulled into sleep by the screams of those who have become detached from their reality. I spoke previously of insomnia; it is not just the memory of Evie and everything that has happened that keeps me awake at night, but also, the pitiful cries that echo throughout this place day and night. It is implausible how humans can make noises that can only be described as inhuman in their nature.

I have had plenty of time to reflect, of course, upon my outburst in the court. If I had not made it then I would imagine that the sentence of death would have been carried out. I think it was but a dream to imagine that the court would ever offer me imprisonment as an alternative to death; which is ironic I suppose, given how that is ultimately what has happened. You may ask why didn't they go ahead and execute me anyway? The answer to that is simple. Despite everything that I have said about the law, we live in a civilised society and it is just not the done-thing to execute someone who is insane and therefore, not in control of their own actions. Rather comical when you think about it really.

I should have held my peace in the courtroom and then with luck, I would have had an eternity to hold my peace afterwards. Instead, I find that I am being punished hourly in ways that I could never have imagined before.

Am I insane? I don't think so. Do you think I am? Perhaps in our way we are all insane to some degree or another; only some of us are locked up for it. I certainly do not deem myself to be on a level with my fellow inmates, who are frightening in the grip that they have lost on their sanity. It amazes me that for all the years that I have been exposed to this place, that I have not become insane; I think it would be easy enough to have done so. The sanest of all people could not help but go insane exposed to what I have been.

Do I still feel that there are changes that are required in society? Yes, of course I do. Imprisonment or incarceration cannot prevent the spirit from being willing, no matter how much of a battering it might take over the years. I argue that our structure of society is entirely wrong. I never really explained it properly in the court, but not just the legal system which leaves a lot to be desired for insisting on punishing love; but also, the whole Sphere structure is wrong. I learnt that thanks to the Pariahs and Aaron, wherever he may be now. Before then, my eyes were closed and I blindly accepted what our parents taught us which is what their parents taught them and so on, back through the generations. We should abolish the Spheres and all live according to our own merits. Yes, we might fall and hurt ourselves, but that is because in many ways, we are like children and we have to learn to walk again. It is inevitable that the transition would see mistakes, but it cannot be as heinous as the mistake that we are living in now. Look around and see the injustice that is seeped into your everyday existence.

If but one person can stand up and ask the question 'why?' because of this account, then I would deem that my time and effort has been well placed.

***

Alpheus I am tired. I have tried faithfully to record my life for you as you have asked me to do so that this record may prove of use to you in the future. I hope that it may do some good one day.

I accepted a long time ago that it was too late for me. My life is done and it cannot be far from over now. Perhaps these crumbled pages will be of use to you one day and they will show future generations what a remarkable society that they have escaped from and they will wonder how it is that we ever lived the way that we do. It is a question that I often ask myself if the truth be known. Regimes do not last forever and empires will one day fall, which once seemed to be so permanent and defiant. If the history of the Ancients has taught us anything, it has taught us that nothing lasts forever.

It is very late now and I am so very tired. Tired from so many things. I hope that I have not missed out too much from this account that I wanted to say, or for what Alpheus would like me to say. It is too late now if he does want me to say more. My hands are crippled now from the writing and the cold has got into the joints. My eyesight has now almost completely failed me from so many hours spent peering at these scribbled lines by poor candlelight. I know that these will be the last words that I ever write and that soon, I will be at a rest that will hopefully put me beyond all pain and suffering.

The only thing that I have left to say is that I have no regrets. Well, that is not entirely true. I regret that Evie became sick and died, but that was out of my control. It would have been so much better for everyone if she had not been sick and had lived, so that we might grow into old age together and die. It was not to be.

Putting that to one side, I do not regret meeting her. I do not regret marrying her. I do not regret the time that we spent together. I do not regret carrying out her wish to die in the manner that she chose. I do not regret a minute of the time that we spent together and I do not regret the punishment that I have received for her. Most of all, I do not regret loving her and I never will; not even when the last breath of life has left my body.

There are times when I wish that I had the courage to follow her by my own hand. It is something that I have debated numerous times over the years since she died and there have been times, when I have probably come close to ending it all. Something has always held me back and I think that is my cowardice. Once you take that step, there is no coming back from it and no changing your mind and I have never had the courage to be able to step over that line. I am not entirely sure why it is that I feel like this.

And now it has come to an end. So long a time. I will not know what to do with myself to occupy the time that I have spent writing this over so many years. I suspect that it is something that will not present me with a problem for too much longer.

I hope that one day you may have the freedom that I have longed for. The problem with freedom is that in order to want it, you first have to know that you are enslaved. It took me some time before I realised the truth of the situation that I was in and how we were all slaves. Perhaps by the time you read this you are free; free to do what you want, say what you want, go where you want and most importantly of all, think what you want. Perhaps that freedom is still a long way away; or perhaps it is that you do not even know that the freedom is something you really need.

My parting words to you are that I wish that you will one day experience the level of love that I have, if you have not already done so. If you have this love then do not waste it. Cherish it, grasp it with both hands and don't let a minute of it pass you by without acknowledging it, for you may never know when it will be taken from you and you will never see the like again.

My blessing be with you, and may you be as at peace, as I hope to soon be.

Dr Roger Michaels
Department of Psychiatric Medicine
University Hospital
Probation Board
HMP Norton
July 28th 2014

Dear Sir/Madam,

As requested, I have conducted a full psychiatric report on the subject, Robert Spencer in preparation for his parole hearing. As you will know, Spencer was admitted to HMP Norton for the criminally insane on March 5th 1997, following his committal at trial for the murder of his wife, Eve Spencer.

As part of the assessment process of Mr Spencer, I have required him to write an account of the events that have happened to him, so that he may gain some degree of therapy from this. As you will see from the attached document, he remains entirely delusional about the events surrounding the murder of his wife and maintains an elaborate fiction of not only the events, but the world in which he thinks he inhabits.

Mr Spencer is extremely paranoid and maintains one of the most detailed fictions of his life that I have ever encountered. Throughout our therapy sessions, he has not acknowledged who I am, but has invented a character for me that he calls Alpheus. Although his account admits to the murder of his wife, he has not only invented a fictional illness that she was meant to be suffering from, but has also invented a fictional society, in which he has become cocooned. The details of this delusion are quite startling.

Nothing of his account acknowledges the particularly brutal murder of his wife; or the subsequent murders of Police Constable Simeon Grant or Doctor Asa Bayley. Indeed, with regards to the last two murders, he appears to have adopted the belief that these were friends of his who helped him in the murder of his wife.

In all the time since his committal, I have to report that Mr Spencer has not shown any signs of improvement in his condition and does not respond to treatment or medication. Indeed, it is my belief that he is actually becoming far worse.

It is my firm belief that his condition will continue to worsen and that due to the nature of his crime and delusion, he should never be released, but should spend the rest of his life in confinement.

Yours sincerely,

Roger Michaels MD FRCP